Dreamers

Dreamers in Time

SARAH COPELAND

BLACK
lace

Black Lace novels are sexual fantasies.
In real life, make sure you practise safe sex.

First published in 1996 by
Black Lace
332 Ladbroke Grove
London
W10 5AH

Typeset by CentraCet Limited, Cambridge
Printed and bound by Mackays of Chatham PLC

ISBN 0 352 33064 3

Prologue

London, December 2313 AD

*T*hey lay there, calm and content after their ferocious love-making.

'After that,' he said, 'you can't still be determined to go?'

'I must,' she replied. 'I know it seems foolish to you, but Professor McGregor is so convincing. I only wish you would come as well. If he is wrong, all we have to do is re-emerge from underground. It won't be too long before everyone stops laughing at us. But if he's right, there will be no one to laugh at us anyway. Please come with me.' Her statement was half question and half imploration.

'You know I can't. I'd lose my job and the debts would mount up. Apart from which, the Russians and Americans are convinced it won't make any difference to the sun. They're agreed it's the only possible way to dispose of the warheads safely. We can't run the risk of another madman getting hold of nuclear waste – the Middle East is still uninhabitable, thirty years on,' he replied.

'But they haven't experimented; all their decisions are based on paper, they can't tell what effect firing all of the planet's nuclear material into a star will have,' she argued.

'The scientists are bound to have looked at it from all sides. It's not as if McGregor even has any concrete idea of what might go wrong. Everything he believes is based on a letter he says somebody wrote to him more than three hundred years ago – the guy's a lunatic! And yet, you're ready to throw up careers and futures because of him. I just don't understand it. Sometimes I think you care more for him than you do for me.' He was beginning to get a little vexed.

They had had this conversation so many times over the past few months and, this time, it was becoming personal much faster than normal. It quickly escalated into a fierce row.

He rose and dressed. 'Go down your bloody mine, then. But don't expect me to be waiting for you when you crawl back out!' He slammed the door behind him.

She lay there, crying softly to herself, sure that he was right but for entirely different reasons.

Chapter One

Nucassel, July 3550PS

She dreamt of herself clad only in diaphanous silk trousers, her breasts exposed and oiled, in a strange, white place. As she walked, a room slowly grew around her: a marbled pool in the centre seemed the focus for dozens of women who stood and sat and lay on divans, dressed in the same transparent pantaloons. The chamber was warm and exotic scents assailed her senses, but underlying everything was the smell of the women. She felt relaxed and apprehensive and these emotions seemed to pervade every part of her body. As she continued to walk, a gentle breeze stirred and she discovered that what she had thought were trousers were two independent legs, which overlapped above the knee, but were not joined. As she moved they danced softly apart. She could not understand how she had come to this place – she knew herself, and yet felt curiously alien. She moved towards an empty couch and sat down to consider her predicament. As she looked around the room, she could

3

see that some of the women had their legs wide apart, idly toying with themselves. One dusky beauty who lay not far from her had eight gold rings protruding from her labia, which could quite clearly be seen as her mons was entirely bereft of hair. Although its movements were barely perceptible, she watched a slender wand move in and out of her velvet tunnel. A part of her wanted to go and offer assistance to the woman, but the lazy part, entranced by the atmosphere of the place, decided to play, too.

Her hand, which seemed to feel like a stranger's against her flesh, found its way beneath the folds of silk. It moved towards her pubis, intent on a little excitement, and it did not seem surprised when it encountered bare skin rather than down. However, *she* was surprised but she could not express her consternation. When her hand moved to part the sweet petals enclosing her bud, it was hampered by a fine gold chain, laced through rings that pierced her labia, preventing all but the most delicate touch. She knew that she should be distressed by this barbaric mutilation, but somehow it seemed only natural. Whilst she was confused, she was also unconcerned.

Somewhere a bell rang out and the women rose and moved towards a stark white wall, which seemed to ripple as she watched it. She joined them. Unthinkingly, they formed a line facing the wall, and waited. No word was uttered, no sound was made. She had no way of knowing how long they stood for. Whether it was for minutes or hours, time seemed suspended.

At last the wall parted, and two men moved towards them. They stood before her, and the other

4

women all faded away. The men turned to face the wall again and without a word or giving any sign she knew that she should follow.

The wall was not a wall at all. Just a dense, heavy curtain of a fabric she did not recognise. Beyond it, seated on an immense heap of cushions raised high upon a dais, was a man she knew but could not name. His bronzed chest was bare but for a magnificent gold ornament. Her escort moved back towards the wall and she fell to the ground, pressing her forehead against cool marble. The man clapped his hands and she raised her head to see him beckon her forward.

In front of the dais was a small table upon which was a bowl of beaten gold, filled with the purest water; water that glistened and sparkled like liquid diamonds. Beside it lay a blade, honed unnaturally sharp, and a cloth. While her mind railed against a barrage of unbearable tortures, her hands knew to lift the knife and kneel at the edge of the dais. She turned to find the bowl and then positioned it between his outstretched legs. She undid the silken rope that wound around his waist and pushed the billowing silks aside until she had exposed his groin. His strong shaft pointed at the heavens, and a tiny bead of dew glistened at its apex. Then, slowly, and with the greatest care, she stroked the blade carefully across his skin. Where the blade had passed was now a smooth track of flesh. She continued to shave him until she reached that small dip, at the union of his body and prick. Her mouth was dry and she was strangely moved by this man who trusted her, without a second thought. Her hairless hole was wet and her labia swelled against their chains. She rinsed the blade and started anew, this time with the pendulous sack of his scrotum. It felt full and hard against the blade's edge. She found herself longing for the time when all was done but for the towering prick, which she would shave lovingly like a sculptor until the lines of his definition were clean and smooth, free of all imperfections. With the cloth from the table, dipped in the water, she wiped away all traces of her work and started to debeard the monster. So slowly the blade travelled, so scared she was of her trembling hands, it seemed an hour passed before it stood there, proud and flawless. She then moved bowl, blade and cloth back to the table, and then he clapped again. The two men came forward, one to move the table, the other bearing a massive sabre. At a nod from his master, the sword-bearer inserted the sabre into the gap in her trousers, lifting it skilfully to sever the bindings around her waist. They fell in silken puddles at her ankles. The other man returned carrying a chair without a seat, and gently pushed her down into it, placing her ankles astride the chair's legs. The men moved behind her, whilst she sat facing their enigmatic master. Her legs had been spread open by the manipulation of her ankles, and she could feel the chains that bound her love-folds becoming taut as her hollow was stretched open.

He clapped a third time and three women entered. The women were exquisite: two were of Amazonian proportions and the third as slender and diminutive as a child. The first two grasped her wrists while the waif knelt between her legs. This child-like woman's breasts were as petite and perfect as the rest of her form, and through her right nipple there was a large gold ring cruelly piercing that sweet young sprout. Attached to this ring was a tiny key. The waif leant forward and her left breast fluttered across her captive's knee, causing her victim to tremble with desire. She took the key between thumb and finger and gently guided it. Expertly, she manoeuvred her pert teat until she located the lock which held the captive lips in bondage. Delicately, she unlaced the chain, her fingers fluttering intoxicatingly against the swollen flesh. She then placed her foot upon her prisoner's thigh: a pretty foot, with its high instep and ruby rings on each of the tiny toes. She unclasped a chain from around her neck, a chain which matched those around her ankles. The Amazons then freed their hold upon their victim's wrists and turned sharply in towards her so that their ponderous breasts pressed heavily against her cheeks. She could hardly draw breath, her heart was pounding so fiercely. Yet she knew that she had been released solely to unbind the gilded ankle which rested upon her thigh. That chain removed, she placed it in the woman-child's awaiting hand. Immediately, the foot upon her thigh was removed. The statuesque captors retook her wrists in their firm, strong hands, while the pretty imp knelt back between her legs. With speed and dexterity, she fastened one end of each chain to one of the tiny rings that pierced her victim's left labia. With a touch as light as butterflies' wings, the chains were passed around the seated woman's rump and through the corresponding rings of the right labia. As one, they were pulled taut, and her inner flaps were pulled tight towards her thighs. Her gaolers locked the chains in place by little padlocks which snapped and held her fast, biting into her flesh. She was left wrenched open

7

like a ripe fig. Then the waif raised her left hand and from her smallest finger she opened a strange hinged ring, removing a tiny band of gold. She wrapped the golden band around the tethered woman's precious bud. The prisoner's swollen berry, collared in this wild manner, grew even more pronounced.

The man clapped and the woman-child went to him and knelt between his legs, while the two Amazons raised their captive out of the chair, their mighty hands under buttock and thigh. They carried her to their master, held high above them. Shaped like a star, the woman's pudendum pointed towards the heavens.

Slowly they lowered her down towards his immense obelisk. The woman-child held him steady whilst the Amazons readied her, the sacrifice, for penetration. In the distance a gong sounded and she, victim only of her own longing, waited for the moment that his flesh was engulfed by hers.

The gong continued to reverberate through her head as she remained suspended and, slowly, she realised that there was no gong, just the sound of the morning bell calling her from sleep.

Ehlana lay there for a moment, hopeful that sleep would reclaim her and allow her to finish the dream, but her body, conditioned over many years to the ordained early-morning routine, would not permit that. So she rose from her pallet and moved towards the window which overlooked the city. It was, she thought, the most beautiful time of day. The sunrise cast soft, pinkish hues that gentled the normally harsh, clean outlines of the white buildings until they almost seemed to pulse with rosy

8

health. No signs or sounds of any life disturbed the empty streets, but still she felt the quiet breathing of the city. All too soon, however, the sun would rise high enough to display the city in its stark, clinical reality.

Ehlana sighed. Her dream had left her disconcerted: barbarian practices had no place in this world and she could think of no reason why her imagination should create them. But she knew well enough not to mention it to her Evaluator. Once, when she was little more than a girl, she had confessed to a strange fantasy and she still recalled the subsequent interrogation and painful re-education session she had been forced to endure. She was sure that any hint of licentiousness would result now in the loss of her Licence. Eight years of study had finally resulted in her acceptance into the Guild of Historians and her first solo trip in the History Machine was scheduled for that very afternoon – she had no intention of jeopardising that!

Realising that she had spent too much time in idle reflection, she hurried to dress and join the others before breakfast was finished.

By the time she reached the Refectory, though, only three remained: Lomai, Mara and Jodai. She had known all three since infancy. They all came from the same hatching. The others had chosen to follow Life Sciences, whereas Ehlana had been drawn towards History. Normally, she felt a little excluded by their close camaraderie, but not today.

'Greetings and well met,' said Mara, as she stood and embraced Ehlana. 'Are you all set for the great day? How far back will they send you?' She was at least five inches taller than her sister-friend, a willowy blonde against red-haired Ehlana.

'Apprehensive, but there's no reason why I should be. I'm returning only two hundred and fifty years – I've been back further than eleven hundred with Magister Tolai. Sadly, I am unlikely to return with any new information: the population then is still two thousand, hatchings are in the seventh month, and the Sleepers still sleep. There. That's all I am likely to learn. I sometimes wonder if it's worth the energy it uses,' replied Ehlana, looking a little downcast.

'But to be the first of the distaff to travel – that must be a wonderful thing. Everything you do, you are the first. Truly, that must make a difference.' Lomai spoke eagerly as he embraced his sister-friend. 'We, poor souls, are not likely to find a wakening for the Sleepers: we can but follow other people's plans and hope that Serendipity chooses one of us to happen on a means to increase the harvest. As it is, your exalted position as the only female Historian grants you the marvellous privilege of a room to yourself – if that is not a good reason for membership of any Guild, I do not know of a better one!'

'Well, we will expect a full report of all that you saw,' said Jodai, always more formal than his hatchmates. He had always been that way and, despite much teasing over the past twenty-three years, they had rarely managed to unbend him. 'When do you go?' he asked.

'Oh, not for an hour yet, and I'll only be gone for two – you won't even have time to miss me,' she replied. As she glanced up at him she suddenly realised why the face of the man in her dream had been so familiar – it was Jodai; her blush was nearly as red as her hair. 'Anyway, I promise I'll bore you

10

to death with all the details, as long as you promise to listen.'

What can be happening to me? she thought. Barbarian dreams with Jodai's face – her Evaluator would have a seizure if she confessed it. Fortunately, the bell began its call to labour and her hatch-mates pressed her hand in farewell, leaving her alone in the immense room. She had time enough to eat breakfast before the next shift arrived, but her imminent voyage had completely overwhelmed her appetite. She decided, instead, to visit the Field, so that she could reliably inform her hatchlings how much it had grown over the past quarter century.

It took less than ten minutes to reach the Field, the streets were almost entirely empty as she walked along. The aroma of damp soil was always strong enough to smell long before the final barrier opened, but as ever she was entranced by the view given through the opening doors: three square hectares crammed with life. All of the seed stock that had survived the thousand years below ground was protected by a great, glassed roof that augmented the sun's light and filtered out the harmful rays. She had always harboured a strange fantasy about this place and, knowing that the Field workers had gone for their stint in the Refectory, believed that she might be safe to indulge it. She moved swiftly to the Moss Garden, raising her shift over her head as she went, and lay face down in its cool greenness. Recently watered, it softly moulded itself around her naked body. The sun's meagre warmth was increased ten-fold by the glass canopy and she felt its heat upon her back, buttocks and legs like a caress, whilst little tendrils of moss stole

11

into every crease of her that they touched. She wondered if she lay there long enough whether it would envelop her entirely, growing deep inside her, spreading its life throughout her form. She rolled over then, onto her back, and gazed up at the roof, vivid flecks of green clinging to her breasts and belly which started to dry out as soon as the sun touched her.

'Ehlana?' she heard a voice call. Quickly she grabbed at her shift, pulling it over her head. As she stood, she saw Jodai emerging from the yellow, green and black of the Sunflower Garden.

'Here,' she called, glad that he had warned her.

'Sora saw you heading for the Field, so I thought to catch you here before you left. I just wanted to wish you good fortune and a safe journey,' he said.

'It is good of you to find me. I decided to pass a half-hour here before I travelled, mainly so that I could tell the three of you how much has been achieved since then. It was the only piece of information that I thought I might bring you. Foolish, I know, but I think I saw it as justification for my trip,' she explained.

'It's foolish for you to think of us at a time like this – your choice of History has at least as much value as ours. Enjoy it for itself. I would, if I had chosen differently. But shouldn't you be going now? You've only just enough time to reach the Laboratory before the tenth hour strikes,' he reminded her.

'It is that late already? Sunfire, if you had not come to find me I would have missed it altogether! I shall see you later.' She pressed his hand in parting and ran towards the door.

Jodai did not follow her, however. He waited

until she was out of sight and then lay down in the imprint of her body that the moss still held.

Ehlana opened the door to the History Lab just as the bell began to toll the hour. Hurrying in, she greeted the Magister, Tolai, and his two assistants.

'Just in time,' the Magister said, lifting his head from his console. 'Then again, we could not really have started without you. Been to the Field, I see.'

Ehlana, flustered, looked down at her shift: little spots of green bespattered its whiteness. 'I thought to bring my hatchlings news of the Field's growth – if my trip allows me enough time to visit it,' she explained.

'Ah, well, it is good to have a purpose,' he responded. 'You have your crystal?' he asked, not bothering to look at her neck. Suspended there on a fine golden chain hung the translucent stone that would allow them to find her and bring her back from wherever in time she journeyed.

'Are you ready, Ehlana?' the Magister asked. 'There's no time like the past, eh, girl!'

Ehlana smiled as she stood on the platform. Holding on tight to her crystal, she offered up a little prayer to the blessed Neil, patron saint of all voyagers into the unknown. Across the room, she heard the call of the History Machine as it thrummed into life. She could feel its voice resonate in her crystal. She closed her eyes as her body became a sounding board and the single note of crystal vibration overwhelmed her. She knew if she opened her eyes she would see nothing now but the void and feel nothing but her fall through time. Strangely, she felt as if she had already travelled more than the destined two hundred and fifty years and the song of the Mother Crystal was becoming more discordant with each breath she took. Yet still she travelled. The noise grew viciously and now there was pain. She could not understand it. Her previous journeys, twenty in all, had never been like this. Perhaps I dream again, she hoped. Her head throbbed wildly and she felt as if she was being torn apart. It was as though the very fabric of her existence was being shredded by her passage through time. She began to pray that her dissolution would be swift, that the agony would end. And she screamed.

Chapter Two

London, February 1979AD

*E*hlana was still screaming when someone slapped her face. She opened her eyes, looking straight ahead, only to find that she confronted herself.

'Who the hell are you?' the mirror-image asked her.

'I think I must be you. When am I?' Ehlana replied.

'You're in my flat, at two in the morning, looking just like me and asking me questions! I can have the police here in less than three minutes. So why don't you tell me what the hell is going on?' her twin said.

'I travelled here. I was going back on my first solo journey and something has gone horribly wrong. It's all so dark here. I don't understand.' Ehlana tried to fight back her panic, but failed and began to slide to the floor in a faint.

When she came round, it was with her head resting in her twin's lap.

'There, don't worry. It's okay, Suzie. Everything's okay,' her double crooned.

'My name is Ehlana and I don't know why I'm here. Who are you? When is it?' Ehlana stumbled over her words, her mouth as dry as if she had swallowed the dust of ages.

'I'm Louise – but my friends call me Lulu. As to when it is, I don't think I understand the question. Or at least I think I might not want to. If you aren't a burglar, and you don't look like one, you're either an alien body-snatcher or my favourite idea at the moment is that you don't belong in seventy-nine. Who's the Prime Minister?' she quizzed.

'Who's the what? If you mean the Magister Prime, Krotai has led the Council for seventeen years. And what's a seventy-nine?' Ehlana replied.

'Shit! I think I need a cigarette. Just stay here while I get one,' commanded Lulu, as she lifted herself free from the still prostrate Ehlana. From the other room she called, 'Do you want a drink?'

'Yes, thank you,' was Ehlana's reply.

'I've got gin, Scotch, tea, coffee and orange juice. Oh, and I think there's some tonic water as well. But I'm out of ice and I don't think I dare offer you any of the lemon that's been in the fridge for at least a month,' Lulu said.

Ehlana sat up and stared at the open doorway. In the distance she could see Lulu staring back. 'Oh, God, you're not temperance, are you? I didn't mean to offend. I can always get you a glass of water, if you'd prefer,' she gushed.

'I must sound foolish, but the only drink I recognise is water. The only thing I have ever drunk is water.' She felt so much like a confused child that Lulu's suggestion that she start with a glass of

16

orange juice was gratefully accepted. Lulu, however, poured herself a very large gin with a very small tonic, grabbed her cigarettes from her bag and moved back towards the bedroom. Ehlana had managed to sit up on the soft edge of the divan by the time Lulu returned.

'Here, try this. If you don't like it, we'll try something else,' she said, grinning. For some reason Lulu couldn't quite fathom, she didn't feel the slightest bit threatened by Ehlana. Ehlana, however, was getting to grips with the strange, thick fluid.

'Sunfire, but this is wonderful. I can't describe it – it stabs my tongue and soothes my throat all at once. What is it? How do you make it?' The training she had thought futile cut through her confusion. This journey was all that the others could never have been and she had only just arrived!

They talked all night, or at least, Lulu had been answering Ehlana's questions through the night. The few questions that Lulu had been allowed to ask had left her more confused than before. They had both agreed that there was no way that either could ascertain the other's correct position in time.

The ringing of the alarm had suddenly caused Ehlana to gauge the passing of hours. When Lulu explained that six hours had passed since her arrival, Ehlana began to realise the exact nature of her problem. She had been analysing only the history and had completely failed to judge the reality of her situation. Not only had they sent her way too far, they probably had no idea where she was and therefore could not set the History Machine to find her. A random search could take months or, worse, years! She knew that they might

17

even fail to find her at all. Overwhelmed by this, she burst into tears.

'Don't cry, Suzie,' said Lulu. 'What you need is sleep. You've come a long way and if any of us travel too far we get this thing called jet-lag – I suppose you've got time-lag! Listen, I've got to go to work, but I'll be back as soon as I can. You go to bed, I'm sure you'll feel better once you've slept.'

'I don't know that I can. I'm so very far away from home and no one even knows it,' was Ehlana's tearful reply.

'I've got a couple of sleeping pills you can have. They'd knock out an elephant – shit, very large grey mammal with big ears and a trunk. Honestly, they're perfectly okay, I have them for those odd nights when I just can't seem to drop off. I'll make you a cup of tea – you'll like it – and then you can just slip beneath the sheets and dream until I get home. Then we'll talk some more.'

'Just one more thing,' Ehlana began. 'You have now twice called me by another name. Who is Suzie?'

'My younger sister, but so much like me that people often assumed we were twins. Once she'd finished school she came up to London to live with me – she'd been living with our aunt since our parents died. I was still flying then and, apart from the company, it was good to have her here looking after things while I was away. We were always very close. But I had a long-haul flight to do just after she'd split up with her boyfriend. I thought she was all right, so I left her. I should only have been gone about twenty-four hours, but the flight got fog-bound in Chicago and by the time I got back to the flat Suzie was dead. She'd taken an overdose. I don't think she meant to kill herself, I think she expected I'd find her in time to do something, but I was too late,' Lulu explained, her face turned away from Ehlana's gaze. 'After that I gave up flying and got a desk-job. I just couldn't bear running the risk of being too far away if anyone needed help again. Anyway, if I don't get my act together right now and get to the shop, I shan't even have a job.' She moved towards the door. Ehlana could now see the tear tracks on Lulu's face. But Lulu was gone before she could think of anything to say. And soon after, Ehlana was fast asleep.

She was dreaming again. Once more, Ehlana found herself in the white, airy chamber. This time, though, there were no other women and she was not free to move around. Instead, she lay naked on a divan. Her wrists and ankles were bound to each corner of the bed and her mouth was gagged with a silk scarf. Slowly, she became aware of someone softly stroking her left instep and the room became suddenly darker. She managed to raise her head and saw a man. It was not Jodai this time, but a total stranger. He smiled at her and started to massage her other foot. She lay back on the pillows and idly considered whether she should make an appointment to see her Evaluator. But it felt too good to do anything other than lie back and enjoy the present experience. Slowly the man's hands began to move up her calves. Then they stopped. A cool, moist sensation was followed by his hands again, moving so smoothly that she guessed he must be oiling her. Again the coolness came, this time upon her thighs. A long sigh slipped through

19

her silk muzzle and she heard a low laugh from the foot of the bed. His hands passed over the sides of her thighs and he moved to kneel between her legs. He stopped there a moment, smiling at her while she looked at him. Unlike her earlier dream, this man had straight, dark hair, a thick, dark moustache and strong shoulders tapering to a narrow, boyish waist. His eyes, too, were dark, but sparkled as if with some mischievous intent. Looking down at her, he threw back his head and laughed.

'I promised I'd do it one day,' he said, 'and now I've caught you.' His voice was warm and deep. He continued to stroke her, first her hips and then her belly. He stopped to reach again for a bottle of oil and then, slowly, his hands moved towards her breasts. She felt her nipples harden even before he touched them, rolled them gently between finger and thumb, but when he bent his head to suck at one she felt as if she was falling again through time. Moments seemed to stretch into hours and she prayed that he would never stop. As he sucked, he moved a hand towards that one part of her he had not yet visited. So slowly his hand moved over the downy patch at the juncture of her thighs that she was too frightened even to breathe, for fear of scaring it away. Softly it parted the fern-like guardians of a secret she had never discovered herself and slid, viscously, between her swollen lips. He kissed her then, hard against the silken folds across her mouth, then little, light, moist kisses all the way down her body from her chin to that small spot he fingered. She knew immediately when his tongue took over the task of masseur – she felt its touch in the core of her being. Insistently, it pulsed against her, forcing her heart to beat in time with its rhythm. Her body racked itself to get that small bud closer to his tongue as it licked and flicked. Her breaths came rapidly as she tried to fight against an overwhelming need to give in. And, finally, she felt herself go rigid against him, wave after wave of pleasure rippling through her body.

As she fell back, afterwards, he moved back up her body and pulled away the gag.

'Oh, God, I love it when you're passive,' he said, and then pressed his lips against her mouth, his tongue slipping, snake-like, past her teeth.

Still kissing her, he raised her buttocks onto his thighs and thrust his stake deep inside her. Her pain was only marginally greater than his, for she stifled her scream by biting down hard on his tongue.

'Shit! Lulu, what the hell did you do that for?' he shouted as he leapt away from her, his hand flying to his mouth.

'Lulu? Sunfire! Then this is no dream!' said Ehlana, waking with a suddenness that surprised her.

The bedroom door opened and Lulu stormed in.

'Jesus, Clem, what the fuck do you think you're doing?' she demanded.

'Lulu? What the hell's going on?' said Clem, looking at his irate girlfriend who stood, fully-clad, and framed by the doorway. 'If she's Lulu, then who the hell are you?' he asked.

'I am Ehlana. I am so sorry, I thought that you were a part of my dream. I had no idea where I was or even when,' Ehlana rambled, more confused than she had been when she first arrived.

'Clem, you go and put the kettle on. I'll be out in a few minutes,' said Lulu as she threw him a robe

21

from behind the door. He put it on and followed her orders.

Lulu sat down on the bed beside a very perplexed Ehlana and began to untie the ropes that held her.

'Listen, I'm the one who ought to apologise. I really should have called Clem and told him I'd got someone staying. He's used to just letting himself in when he's in town and I guess he couldn't resist the temptation. He didn't know it wasn't me,' she explained.

'But what did he do? I know my dreams are barbarian, but how could he have known to get into my dream? Do you have dreams like that?' asked Ehlana.

'Dreams? If I'm lucky, but I prefer the real thing!' answered Lulu.

'You mean that it happens like that often?'

'As often as it can. Let me get this straight, you don't have sex?'

Ehlana looked blankly back at her.

'Sex: you know, procreation, mating, fornication. How do you reproduce?' Lulu looked as puzzled as her twin.

'The gametes are harvested at birth and then, in the spring after the donor dies, cross-pollination takes place in the Laboratory ready for the next Hatching,' Ehlana explained, as if to a foolish child. 'How else can it be done?'

'Exactly the way you were just doing it with Clem. Except that I think our way is a lot more fun. Christ, you must have travelled thousands of years. Doesn't anybody do it where you come from?'

'Not that I'm aware of. But why would you do it often, when it is so painful?' Ehlana replied. How strange, she thought. Atavistic memories are con-

22

sidered to be so very rare. I wonder how many of us have them without even realising what they are?

'Hell, no, it only hurts the first time. Listen, I've got some stuff to sort out with Clem. I bought you this: a single volume that purports to give the history of the world. I don't believe it can be very precise in so few pages, but otherwise I would have had to stagger home with a full set of encyclopaedias. You sit and read; I'll go and organise a cup of tea.' Lulu handed her the book, surprised that Ehlana just sat there, looking at it as though it might bite her. 'Anything wrong?' she asked.

'No. It is just that I have only ever seen these in the museum. They are sealed away in airtight containers so all that you ever read are the same two pages. It seems wrong to be holding one, that is all,' Ehlana replied.

Ehlana, left on her own, was torn between the book and her body. Initially, her body won and she stood for some time staring at herself in the full-length mirror on the front of Lulu's wardrobe door. Did she look different now? Her experience certainly made her feel different. She cupped a hand around her left breast, gently rubbing its nipple as Clem had, and marvelled at its hardness. Her other hand slipped down between her legs to play between her still moist folds. She could have stood there for hours, but her training called her back and she sat, cross-legged upon the bed, and began to read.

Some time passed before she realised how thirsty she was – the promised tea had never appeared – so she decided to go into the living-room to find Lulu.

23

She did not have to look too far. Lulu was naked, kneeling astride a prostrate Clem.

'Thought you'd caught me out, did you, you bastard! I'll teach you to try and tie me up,' she moaned, as she rocked to and fro over his body, her eyes tight shut. Ehlana was fascinated by the gentle swing of Lulu's breasts and watched them as if mesmerised. Slowly, she walked towards the bodies, drawn by the lodestone of pendulous flesh, and reached out to touch Lulu's nipple as Clem had touched hers. She traced each tiny wrinkle on the brown, stiffened flesh.

Lulu looked up then, her tongue darting out between her red lips as if to moisten them.

'Well, twin, how do you think we should punish this man of mine for his audacity?' she asked Ehlana.

'I am very new to these games. I think I need instruction!' Ehlana replied.

'Shit! There's only so much a guy can take, Lulu,' said Clem, sounding quite desperate.

'If you hadn't tried to be clever, you wouldn't be suffering the consequences, would you, darling?' replied Lulu, caustically. 'Anyway, I don't think we want to listen to you whining. The only solution that I can think of requires your assistance, Ehlana. I think you need to sit on his face and then he'll be too busy to complain. Kneel down, facing me. You can put your hands upon my shoulders to steady yourself.'

Ehlana followed her tutelage obediently.

'Now,' said Lulu, 'slide back along his chest until you can feel his tongue against your clit. There, that's it,' she said, as a beatific smile appeared on Ehlana's face.

Lulu recommenced her gentle rocking as Clem's tongue repeated its earlier ministrations. Ehlana, curious, put a hand down to where Lulu and Clem's bodies met, her fingers luxuriating in the damp forest they found. Gingerly, she moved a digit to find the nub of flesh Lulu owned, which she knew must be twin to that on which Clem suckled. Finding it, she started a gentle massage, trying to ape the movements Clem made against her own.

'Aaah,' groaned Lulu. 'Whatever you do, don't stop. I couldn't bear it if you stopped.'

Encouraged, Ehlana increased the pressure of her touch and, at the same time, pushed herself harder against Clem's mouth. Lulu bent forward, caught Ehlana's left nipple between her teeth and bit softly.

'Sunfire,' murmured Ehlana. 'How could we not know of this?' She felt as if her very existence hung between two mouths, each gently pulling at her, drawing her essence into themselves.

Lulu ground harder against Ehlana's finger, demanding more and more. She had stopped rocking and it felt to Ehlana as if her finger was trapped in yet another mouth: harder but still damp and warm. She felt Lulu start to shudder against her hand, her breaths torn from deep inside her.

'Now! Do it now! Don't stop, please don't stop,' Lulu shouted, rubbing herself maniacally against Ehlana's hand. Suddenly, she slumped forward against Ehlana, a great, ragged sigh bursting forth. Instinctively, Ehlana moved her hand away.

'Just let me get my breath back, and we'll swap,' said Lulu, grinning wildly. She half rose, half rolled away from Clem and granted Ehlana her first true look at the thing that had hurt her. It towered up from between his legs, its great head looking angrily red. At its tip she saw a single, pearly droplet and she could not resist leaning forward to lick it away. She felt Clem's moan throughout her whole body, starting as it did in her own moist cleft. Prompted by his reaction, she leant further forward, taking the large head into her mouth, sucking on it as Lulu had sucked on her nipple.

'Not too much of that,' warned Lulu. 'He's not allowed to come until you've fucked him. Actually, I think it's probably time that you did. Give me a hand and I'll help you stand up.'

Ehlana was pleased of her support, as her legs felt decidedly weak.

'Now, turn around and kneel with your legs either side of his hips. I promise it won't hurt you this time, at least I don't think it will, certainly not as much as before.' Lulu knelt down beside her and expertly steered Clem's penis between Ehlana's swollen labia. Ehlana flinched, her muscles spasming nervously around Clem's distended head.

'Oh, god, Lulu, I can't take much more,' Clem whimpered.

'Shh, baby, not long now, I promise,' she crooned back at him. 'Relax, Ehlana, he won't hurt you this time. Just ease down slowly, swallow him deep inside you, as far as he can go.' She massaged Ehlana with her voice and her hands, 'There, doesn't that feel wonderful?' Ehlana could manage no more than a groan in reply. 'Now, slide yourself gently up and down his shaft. Sometimes it feels really good to slide it nearly out, just holding on at the end – you can feel his pulse throbbing there. Then I like to gobble him up again, all the way down to his balls.' Clem let out a strangled cry. 'Not yet, baby,' she told him. Then, to Ehlana, 'Not too fast or he'll be there before you.' As she had threatened earlier, Lulu then straddled Clem's face, coaxing him into action.

One of Clem's hands moved around to cup Lulu's breast and the other started drumming an insistent rhythm against Ehlana's tumescent bud. Ehlana tried to move in time with his rubbing, which became faster and stronger each time she slid along his pole. Wildly she rode him and his hips rose to meet each thrust.

'Now! Now! Now!' screamed Lulu. Unmistakeably, Clem's resistance flew away and an incredible throbbing filled Ehlana's void. An invisible force tore through her very soul and hurled her, panting, down against the other steamy bodies.

Almost in unison, Ehlana and Lulu rolled off Clem's exhausted frame. He seemed able to do nothing but breathe, and even that sounded laboured.

Eventually, he crawled away from them. 'I need a bloody drink,' he said. 'Anybody else want one?' Lulu began to laugh, an infectious sound and soon Ehlana joined her. The relief she felt was immense, as though she had been waiting for it all her life. Perhaps she had, she thought.

The strangeness of the society she visited took her by surprise. They had so much that they took for granted: books, for one; the odd, but wonderful, habit of immersing the entire body in warm water in order to wash – profligate, but marvellous; a variety of grains and vegetables that took her breath away. She did not think, though, that she would ever become accustomed to the eating of flesh: she could still recall her nausea as Lulu explained what she ate.

Five days passed before Ehlana felt the tell-tale vibration begin in the crystal at her neck. Part of her rejoiced at being found and another part was loath to leave this place. She had hardly slept, so keen she had been to explore all aspects of life. Lulu and Clem had arranged it so that she was never idle and had taken her to see so many new things. But she knew it was only a matter of minutes, if that long, before she was drawn home. She had previously warned Lulu that her departure, once it started, would be swift. A warning cry left her throat and Lulu ran to her.

'Already? I'd hoped for longer. There's so much more for you to see,' said Lulu. 'If you find a way, come back – you'll always be welcome. Oh, here, take your book, and Clem left these for you – as souvenirs.' She pressed several small packets of seeds into Ehlana's hands. Tears were starting to well from Lulu's eyes, 'Bye, twin. Be good.'

The pull back to her own time was both strong and painful. Ehlana found herself incapable of uttering a word, it was all she could do to grasp the book and push Clem's gift into the pocket of her borrowed jeans. She just had time to pull her Guild Ring from her finger and hurl it towards Lulu before the room disappeared, replaced by the black void. Hugging her book tight to her chest, she prayed she would not drop it.

Chapter Three

Nucassel, August 3550PS

*T*hree people caught her as she fell from the
platform. Her return voyage had been no less
painful than her outward journey. By the time she
regained her senses there were many more in the
Laboratory than she remembered being there at the
moment of her arrival.

'Ehlana, dear child,' cried Magister Tolai as he
threw the door open and strode in. 'We had nearly
given up hope. When have you been, girl, and what
do you hold in your hand?' The interrogation
started then.

More than four hours passed before they allowed
her to return to her room. Her Guild-brother,
Liranai, walked her there and Ehlana was hard put
to make him leave. She craved some time alone,
but she had not been back long enough to draw
breath before there was a pounding at her door.

'Ehlana, it's me, Jodai,' she heard. 'Please let me
in!'

She opened the door and was swept up in his arms as he rushed in.

'I thought you gone forever. Where have you been? What happened?' He put her down on her feet and stepped back. 'Forgive me, I don't know what's the matter with me. I've felt strange ever since you left. If you would prefer that I return at some other time, I shall not mind.'

'No, Jodai. There's no problem. Sit and we'll talk,' Ehlana replied.

The hours passed, until at last she had told him everything, apart from the thing she still had not worked out how to explain.

'My only sadness,' she said, 'is that I did not bring you anything.'

'Sunfire! It's just so good to see you. But what are you wearing? I've never seen its like.' Ehlana had entirely forgotten that she still wore Lulu's shirt and jeans. In their excitement over the book, none of her Guild brethren had even noticed her strange clothes and she had been so busy answering their questions that she had completely overlooked Clem's gifts, which still lay crammed into her trouser pocket. Reaching for them, she opened a packet and laughed.

'Oh, Jodai, I did bring you something. Look! Seed stock! I do not know if the journey will have harmed them, but you saw how the book looks no older than it did when I received it.'

Like a small child, filled with wonder, he studied the pictures on the seed packets and, almost reverently, opened their paper wrappers to peer, without touching, at the treasures inside. She pressed his hand and he looked at her, unable to speak.

'They were a gift from a man I met,' she

30

explained. 'In a lot of ways he reminded me of you. It is appropriate that he thought to give me them, of all things, and I believe he would be glad that I give them to you.'

'Oh, Ehlana,' was all Jodai could say, overwhelmed.

'If you want to go, I understand, but don't leave it too long before you come again. There are other things that I would like to share with you,' she said.

He pressed her hand in parting and left, closing the door behind him.

The next few weeks were chaos, there was so much information she needed to pass on. She spent most of her time with Magister Tolai and her colleagues. Each new thing she recalled was painstakingly investigated and, at last, the Magister decided that the most likely reason why she had been taken from her prescribed route was because she was female. Certainly, no such thing had happened to any other Historian and the only common factor was that they were all men. She asked why she had not been affected on other journeys. Tolai concluded it was because on her previous trips she had always been accompanied: this time she had travelled alone. For some reason, the History Machine had appeared to send her to the closest link in her time-line, metaphysically rather than temporally.

Tolai explained that because they had no other source to draw on, it would be of great benefit if she were prepared to travel solo again. The Magister also warned her that because of her strange influence upon the History Machine, she ran the risk of being lost to them permanently. As a precaution, Liranai had suggested she wear a larger crystal

– he believed it might make it easier for the Machine to track her.

'Whatever decision you reach, Ehlana,' the Magister said as he walked her back to her room, 'there will be no loss of honour. You have already done much to further our studies. Once your news spreads throughout our community we are bound to have more females sign up for History classes. We certainly have many years work to do already from what you brought with you, so you do not need to worry if you decide not to travel again. I will leave you to make your decision.' It had not occurred to Ehlana that she would have a choice – they would have had to restrain her to stop her!

Ehlana had already made up her mind, but felt in need of some respite. She knew that no one would rush her and took advantage of this. She also knew that she might not be able to return to her own time, and used this as an opportunity to do the one thing she wanted to do before she left. Now all she needed to do was find Jodai.

Dressing again in the comfort of Lulu's clothes (comments had been made, but she chose to ignore them), she was just about to leave her room when there was a knock at the door.

'What timing!' she said as she opened the door to find Jodai standing there. 'I was just coming to find you.'

'And I was just coming to find you. Liranai said that Magister Tolai was taking you home.' He held a small pot towards her. Nestling in the middle of the soil was a vivid, green shoot. 'Look. They are all growing. Only three failed to germinate. I smuggled this one out to show you. Magister Pula would have me hung if she knew, but as she would not grant me permission to bring you to see them, it was my only alternative!'

'I am so pleased. I was afraid that the journey would have killed them and then all you would have been left with were the pictures on their packets. Which one is this?' Ehlana asked.

'Orange. I remembered you speaking of the drink. I promise that, if its bears fruit, you will drink it again,' he replied, looking so serious that Ehlana nearly laughed.

'Come and sit. I need to talk to you,' Ehlana said. 'I will be travelling again soon and I cannot be sure that I will return. It seems so long since my last departure, when all was certain. But now, who can tell? There are some things I have told no one and I need to be sure that, if I tell you, you will not break my confidence. Can you give me your word?' she asked.

Jodai looked at her carefully. 'I swear it,' he replied. 'But are you sure you prefer me to hear, not Mara or Lomai? I should not be offended; I know you have always got on more easily with our other hatchlings.'

'No. If anyone, it has to be you. But it may offend, and I would not do that to you lightly. If it becomes unbearable, you must tell me to stop, but you have to promise never to tell anyone,' she said.

'I vow by the Sunfire that I shall never reveal a word,' he said solemnly. 'Is that enough, or would you have me cut my tongue out too?'

She smiled. 'Your word is enough.' She moved towards the window and looked out over the city. 'Before I travelled, I had strange dreams. Barbarian dreams. I dreamt of naked bodies, of weird intimacies, of another's flesh pressed close to my own. Sometimes strangers, sometimes friends. Even though I knew they were wrong, I did not go to the Evaluator. As I told you, I met two people when I travelled: a woman and a man. And while I was in their time, I did with them the things that I had dreamt of. Oh, Jodai, it was magical. Even now, my skin burns with remembrance of it.' She turned to look at him, and he looked away. She swallowed hard. 'If you would rather that I do not continue, I need not,' she said.

'No. I too have had those dreams. I thought I was the only one. But, it was always the same people that I dreamt of. I did go to my Evaluator and he convinced me that it was improper. "An abuse of my hatchlings", he called it.' He still could not look up to meet her gaze.

'He was wrong. It is no abuse, believe me. It is the most natural thing in the universe, but somehow we have forgotten that.' As she spoke she started to unbutton her shirt. 'I need you to help me remember, Jodai. I need to feel your body pressed close to mine.' She could see Jodai swallow hard as he sat, perched, on the edge of her couch. She slid the sleeves from her arms and walked towards him, bared from the waist up. Standing in front of him, she took his left hand and cupped it against her right breast. Beneath his trembling palm she felt her nipple swell, engorged and taut. She pressed his hand closer against her skin until he could not help but notice the hard peak. Glancing down into his lap, she could see his own tumescence straining against the fabric of his robe. She held her other breast and stroked it, drawing her fingers back and forth across the stiffening flesh of her nipple. Jodai appeared fascinated at the way the lines and furrows developed as it hardened and, finally, reached out to gently trace its outline with his index finger. Ehlana let out a deep sigh. It seemed as though a million years had passed since another's hand had touched her this way.

Emboldened, Jodai leant forward and licked wetly around her distended nipple, flicking it lightly with his tongue. She pushed his head down hard on to her breast and, instinctively, he started to suck. Ehlana nearly fainted – she felt as if he suckled on her soul. Swiftly, she undid her jeans and wriggled out of them until she stood there, naked. Stroking his hair, she spoke.

'Stand up and take off your robe. I need to hold you and feel our bodies close together.'

Silent, but obedient, he did as she had asked. The meagre light from the sun seemed somehow to turn his naked form to gleaming alabaster. Ehlana stretched forth and touched his strong chest with her hands, running her fingertips along well-developed pectorals and over his suddenly hardening nipples.

'Look,' she said. 'They behave the same way as mine!' Reasoning that what had felt so good for her must therefore feel as good for him, she bent forward and caught the pale brown nut of his nipple gently between her teeth while she flicked her tongue across its tip. Jodai threw back his head and howled as the fires of his first orgasm ripped through his body, his seed pumping out over her thighs.

She pushed him, unresisting, back upon the couch. Her lips still nuzzled at his flesh while she clambered across his thighs, his deflating prick sliding wetly beneath her belly. Creeping upwards she changed her attention from his nipple to his mouth, kissing him first with little, dry pecks which became stronger as her need for him grew. At first she encountered his teeth, but he soon opened to her, their tongues duelling within. As their embrace continued, she felt the first, gentle stirrings of his other sword. Fearing it anxious for encouragement, she slithered down along his body until her mouth found the swollen, pink head. She sucked it in, hungry for the feel of its roundness against her tongue. Slowly, she slid her mouth over his silken shaft, pushing herself down until her nose brushed against the blond curls at the base of his prick. She could feel his pulse throbbing within and she knew it would not be long before he peaked again. His hand came down to lie gently on the back of her head and he stroked her hair as she moved lingeringly over his shaft. She snaked a finger down to rub gently against his tiny wrinkled hole – as Clem had liked – and nearly gagged as he wrapped his digits in her hair, pushing his whole length deep into her mouth while his juices surged. Afterwards, as he lay there panting, she stretched out alongside him. She opened her legs wide and, with her left hand, softly parted her swollen labia to reveal the hard bud that stood there proudly. With her right hand she reached for one of his, placing it over her left.

'Here,' she said. 'Touch me here. Give me the same feeling I gave to you. Rub it, slowly, gently. Oh, yes, just like that.' Jodai, slightly recovered, was now leaning on his side, gazing down at her body beside him, as he languidly ran a finger around and around her clitoris. Her hand still held her labia open and, leaning forward to inspect this special place, he decided that it merited a closer look. Kneeling between her legs, he stared in fascination. From her own knowledge of Lulu she knew intimately the strange, damp seashell shape that confronted him; she felt him push back the hood that tried, unsuccessfully, to cover her exposed, erect bud; an exploratory finger wormed its way inside her, slipping warmly between her silken folds. Bending lower, his tongue flicked out to taste the route from hole to tiny hillock, then returned to feast upon sweet juices. As he sucked and licked, she sneaked a finger down to continue the massage she knew was required. But no matter how hard she rubbed, she could not find the release she sought.

Pushing his head away from her groin, she said, 'Roll over on to your back. I'll show you something else we have forgotten.'

As he complied with her command, she positioned herself again astride him. During his earlier oral ministrations his prick had regained its former appearance and rose stiffly above his belly. With consummate ease she impaled herself upon his swollen wand and began to ride upon him, slowly at first, then more insistent and, finally, bucking wildly above his trembling form. This savage friction culminated in their simultaneous explosion, Jodai calling her name aloud whilst she collapsed upon his chest, weeping with relief at her deliverance.

'Sunfire,' breathed Jodai. 'What have we done? My dreams never erupted like that. Did I hurt you?'

'No, no pain – only pleasure,' was Ehlana's reply, as she lay exhausted beside him. 'As I understand it, the act was procreative, but in the time I travelled to it was almost purely a recreational pastime.'

'I cannot understand how we were persuaded to abandon it,' Jodai mused. 'When do you plan to leave?'

'Tomorrow, I think. At least I will if I can persuade the Magister,' she replied.

'Can I come to you again tonight?' he asked, an expression of hope written clear across his features.

'Oh, Jodai. One part of me desperately wants to say yes, but I have no idea what we risk if we are caught. There must be some reason why the subject has become so taboo that none of us have even the vaguest idea of its existence. We must steal our moments when we can, not go courting disaster.'

'Sadly, I must concur. Whilst you travel, I shall endeavour to find out when we lost the art, and why. But I do not think I can bear it if you do not return soon,' he added, ruefully.

'Whether it be a day, or a million years, I will come back to you,' she vowed, pressing his hand against her breast, no longer bared, but covered by the ochre shift they all wore.

'Go now, before I beg you to stay.'

'Farewell and travel safely, my dearest hatchling,' he called from the doorway. 'Until your return.'

Alone again, she stood at her window, watching the sun set. She shivered a little, gazing out at the stark lands beyond the city's dome, so different from where she was journeying to. Too early to sleep, she decided to visit the Field. All her life it had been the one thing guaranteed to lift her spirits, but she had avoided it since her return.

The streets were almost empty as she walked. It

would be nearly dark outside when she reached her goal. The Field, however, was brightly lit when she arrived. The lights would stay on for another four hours yet, giving the plants the extra time they needed in order to survive. She stood at the portal and her heart ached. With Lulu she had journeyed outside the other's city, to a strange land: trees and grass and fields as far as the eye could see, dotted about with buildings. The whole so vast and huge and green that Ehlana had almost panicked. When she explained to Lulu that little more than a hectare of such land existed in her own time, she was overcome with grief that they had lost so much. They had sat in Lulu's car and a proposed trip that afternoon to a place called the zoo had been cancelled. Lulu never did tell her why, but from her friend's demeanour she had surmised that it would cause her more heartache. She had not described the full extent of their loss to anyone since her return, but standing there, consumed by a fierce passion, she pledged that she would do all she could to find some hope for the Field.

The following morning, she rose early, donned a clean shift, her crystal and her determination, and went to the Laboratory. Magister Tolai and two of his colleagues were already at work.

'Magister, my mind is made up and I am minded to travel. Would you have any objections to sending me now?' she asked, her formality overcoming her fear of the pain she knew might accompany her journey.

'If you are decided, Ehlana, then I would not dare to stop you.' He led her over to the platform and helped her to step upon it. 'Where is your Guild

39

Ring, child?' he asked, gazing at the hand that he held.

'Oh, Magister. I left it as a gift when I travelled last – it was all I possessed to give – save for my crystal and I knew I could not be parted from that. I am sorry, but I had not thought to report its loss.'

'No matter. Take mine, you might have need of gifts again!' Then, more seriously, he said, 'As you know, last time we did not know when you were and it took us some while to find you. I have no reason to believe it will not be the same again.' He had moved back to his apparatus, and put forth a hand to caress the History Machine. 'But, so long as the crystal still sings for you, we shall hunt until we find you. Farewell and study hard, my daughter. Our hearts and hopes travel with you.' With his parting words he threw the switch that powered the Machine and the Mother Crystal's song began.

More quickly than she recalled, the pain began to mount inside her and her moan rose in increasing crescendo. She hoped, in that small part of her mind that still functioned, that becoming 'lost' did not suspend one in the pain-filled void for ever. Already her journey seemed longer than the previous one and above the crystal's discord she could hear her own voice, a thin, wailing scream.

Chapter Four

London, August 1984AD

She landed, awkwardly, on a warm green carpet of grass. Bending down to rub her wrenched ankle, she was first startled when a hand fell on her shoulder and then immediately reassured by a familiar voice.

'Ehlana? Is that really you?'

Straightening and turning all at once, she found herself gazing, eye to eye, at a woman a little older than herself. Whilst she and Lulu had before been virtual twins, the resemblance they shared now was tinged with difference. Mere weeks had passed for Ehlana, yet for her friend clearly some years had gone by.

'It is me. How long have I been?' she replied.

'It must be at least five and a half years. We'd almost given up hoping that we'd see you again. Come on, we'll go back to the flat and find Clem – he's going to be amazed!' Lulu grabbed Ehlana's hand and started towards an opening in the black-rodded fence that stood between them and the

41

sinuous line of slow-moving metal that snaked on the road beyond. Darting between the cars, she dragged the reluctant Ehlana across and down a side street, running all the while until they came to a larger road where the traffic moved swifter. A black vehicle with an amber light responded to Lulu's frantic gesticulations and pulled to a halt beside them.

'Nevern Square, SW5,' she told the driver, opening the door and drawing Ehlana in beside her in one continuous movement. 'So, how have you been? What's new since you were last here?'

'So little,' Ehlana replied. 'I have been gone for less than six weeks.'

'Well that accounts for why you look so much better than I do. I thought it might be all that pure living that kept you looking so great. Either that, or I'm way too depraved for my own good!'

Ehlana, looking bashful, replied, 'My life is no longer so pure. I returned and shared bodies with one of my hatchlings. Once awakened to the possibilities, he grew to enjoy it even more swiftly than I, suffering neither pain nor discomfiture.' She shivered, a frisson of remembered pleasure passing again throughout her body.

'Explain again about your hatchlings, would you? I still don't entirely understand the relationship,' said Lulu.

'The size of each year's Hatching is dependent upon the number of deaths during the preceding twelve months. A gamete from each of the deceased is fertilised and the resulting zygote is incubated. There can be many zygotes, few or even none. Incubation takes nine months and the resultant infants are reared together until the age of eight.

There were four in my hatching. Close friendship between hatchlings is normal and often all elect to follow the same vocation. I was the sole Historian in my group,' she explained.

'Why so rigid? Why not allow the parents to share time with their kid?' Lulu interjected.

'To maintain the population level. Two thousand is the number and cannot be exceeded. As to parents, we honour their works and acknowledge that in their passing they gave us life. All things are as they must be, as the Sleepers decreed,' Ehlana replied, reciting each statement like a catechism.

Lulu opened her mouth, but the taxi pulled to a stop before she had a chance to formulate her next question.

They clambered out and Lulu duly paid the driver. Opening the front door, she tore up the stairs, shouting loudly for Clem. By the time they reached the third floor he was hanging over the banister looking down towards them.

'Where's the fire, then?' he said, not noticing Ehlana who was following quietly behind.

'We've got a visitor!' exclaimed Lulu.

'As long as it's not your mother, I don't mind,' he replied caustically, then, 'Oh, my god, Ehlana! When did you get here? How long will you stay?' His questions tumbled haphazardly at her, whilst she stood there unable to reply. Five years had etched lines on his face and turned his dark hair grey at the temples. He threw his arms around her waist, lifting her up and drawing her close. 'Hell, but it's good to see you again.'

Lulu bustled them good-naturedly into the flat. 'Come along, children, we can do all this so much more comfortably sitting down than we can in the hall. I'll get us a drink while you get over the shock!' Lulu moved towards the kitchen, leaving Clem and Ehlana alone. After his initial exuberance, he seemed a little distant now.

'So how long can you stay this time?' he asked. 'I don't want to run the risk of you going again without giving me the opportunity to say goodbye. Did any of the seeds grow?'

'Jodai told me that only three failed to germinate. I saw one of the seedlings before I left,' she replied.

'Five years for a seedling? At that rate you won't get an orange for decades!'

'Time has passed slower for me. I was only home for six weeks. In fact, the difference will be much cause for learned debate when I return. It was agreed that they would attempt to discover my location but not pull me home until twenty-eight days have passed, providing that they manage to find me in that time. It is possible that I could be here for as long as three years, on that basis, or even longer if they cannot find me. How much of my return before was blind chance is unknown. I could not even be sure when I would travel to this morning, far less imagine that I would journey here again. I am much pleased that I have. It is good to see you again, my friend,' she said gently, leaning forward to touch his hand in greeting.

Lulu returned then with a tray. 'Do your magic stuff with this, then,' she said, handing Clem a large green bottle. Droplets of moisture glistened along its length and its apex was covered with gold. Deftly he shredded this and removed the metal cage beneath. A loud pop was followed by a cascade of golden liquid which he expertly caught in a tall, slender glass. Ehlana stared, transfixed by his wizardry. 'It's champagne,' explained Lulu. 'It's the only thing to drink back here when you want to celebrate. Purists only ever drink it on its own, but it's good with orange juice, too. Here try it straight, first, and then with the orange juice if you want to.' She handed Ehlana the first glass.

Ehlana sipped: it felt as if liquid laughter filled her mouth, a myriad tiny bubbles exploding against her tongue before they slid mischievously down her throat. Then she greedily emptied her glass.

'Not too fast or you'll end up forgetting your name!' Lulu admonished as she poured her another glass. 'Maybe you'd better try it this way,' and she topped it up with orange juice.

Ehlana sipped again. 'I think I would have to drink a great deal more before I selected my preference. This way definitely adds another dimension to the fruit!'

'So, where are you going to take us two girls tonight?' Lulu asked Clem.

'Much as I'd like to have you both to myself, we've already promised to see Richard and Tom at Trader Vic's, so I guess we'll start there and then see how things grab us. Okay?'

'Mm, suits me,' Lulu replied. 'I'll fill you in on all the details, Ehlana, while we try and work out what to wear.' She refilled Clem's glass, picked up her own and walked towards the bedroom. 'Come on, Ehlana, and don't forget your drink. We've only got two hours to get ready!'

Ehlana followed and sat, as directed, on the edge of Lulu's bed, sipping obediently from time to time as Lulu whirled from wardrobe to chest of drawers and back again, each visit adding another item to the rapidly increasing piles of rejected clothes on the floor. Occasionally something would satisfy Lulu's obscure criteria and make it as far as the bed for later consideration, but for the most part dresses, skirts and shirts made it only as far as the floor. Ehlana did offer to start returning the unwanted items to their appropriate places, but Lulu quashed that idea.

'Until the cupboards are empty, I can't be sure that I've looked at every possible combination. If you put them back, I'd only end up taking them out again. Don't worry, it won't take me ten minutes to tidy up once I've chosen. If you go and have a bath, I'll be finished by the time you get out.'

Dutifully, Ehlana had begun running a bath, returning more to watch the Wardrobe Mistress at work than to fetch her glass, but Lulu chased her off. 'Have your bath; I'll have narrowed it down to two or three options soon. It'll be your decision after that.'

The warm water lured Ehlana with its siren-song and she slid in and lay back, trying to assimilate all of the new information she had so far gathered. Six weeks or five and a half years had passed: did that mean time moved more slowly where she came from, or were there other factors? The only thing materially different between the two journeys was the size of the crystal she now wore. Before, it had been the standard one carat issued to all graduate Historians; now it was twice that size, especially cut by the Magister, in the hope that the larger crystal would be easier for the Mother stone to find. Before, she and Lulu had been identical; now she must resemble far more the sister that Lulu had loved and lost. Even the journey here, was it Lulu that drew her? The men from her time travelled to their closest kin living at the time they travelled to. Did she travel to the kin she resembled most closely, no matter when that twin existed? There must be a stronger reason than history allowed, or else a second random jump should have taken her almost anywhere else in the past. The possibilities raced in her mind: so many gaps still needing to be filled. And then that small gap between her legs began to ache, perhaps in sympathy – or was it anticipation? She knew that this time she could not expect to share with Clem; the first time had been an accident, the second time his punishment by Lulu. A third time had not arisen. She had understood little of what Lulu had explained with regard to close relationships, but enough to know that sharing such as they had done was rare. Her previous visit, and her games with Jodai, had left her hungry for more. Then Lulu came in and broke her reverie.

'Come on, my turn next. I need you to go and try on what I've left on the bed. See which you like best. If there's nothing there that suits you, I'll just have to start again.' Lulu started stripping off as she spoke, so Ehlana washed hurriedly, rinsed the soap away and stepped out of the water. Wrapping herself in the towel Lulu handed her, she went back into the bedroom to look at what Lulu intended her to wear. Two short dresses and a long one lay waiting for her: one black, one blue and the other a striking green. Discarding the towel, she picked up the first one and held it against her body while she stood before the mirror: too short; the second, so blue that it seemed to wash the colour from her face; the third, however, looked promising. Dry now, she undid its fastening at the back and stepped into it, drawing the sleeves up along her arms, wriggling it over her body and, after an age, fastening it tight around her. The dress fitted like a glove. The cut was immodestly low, raising the curve of her breasts and barely covering her nipples which, at the first fluid caress of the gown's fabric, had grown tight and hard, straining against the confining bodice. From beneath her breasts the gown hung almost to the floor, a verdant silken sheath that rippled as she moved, undulating around her form.

'Somehow I thought it would be that one,' said Lulu as she emerged from the bathroom. 'It looks even better than I imagined. All that's needed now is a little war-paint before we go out and conquer new territories. Sit here in front of the window and I'll see if there are any improvements to be made.'

Ehlana sat patiently while Lulu fetched brushes and powders, offering her face up to be painted on demand. On her earlier trip she had been fascinated to watch Lulu sitting each morning to apply the magic ingredients without which, she was told, Lulu felt undressed. She had never managed to comprehend how a little smear of colour could do so much to alter Lulu's entire appearance.

'Done,' said Lulu, and put forward a hand to draw Ehlana again towards the mirror. From beneath her russet curls peeked a face she barely knew, her lips drawn to a ripe red fullness against the whiteness of her skin, her cheek bones high-lighted and raised to an angular prominence. She lifted a hand to touch her face, half-convinced that the stranger she watched in the glass would fail to touch its own, but instead it mimicked her absol-utely. Even having seen Lulu's artistry at work before had not prepared her for the shock of trans-formation. 'Right, you can go and stun Clem, but make sure he manages to open another bottle. I'll be as quick as I can.'

Clem was reading a paper and only glanced up initially. Then he looked again.

'You do not find it a little too revealing?' Ehlana asked, more from a need to break the silence than from coquetry.

'God, no!' he replied. 'Just quite astonishing. I bought that dress for Lulu in Hong Kong and – '

'And it never looked quite that good on me, did it, darling?' finished Lulu from the other room. 'You can get me a drink, it'll give you something to do with your hands, and let Ehlana watch the news on Channel 4. There's paper and pens on the table, so you can make notes for later questions. Not that there's anything particularly spectacular happening at the moment, August always tends to be the silly season as far as news goes – nothing happens, so they have to invent it: rescuing dogs from trees and cats from old ladies, that sort of thing. Oh, and you'd better fill her in on Richard and Tom.'

Clem did as he was told. 'We went to the same school. I've known them both since we were eleven. They're identical twins – closer than you and Lulu in looks – and considered quite eccentric. They are also marvellous company and very entertaining. The easiest way to deal with their idiosyncrasy is to try and imagine that they're only one person, at least that's what they suggest.'

Ehlana looked confused and Clem didn't try to explain further. 'You'll know exactly what I mean once you've met them.' He brought his drink with him and stood behind her chair for a long while, silent. Ehlana imagined him leaning forward, coming closer, his breath warming her where it touched her skin, his lips brushing her neck. She could not move with the tension she felt as she waited, her breathing shallow and a magical sensation shifted up and down her spine. For one brief instant she felt the warm breeze from his mouth and then he was gone, walking swiftly into the bedroom. Ehlana sighed and turned her attention to the television.

After a short while, she became immersed in the news: surprised that a woman now held power in a country formerly so dominated by male politicians. Clearly significant progress had been made in less than six years! All too soon, Lulu emerged from the bedroom in the very short black dress that Ehlana had first discarded, her legs stretching long and tanned to be finally punctuated by the black, painfully high-heeled shoes that she wore.

'Clem's having a shower. But I've told him not to make me wait more than five minutes or we'll go on without him,' Lulu said, a broad grin on her face.

It was twenty minutes later when he reappeared, during which time Lulu and Ehlana had emptied the second bottle. Ehlana felt light-headed and extremely glad that her feet had proved too small for any of the shoes Lulu had made her try on. A sudden vision of herself teetering wildly on the blade-thin heels, followed by the inevitable collapse into a great green puddle, caused no little mirth, particularly when she was persuaded to let Lulu in on the joke.

* * *

50

They were still giggling when they got out of the taxi. Clem ushered them into the darkness of the club, though Ehlana's eyes grew quickly accustomed to the light. Great plants swathed the walls in greenery and the air was moist and warm. A shout went up from a table hidden in the corner, and the three of them moved towards it. Introductions were made, Ehlana being introduced as a close cousin of Lulu's.

'How charming,' began Richard.

'. . . to make your acquaintance,' finished Tom, or at least Ehlana believed so, it could easily have been the other way around. She had understood the closeness of their kinship, although no such thing existed in her own society. But she had not expected such a studied duplication. They wore the same clothes and had the same coiffure, and yet, there were subtle differences: one parted his hair to the right, the other to the left. Each wore a flower on his lapel, but on the opposite side; time bands identical, but worn on opposite wrists. Each truly mirrored the other in the minutest detail. Drinks were ordered.

'Sit here, between us and see if you can spot a mistake,' said one. Tom, she thought.

'We did make one once, but a long time ago. Apart from which, there is nothing so divine as being studied by something as pretty as you,' said the other, 'as it allows a suitable reciprocation.'

Sensing Ehlana's confusion, the first explained. 'What my brother means is that we have ample opportunity to study you as you watch us, and no one can find cause for complaint at our obvious devotion to the view.'

'I still don't understand entirely,' replied Ehlana.

51

'What he means is that it's usually considered rude to stare,' the other continued, 'but by giving you permission to do as you will with us, you must automatically grant us permission to ogle you. I believe we have the best part of the bargain.'

'Do you often dress to confuse?' Ehlana asked.

'Always,' replied one of them. 'It started before we were born. At the risk of boring you, and certainly boring these two,' he gestured towards Lulu and Clem, 'I would explain that our father, having brought our mother to bed with six consecutive daughters, was so desperate for a son that he planted us both together in her belly.'

'Since our emergence from there thirty-one years ago, we have spent less than three hours apart,' continued the other. 'Our friends think it mere eccentricity, but few realise that without the other we each feel incomplete. Together we are more than two; apart we are less than one.'

'Forgive us if this sounds nonsensical, but it is easier if you understand this now rather than aim to treat us as individuals,' finished the first. 'If nothing else, be thankful that our mother did not have triplets, otherwise there would doubtless have been a Harry also to contend with!' The joke fell a little flat on Ehlana and the twins looked disappointed that their punch-line had failed.

Eager to break the silence that had fallen over the group, Lulu spoke to the brothers. 'So, where are we going to eat?'

'Richard booked a table at Langan's for eight o'clock, but if you don't feel like it we can always go somewhere else,' suggested Tom.

'No, that sounds great. Apart from which, I know how you two love to make a grand entrance,' Lulu

52

replied. They talked generally as they drank, mainly of people that Ehlana had not met, and of Richard and Tom's fledgling company which, as she understood it, earned vast sums of money each time the brothers decorated someone else's home as if it were their own. Understandably, this was beyond Ehlana's comprehension.

'Ah,' said Richard. 'If you saw our house you couldn't help but love it and want yours done in exactly the same fashion. Maybe we should come and visit you at home, we adore country cousins.'

'Are we walking up Piccadilly?' asked Lulu, quickly changing the conversation. 'If so, we really ought to leave soon. There's no way I'm running – these shoes are strictly ornamental!'

Clem went off to pay the bill and the twins stood up, each offering an arm to Ehlana. A little more inebriate than when she had arrived, she placed her own in theirs gratefully and they walked towards the doorway.

'Green Goddess with Bookends – walking works of art by Richard and Tom Godden,' stated Clem as he returned. 'How's that sound for a new trade, boys, if the bottom falls out of interior design?'

'Too much like hard work and we could only be on show one place at a time. I don't think we'll rush to patent the idea,' replied Richard. As they continued walking up the broad, busy road, Ehlana tried unsuccessfully to see what Clem had meant by glancing slyly in the large glass fronts of the buildings they passed.

They reached the restaurant, sat down and ordered. It was loud and bustling, none of the hushed tones Ehlana knew from the Refectory. The large white card she was handed listed more dishes than she could count and she did not know what most of them were. In the end, Lulu guessed her difficulty and asked the twins for some suggestions.

'You're quite sure you wouldn't like meat or fish?' Tom asked. Ehlana nodded vigorously. 'Well, then, I would suggest you have the spinach soufflé to start, it's quite wonderful. And to follow, we'll have to ask Michael if you can have a double helping of the stuffed artichoke heart. It's delicious, full of mushrooms and cream and smothered in hollandaise sauce. How does that sound?' She was quite happy to have someone choose for her: left to her own devices she would still have been studying the enormous menu when the Sunfire came.

The soufflé melted on her tongue, its salty sauce was the perfect complement to the fluffy substance. The artichoke heart was almost indescribable: a rich, yellow sauce covered the dark brown mix of pulped mushrooms and cream, which in turn filled the bowl of a pale green vegetable. A hint of lemon suffused all three and, in combination, proved a delectable choice. Food in her own time was a balanced preparation of nutrients, not a gastronomic event.

A dozen different people came up to their table during the meal to greet the twins and various celebrities were pointed out. The brothers were confused to discover that Ehlana had never heard of any of them.

'Where is it you come from? We shall have to move there if it means one can avoid all knowledge and mention of Terry Wogan!' exclaimed Richard.

'You're unlikely to believe her, even if she could explain it,' answered Lulu.

54

'Try us – we love having our credulity stretched,' replied Tom. 'Go on, Ehlana. Amaze us.'

Ehlana began, hesitantly. 'You must first understand that most of my information is mere hypothesis, but based on the very few facts that I have, I shall be born in approximately three thousand and eight hundred years time. In my own time I am an historian and, for research, my Guild brothers and I travel through time. Normally this has been restricted to a journey of some few hundreds of years. For some reason I am able to travel much further than anyone else. The destination for my colleagues is always determined by ancestry: whichever time they travel to, they will emerge in close physical proximity to a living relative. Judging by the similarities in my appearance to Lulu, it would seem this rule applies to me also. However, my last visit here was five years ago, your time, but six weeks in my own. As yet, I have no real answers to that particular difference. I could continue explaining for some hours, but hope that I have answered most of your questions.'

The two brothers stared at her.

'It's for real,' avowed Lulu. 'I know it sounds preposterous, but I believe her. Clem does, too.' Clem nodded his agreement.

'Well, that'll teach us to ask questions!' exclaimed Tom. 'So, what does your boyfriend think about you jumping around all over the place without him?'

'I do not understand the term. Please explain,' Ehlana asked.

'Boyfriend: lover, partner, suitor, husband. Any of those help?' She shook her head. 'Mate, consort, spouse? Person you live with, share a bed with, usually of the opposite sex, but not necessarily.'

'If you speak of sharing bodies, it is neither necessary nor usual in our society. I do not know why, but my hatchling is trying to find out,' she replied. 'For my part, I am interested in learning all I can of the sharing. It is an alien concept to me, but uniquely pleasing.'

Richard raised an eyebrow and stared inquisitively across at Lulu and Clem.

'It was an accident,' said Clem, a defensive note in his voice. 'I thought she was Lulu – they looked even more alike back then.'

Richard took Ehlana's hand in his and spoke solicitously. 'To have travelled so far and to be dependent upon those two for your education in matters sexual is an utter tragedy. They have spent far too long together to appreciate it in all its glory. You must consider allowing my brother and I to continue your instruction. We shall attempt to answer your every query.'

'You must forgive me if my questions seem awkward,' Ehlana said, hoping she appeared neither too forward nor too ignorant. 'But you must also understand that I come from a place where all dwell singly and desires of the flesh are no more than rare dreams: confined to sleep and, for the most part, forgotten with the daybreak.'

'Talking about daybreak,' said Lulu, 'I've got to work tomorrow. If you four want to go clubbing, that's fine by me, but I really must go home.'

'I'll come with you,' said Clem. 'Ehlana, you can take my key. I'm sure we can rely on the twins to make sure you get back safely when you're ready – that's if you want to?'

'So long as I am not inconveniencing any of you,'

Ehlana readily agreed. 'I must admit I have never felt less like sleeping.'

'Wonderful. Then it's settled. You two go home and we shall entertain this delightful voyager as best we can and deliver her back when she's bored with us,' promised Tom.

Lulu and Clem left her then, but the alcohol removed any trepidation she might have felt at being abandoned with relative strangers.

'We'll take you to Heaven, a club around the back of Charing Cross. You'll love it, full of strange and wonderful things. We like it there because no one seeks to presume that they know what we are and if we choose to share the enigma they just accept it graciously,' said Richard.

'I will come, gladly. But I do not understand what you mean,' she replied.

'Sexuality is strictly classified here: heterosexual, homosexual, bisexual, autosexual,' he explained. 'Everyone has to belong to one division or another. We have spent most of our lives trying to be all four and confound society. The code governing behaviour in any of the divisions is one of morals: we have no morals at all, much, I imagine, as you do not. We disregard morals, you have never had them. We have but one code we apply: neither will do anything without the participation of the other. It has been a long-standing joke amongst our friends that we are never likely to find the right woman and settle down.'

'Clem calls us "serial philanderers", never remaining constant to anyone; except that he forgets we are entirely faithful to each other,' finished Tom.

The conversation continued, Ehlana making what she could of it, in the taxi that took them to a strange, dimly lit alley. A gaudy neon sign illuminated the cavernous entrance to Heaven. Inside, it heaved with bodies: male, female, androgynous. An insistent rhythm pounded throughout, encouraging all to 'relax,' which as Ehlana soon realised, was the title of the song. Again, a multitude flocked around the brothers, kisses and greetings exchanged. Suddenly, Tom turned and looked at Ehlana.

'Sorry, this wasn't such a good idea. The last thing one gets to do here is talk. Would you like us to go somewhere quieter?' he asked.

'It is a little daunting,' she half-shouted back.

'Well, we can either go to another club, or take you to our place, or take you back to Lulu's. It's your choice.'

'If it is no burden, I should love to see your home,' was Ehlana's reply.

'It would be a pleasure,' said Tom. 'I'll just grab Richard and we'll be on our way.'

Another taxi, again squeezed pleasantly between the two brothers on the big, back seat. Their house, when they reached it, looked exactly the same from the outside as all the others in the street. Inside, a lofty hallway led up to three dark wood doors and a long wooden staircase.

'Although some of it looks a little like Bluebeard's castle, you're free to look wherever you want,' said Tom. 'We'll go and organise something to drink and then track you down – a bit like hide and seek, except that you don't have to hide.' They went through the door at the far end of the hall. Tempting as it was to follow, she took them at their word and went through the doorway on her left.

She entered an immaculate sitting-room, with

two large sofas on either side of a table, an open fireplace and a magnificent red and gold cupboard. To her right was a concertina-type door which opened into a room with a long table and eight chairs. Another door led her back into the hall. The third door must lead to their kitchen, she decided. Then she went upstairs. Another door at the top of the staircase led into a bedroom of such opulence it made Ehlana gasp. Kicking off her sandals, she walked across a carpet so deep that its pile enveloped her toes and her feet left their imprint in it. An enormous canopied bed filled most of one wall and beyond it a wide glass door gave out on to a garden. She unlocked it and walked out. The surface felt cool and damp against her bare feet and as she walked a strange, fresh scent assailed her nostrils. Eventually her eyes adjusted to the darkness and she saw it was a terrace, grassed and planted, built on what she supposed was the kitchen roof. The real garden spread out below. She was still standing there when her companions arrived with the promised drink.

'Found you,' said Richard. 'Now you have to pay the penalty. Come back inside and sit down while we make up our minds what to do with you.' She did as she was directed. Tom sat beside her on an ottoman and Richard opposite in a chair he had drawn close. They proceeded to tell her of their work. Accidentally, or so she thought, Tom had caught her elbow with one of the wild gesticulations he used while explaining and, as a result of this, a small quantity of wine from her glass trickled slowly down her breast.

'God, but you can be clumsy, brother. Ehlana will consider us a pair of idiots. I suggest you clear up the mess you have made or, if you will not, I shall,' Richard admonished. The other looked at him, one eyebrow raised quizzically. 'Let me take your glass whilst my brother tries to atone for his awkwardness.' Richard reached over to snatch it gracefully before Ehlana could refuse. Meanwhile, Tom leant forward and, expertly and with no hint of his former ineptitude, began to lick away the red wine which still dribbled slowly over her round, white breast. At the first contact, Ehlana could not restrain a gasp and looking up she found Richard staring intently at her.

'If you are not unwilling,' he began, 'I would suggest that we play a special game together. My brother and I call it "chimaera" and we find it very enjoyable.'

'Provided that it does not require a great physical distance between the players, I find myself amenable,' Ehlana replied, Tom's tongue still moving over her breast, all trace of wine long gone.

'Indeed, proximity is a fundamental requirement,' Richard said, a gentle laugh in his voice. He moved behind her and she could feel his hands working at the back of her dress. As he progressed downwards, her breasts burst out of the confining silk and Tom at once began to suck on a now exposed nipple, a hand rising deftly to massage the other.

'This chimaera,' Ehlana asked, 'how is it played?'

'Not so much played, rather made. The chimaera was a beast in ancient Greece composed of three different types of animal. That is the beast we intend to create: three bodies and one animal. Had we considered it, we should have asked Clem to ape Bellerophon and come to be our slayer! But I digress. If you would stand, I can undress you and then myself. Once I am unencumbered, I can take my twin's place,' he said. Ehlana, obliging, stood and he moved first one sleeve and then the other from her shoulders, gently kissing each new-revealed morsel of flesh. At length the gown cascaded down to form a lush green pool of silk around her ankles. Behind her, a kiss began at the nape of her neck and continued down towards the small of her back. A shiver shadowed his mouth along the length of her spine. The kiss stopped but only to permit his tongue to continue straight and hard along the fine valley formed by her buttocks. As he gently prised the flesh apart, Ehlana could feel the soft stabs of his tongue against the tight virgin hole of her arse and she found herself yearning for a deeper penetration there. His hand slipped between her legs, an inquisitive finger seeking out that little nub of flesh and, finding it, commenced a rhythmic caress. Before her, Tom had managed, quite adeptly, to remove his clothes without having had to part company with her flesh. Wrapped up in the exotic sensation of two mouths upon her body, Ehlana allowed them to move her onto the wide expanse of the bed, whereupon they lay either side of her, their hands travelling in exploration. Each of their mouths found a hardened nipple to suckle on. Instinctively, their motions and pressures were identical and to Ehlana it seemed as if they drew her into themselves. Meanwhile, the brothers' hands had met at the soft down which covered her mound. One hand gently spread her swollen lips apart while another began to stroke her clitoris. Looking up for the first time, Ehlana discovered that the roof of the bed was one enormous looking-glass and she nearly lost herself within its reflections. It was as though only half of her were there: the twins lay mirroring each other's movements so exactly that they seemed more one than two. A finger slid into her velvet-smooth tunnel, withdrew, and slithered down towards the dry mouth of her anus. Moistened, it insinuated itself through the guarding ring of muscle and moved slowly in and out of the tight flesh, its movement echoed in her other, humid hole.

A low moan issued from Ehlana's throat as a head slid down her body to nestle between her legs. Above her the mirror revealed a pretty picture: one blond head at her breast and the other, licking gently where fingers played, her long red hair a streaming banner across the pillows. A dull ache pulsed and she begged the twins to calm it. At last, a twin moved from her breast and lay his long, strong body beside her.

'Mount me, sweet lady. Pass a leg across my hips and ride me,' he implored her. 'Take me up inside you and let me feel your flesh surround me.' Ehlana moved as she was bid. 'Slide down my shaft until you can move no further, then press your body hard against mine, until we are fused together.'

At length they lay still: he supine beneath her, she crouching above him, his thick weapon deep inside her. She felt a tongue flick heavily against the sensitive muscle of her bottom, its tip pushing wetly at her tight ring. Then a finger joined it, then another, pulling her gently apart. The tongue reached deeper and deeper, exquisitely intrusive, and then it moved away. The pressure from his fingers increased slightly as he prised her ever more open. Then a new sensation, his prick beginning to fill her other hollow. As he moved closer, she could feel the incredible tension created in the thin membrane that divided the two brothers. Beneath her, one groaned as the other moved until he could move no further. And then, in gentle symbiosis, the men set up a rocking motion, not the wild thrustings she had known from before, more a seesawing: one withdrawing as the other went deep.

Pierced between the two, Ehlana could do nothing to aid their motion. Strong hands held her hips firmly in place and began to push her down until her clitoris ground hard against the supine man's pubis, pinning him onto the bed until he could no longer move. Slowly at first, the man behind increased his thrusts, moving harder and deeper inside her, friction building hotly against the other's imprisoned prick.

It seemed almost to Ehlana that the two made love to each other, that she was no more than the vehicle that permitted their tryst. Fingers dug hard into her back and nails raked her skin as the man beneath fought madly to control himself. His breath came in ragged bursts, his eyes tight shut and his mouth agape. Ehlana leant forward and pressed her lips against his, her tongue snaking forward into his mouth. He sucked hard on the intruding flesh and her clitoris throbbed with jealousy. The mad friction behind her continued, little grunts of pleasure accompanied each thrust. And then it stopped: she felt the pulse of his coming, his head pumping as he held her hard against him. He withdrew almost at once and moved, limply, to one side. The other rolled her over, without slipping from her wet, aching hole, and raised her legs high over his shoulders. His hand found a route to the

63

place where they joined and a finger teased her stiff bud out from between her swollen lips. He moved deep and hard inside her, his tight balls slapping against the gently aching entrance his brother had so recently filled.

'Now it is my turn to ride. I shall fill you and fuck you until you shudder beneath me and only then shall I find release,' he said. 'I can feel you tighten against the force of my prick as it slides in and out of you. Oh, god, you're so hot inside I can feel your burning. Come: let me douse the flames; feel my hardness deep inside you. Please god, come so I can. Now! Come now!' His voice rose and rose until, at the moment Ehlana could no longer hold off her orgasm, he shrieked and held her tight against him. Almost as soon as he had come, he slid off her to lie, panting, at her side. His brother moved swiftly to graze between her legs, his tongue licking and probing deeply, as if determined to seek and separate all traces of his twin from Ehlana's own wetness. When he was done, he moved to kiss first his brother, and then Ehlana, his tongue carrying the taste of their sex to each mouth that he covered. As his tongue explored her mouth, his eager prick buried itself in her hot, moist flesh and he began again the relentless friction.

It seemed to Ehlana that each took her continuously through the night, pausing only to clear gently away with their tongues the evidence of a brother's passing. Eventually, she begged for rest, her bruised and swollen flesh could take no more. Each new caress against her sensitive skin burned like fire. They granted her request on the condition that she tell them of her home. Their questions, and her answers, stretched the night finally away. The sun was already rising before she had finished her tale.

'Each Guild strives continuously for a way in which to increase the yield. For my part, it always seemed that the Historians contributed less than any. Two of my hatchlings work in Agronomy and labour long to achieve little. It is strange that the most significant event in two thousand years was the return of a Historian with unexpected seed stock!' Ehlana explained.

'You could always try and stop the solar flare happening in the first place,' suggested Tom.

'How do you mean?' quizzed Ehlana. 'Even if I was there, I doubt anyone would listen to me.'

'Well, maybe not directly. But what about the Scotsman who persuaded the survivors to join him underground? Might he have done more if he'd known more?' continued Tom.

'I do not know. It is so long since I studied his life, I cannot recall any details. But it is worth investigating. It certainly seems the freshest approach to our age-old problem,' she replied.

'Good grief, brother, you could go down in future histories as the saviour of the planet! What irony that would be!' said Richard, amused by the image he had conjured. 'There again, maybe this could be one for Malcolm?' He looked at his brother inquisitively.

'It's possible,' Tom agreed. Turning to Ehlana, he explained 'Malcolm is our latest customer. He's a pedologist. Richard thought that meant he was a self-confessed deviant and nearly refused the commission until I made him look it up. As it is, we have his enormous old house in Islington to transform and lots of money to do it with.'

'I understand pedology,' replied Ehlana, 'but find it strange that with such plenty you would have need of soil scientists. Deviant, I know not.'

Richard laughed and slapped his twin's buttock. 'Deviant is what we are! It covers, in varying degrees, anything outside the normal mores and it's much more fun than pedology!'

'The plenty you see is confined to small pockets of the planet. Nearly three-quarters of the population lives less well than you do in your own time,' Tom explained. 'Unfortunately, population control seems the only solution – it certainly seems to work in your time. Malcolm specialises in making arid areas – deserts – fit for cultivation. He must be quite successful, as it appears to make him a great deal of money. When you travel can you take anything with you?'

'Certainly from here to there,' replied Ehlana. 'I cannot see that the reverse would not work. Why?'

'Bring a soil sample next time you come, then,' said Tom. 'We can get it to Malcolm and, using our technology, he might be able to find a way you can use it. That way, I could, or at least Malcolm could become the saviour of mankind. I don't think I could bear living with Richard's ego if his Scottish connection worked!'

'Ego?' said Richard. 'I don't know what you're talking about! I do know, though, that if we don't get up soon, we'll miss our train to Suffolk and, with it, the opportunity to showcase ourselves to two hundred of Madame Cholmondeley's richest friends at her "discrete little luncheon".'

'Hell, I'd forgotten that completely. Any way we can get out of it?' he asked his brother. Richard shook his head in response. Tom turned to Ehlana and ran a hand slowly along the curve from her waist to her thigh. 'Regrettably, much as I would rather spend at least the next three days in bed with you, we must run. We'll call you at Lulu's once we get back home and, if you like, maybe we can play some more.' His expression was both hopeful and questioning.

'I would like that,' she replied. 'And perhaps a meeting with your scientist friend – there might be information that would help him, but I would have to seek it in my own time.'

The brothers were already up now and Ehlana lay on her belly, watching them dress. It was a most bizarre procedure: they used no mirror but each other. They corrected inconsistencies only by watching the other's actions. Surprisingly, it seemed to work well.

They called for a taxi to take her back to Lulu. Tom was on the phone when she left, but Richard walked down with her. He opened the black door and, once she was settled inside, stretched in to kiss her on the cheek.

'It was wonderful,' he said. 'I promise we'll call when we get back. Don't do anything we wouldn't, or if you do, tell us all about it afterwards!' He thrust a crumpled piece of paper into her hand. 'Make sure the driver gives you change from that!' he called out as the cab pulled away. Sitting back on the wide seat, Ehlana realised that she had hardly seen much of their house, apart from their bedroom. She wondered if Lulu would guess that she had done more than admire the curtains. Yes, she decided, Lulu knew before she left her the previous night. In fact, Lulu had seemed quite keen that she should go. Not for the first time, she wondered at the constraints that 'relationships' placed on sharing and why they continued trying to make them work.

By the time she arrived at Nevern Square, Lulu had already gone to work, but she had left Ehlana a note with a list of things she might like to do until her return. The last suggestion was sleep, followed by a large exclamation mark. Lulu had definitely known! Sleep, however, was an attractive idea. She regarded her green-sheathed reflection once more before she reluctantly shed the silk gown and returned it to the confines of Lulu's wardrobe. After a cool shower, Ehlana lay down on the bed and dozed as the warm breeze from the open window played across her body.

Lulu woke her a few hours later. The sky outside was overcast and the air in the room was oppressively close.

'It's going to storm,' explained Lulu. Ehlana looked at her blankly. 'Shit! I'm out of practice! Storm: noun; atmospheric disturbance normally accompanied by thunder and lightning. They're generally rather good fun, but preferably not when you're standing under a tree – people have died that way – the tree draws the lightning and earths it. It's natural electricity: wild and unstable. I don't want to spoil it for you – you'll understand it better when you see it. Storms also tend to be rather wet, but you must remember rain from the last time you were here. Anyway, I want to hear about what you got up to last night! I've never known anyone well enough to ask them what it's really like in bed with Richard and Tom, and I'm dying to find out. I'll go and put some coffee on – join me as soon as you're ready. Help yourself to anything you want to wear. Nothing's moved much since you were last here. That's fine for you, it was only six weeks ago, but it makes me a bit of a slob in my own time!'

Ehlana did as she had been asked and, as they watched the storm unfold through the window, she satisfied Lulu's curiosity at the same time learning more about weather. Lulu appeared quite impressed by her account.

'I always wondered. They never seem to see very much of anyone, and I just thought that maybe they found women a little boring after a while. I hadn't realised quite how mutually dependent they are. Still it sounds like a great time was had by all. Clem and I came back to a furious row. I rather think it was my fault, but he certainly didn't make it any easier. Anyway, he stormed off and I haven't heard from him since.' Ehlana looked concerned. 'Oh, he'll come back. If nothing else, he left his credit cards behind and he's not going to get too far without them. Apart from which, sex is always better when it's repairing the damage after a row,' said Lulu, reassuringly.

However, Ehlana did not see Clem again. The days rushed past at an increasing pace: Malcolm, the soil scientist, was in a place called Cairo and would not be back for several months, but Richard and Tom took every opportunity to squire Ehlana. She enjoyed their company, but it made it difficult for her to do much apart from party! When her crystal at last began to tremble at her throat, she bemoaned how little work she had actually done. She was dressed and ready for another evening out with the twins, this time to the theatre. An opening night, she had been told, for an extravagant production, the set of which had been designed by the brothers. She had hoped it would all become clear once they arrived there, but it seemed now that she would never know. Lulu had not yet arrived home and Ehlana felt a twinge of guilt that she would be departing in Lulu's green silk gown which had been but loaned, not given. There was, however, no time in which to do anything about it.

Chapter Five

Nucassel, September 3550PS

*F*or a while she stood there swaying, until at last someone held her steady. It was as though the physical contact reminded her of who she was and, as she waited on the dais, she pulled the Guild Ring from her finger.

'This one I did not leave behind, Magister, but I thank you kindly for its loan.' She passed it to the Magister and he slipped it on.

'I thank you for its safe return,' Tolai replied. 'Take my hand and step down, child. There are many questions you must answer.' Her interrogation began. Indeed, the first few days of her return were taken up almost entirely in the passing on of information. The item which caused the greatest interest was the difference in time between her two journeys. The Magister was also puzzled by the time lapse differential. Four weeks had passed in both worlds since she departed from her own time: it seemed therefore that time must move at the same speed. He agreed that the increased size of

71

the crystal she wore must surely be the cause of her relatively shorter journey backwards and proposed further experimentation.

Ehlana did not see Jodai until the third evening of her return. He slipped quietly into her room one evening just after sunset, looking, Ehlana thought, a little uncomfortable. She embraced him and felt him flinch beneath her arms.

'What ails you, dearest friend and hatchling?' she asked.

'Nothing,' he replied. 'Though I have a little success to report.'

'The seedlings?'

'No, though they fare well. It concerns the sharing of bodies. It seems we are not the only ones troubled with strange dreams and urges.' Ehlana looked at him expectantly. 'As I promised, I have been trying to discover why our desires have become so suppressed and began my research with the Evaluators. I reasoned that I might as well face the danger early on, rather than run the risk of being reported. Do you recall Emora, a tall, dark-haired girl some five years our senior?' Ehlana nodded. Jodai continued. 'I knew she was apprenticed to the Evaluators and discovered that she had graduated about two years ago. I sought her out and invented a most disturbing dream. At first she would not listen, insisted that I see my allocated Evaluator, but I told her that I could not, for my dream had been of her. She seemed both angered and flattered at the same time, but in the end she relented and allowed me to describe it to her.' He paused for a moment and then continued. 'I believe she is now interested enough to do a little research of her own.'

'You can't finish there! At least tell me what you told her!' Ehlana thought she might have sounded a little petulant.

'Well, understand at least that it was just an imagining: I did not truly dream of her, although I enjoyed the creating of my tale. I told her I had dreamt her all dressed up in black: a tight, shiny fabric that clung to her every curve. That in my dream she had bound me tightly hand and foot and hung me by the wrists from a hook so high on the wall that I could not place my feet flat on the ground. That then she had produced a long, black blade and sliced open the back of my robe, leaving me exposed to her mercy.' He paused and Ehlana waited, breathless, for him to continue.

'And then I told her that I dreamt she beat me with a long, black, knotted cord until my back bled.'

'So what did she say to all that?' Ehlana asked, impressed not only with his inventiveness but strangely aroused at the thought of his imagined vulnerability.

'She made me tell it again, but this time she made me do it.' He stared down at the floor.

'You mean she tied you up?'

He nodded.

'And whipped you?'

He nodded again.

'Sunfire! Jodai, when?'

'About an hour ago,' he replied.

'Can I look?' she asked. 'I mean, will you let me see if it needs dressing?'

He nodded a third time and gingerly pulled his robe over his head. Ehlana counted twelve broad red ribbons across his back, their edges lined with

73

little flecks of dried blood. She hurried away to find water and a cloth with which to tend his wounds. These found, she started dabbing at the livid marks.

'Oh, Jodai! I had not intended that you should suffer in my quest for information,' she said apologetically.

'Strangely, I felt little pain – it is only now that it irks me. At the time, I must confess, I found the experience pleasurable. When I told my tale the first time, my staff stirred and when she beat me I thought it might explode. Even now, with the retelling, it hardens again.' As he spoke, he turned to face her. She had no excuse to doubt how much the experience excited him: the pale skin was stretched tight around his turgid flesh and, here and there, dark veins stood in prominence. She reached out to gently stroke his reddened head.

'Did you both miss me, then?' she asked, tenderly.

'Both?' Jodai looked puzzled.

'You and this one.' She leant forward and planted a kiss on its tip. 'Or did you hardly notice I was gone?'

'We missed you!' he replied plaintively. 'Many times did I wake with an image of you in my head only to find this tyrant in my hand, demanding attention. Often did we both wish you here!'

'Where?' said Ehlana, who knelt before he had a chance to reply and greedily sucked his heavy flesh into her mouth.

'Oh, right there,' replied Jodai, his voice catching in his throat at the first touch of her tongue. 'Other places too, but they all seemed to involve his total immersion in some portion of your body.'

Ehlana detached herself and laughed, then stood

and lifted her robe over her head to stand naked in front of him.

'And did you spare a thought for us in all your travels?' asked Jodai.

'I did, and I learnt new games to play,' Ehlana replied. 'But for the best of these we lack a companion. Still, there is much we can do together.' She moved towards her pallet and lay down on her back. 'Come, lie beside me and I shall tell you of what I have seen and done.'

Jodai moved tight against her side, raising himself on one elbow in order to feast his eyes upon her form and at the same time to touch what he saw. Softly at first, and then harder, he pinched the soft pink bud of one nipple until it hardened beneath his fingers. Once it stood proud and defiant he concentrated on the other, not wishing to offend it with his lack of attention. Ehlana groaned as the sensations surged down from her breasts to her groin. Now it was Jodai's turn to laugh.

'You did miss me,' he said. He slid his body along hers until he reached her calves. She lifted her left leg high over him and brought it down to rest, framing his kneeling form between her two long limbs. She readied herself for imminent penetration but instead he bent forward and pushed her labia wide apart with his fingers before his tongue stretched out to toy with her exposed and swollen nub. At first he licked and flicked against it gently: almost unbearably soft was the touch of his tongue against her most sensitive part. Then more insistent and the ache she felt deep inside grew ever more intense. He pressed his face hard into her, his tongue travelled further and faster until she could take no more and shuddered to her climax under his mouth. He raised her hips then and feasted on her sweet nectar.

At first, neither of them noticed the figure in the open doorway, then Jodai looked up from between Ehlana's legs and froze. Ehlana turned and saw Mara, who stood there baffled and bewildered.

'Come in, dear sister-friend and close the door. There is much here you can learn and enjoy, if you wish to,' said Ehlana. For a moment the girl did not move: confusion fought with her curiosity and, at last, the latter won. She moved into the room and shut the door behind her. Ehlana unwound herself from her lover and sat on the edge of her bed. 'Jodai and I practice an old art, one long since lost and only recently rediscovered. But if you want to join us, even just to watch, you must remove your robe.'

'I know what you do, or at least I believe that I do: I learned of the ancient breeding rituals in the third year of my apprenticeship,' said Mara. 'But I do not understand why you do it. Procreation is impossible.'

'Ah, but we do not seek to increase our numbers, merely our understanding of the other's body,' Jodai explained. 'Mara, the pleasure becomes so intense I cannot describe it.'

'Pleasure? But how?' asked Mara. 'All hatchlings have their gametes removed at birth. I read of a study initiated by the fourteenth Magister Prime which conclusively proved the absence of carnal desires in post-solar flare man.'

'I think it not an absence, merely a dormancy,' said Ehlana. 'For my own part I had dreams and visions long before I discovered the reality. I travelled back many years before I found it, and there it seemed as natural as breathing. As it is, you graduated as a Physician and yet it falls to us to finish your education!' she said, a wry smile on her face. 'Have you ever looked at yourself naked?' Mara shook her head. 'Well, look at me then. Jodai, remove her robe: she seems to have forgotten my primary condition.' He obeyed her and Mara did not demur. 'Now, I'll try and make this a simple lesson and deal with the matter by rote.' She stood up and moved towards Mara. 'First, and most obvious are the mammary glands: they serve no function within our society. And yet they do have a function. The gentlest of touches produces a strange thrill.' Ehlana cupped Mara's breasts in her hands, as if raising them for inspection. 'Different pressures produce different sensations: one of the most interesting is when someone takes this hardening tip between their lips.' She bent her head and sucked once, softly. 'If my assistant would care to help?' she asked looking directly at Jodai. He bowed, formally, and put his mouth where hers had been and continued what she had started. 'You will no doubt begin to notice a strange phenomenon shortly: a nerve which you know physiologically does not exist appears to run directly from your nipple to this little spot, here.' Ehlana inserted a finger between Mara's already moist labia and touched the hidden treasure inside. 'If you sit on the edge of the bed, my explanation would be easier.' Mara sat without argument and Jodai went to kneel behind her, reaching round her back to play with her pert teats. 'Spread your legs wide apart and I shall continue.' Mara obliged and Ehlana knelt between her open thighs.

'As I was saying, there is a strange communion between these pieces of erectile tissue: what the one feels here – ' This time she caressed the little bulb of exposed flesh with a slow, circular movement. ' – is shared by the other in a mysterious way.' Jodai, attentive and enthralled at this unexpected opportunity, mimicked Ehlana's caress on the skin beneath his hands. Mara leant back against him, her eyes closed. Ehlana bent forward and flicked her tongue across the tiny bud. Mara groaned. 'And then, one must not forget this little void.' She slid a long, slim finger into Mara's virgin hole, which was so slick with excitement that it had an easy entry. Then she drew it out and gave it to Jodai to suck on. 'There,' she said. 'Those are your parts explained. If my assistant would step forward, I shall now demonstrate the other half of the equation.' Jodai came to stand beside Ehlana and she continued.

'As you can see, the normally somnolent penis, given only a little stimulation, turns into this: ideally designed to fit and fill almost any orifice!' Jodai grinned inanely, a little awkward at this close inspection. 'Thereafter it is all a matter of friction, and oh, how sweet it is! The first time can bring pain, but it is soon forgotten. Any questions?'

'A few,' Mara replied. 'Does it not tear you to take him inside?'

'Only once: if Jodai will lie down, I can show you,' said Ehlana. He lay, eagerly, and Ehlana straddled his hips, slowly impaling herself on his swollen, red head, sliding down until she could move no further. Mara moved closer to better examine the extent of their fusion. Ehlana knelt, speared and unmoving beneath the other's gaze; Mara stretched out an inquisitive finger and gently rubbed at the erect and protruding bud of Ehlana's clitoris.

'Ah,' moaned Ehlana, her own sex tensing against the stiff flesh deep inside her. Beneath her, Jodai groaned at the strength of her grip. Emboldened, Mara increased the pressure of her massage. Ehlana writhed and ground her hips hard down, pushing Jodai deeper into the bedding. Mara watched, fascinated, never ceasing the tiny circular motions that her finger made. Almost imperceptibly, Ehlana began to ride the shaft that pierced her, not daring to move too far in case she lost the wonderful contact with Mara's cool hand. Jodai strained against her, eager for more.

Mara's hand worked faster, drumming an insistent rhythm that pulsed deep inside Ehlana. No longer able to defer, Ehlana's inner muscles spasmed along the length of Jodai's hard prick and she shuddered to her climax. Jodai lay beneath her, desperate for the greater friction he required. Despite his protests, Ehlana moved off him and sat on the edge of the pallet.

'Well, hatchling,' she said, 'did you see anything to interest you?'

'Much and greatly,' replied Mara. 'Between my thighs is a hollow ache that I have never known before. I beg you to alleviate the pain, for I fear it is not one that I can cure for myself.'

'To free you from the one pain we must inflict another, though it is swift to pass. If you desire it done, you need only ask,' said Ehlana.

'Do it,' was Mara's dry-mouthed reply.

'Then sit down on the edge of the bed, open your legs wide and lie back. Together we will work to ensure that your suffering is sweet,' Ehlana promised.

Kneeling between Mara's thighs, Ehlana bent her head to examine the scene before her. With deft fingers she parted the fleshy lips that obscured her view. The little hole seemed far too small to accommodate Jodai, but it was already wet from earlier excitements. Slowly, Ehlana inserted a finger, pushing until it encountered stiff membrane. A second finger joined the first, and then a third. Mara squirmed against her hand, her moan purely of pleasure, unlike her sigh when Ehlana's hand withdrew. Using both hands to pry the flesh apart, Ehlana leant forward to taste the sweet moistness where her fingers had recently been. Mara writhed against the gentle probings of her tongue. Ehlana's thick muscle then tasted the route all the way to Mara's small bud, tracing rings around it once she found it. Jodai stood watching, his shaft in his hand. Ehlana stood up and moved to the side.

'Now, brother, for your part. Kneel as I did.' Obediently, he did as she ordered. She took his prick in her hand, running a finger across the broad, red tip. Adeptly she steered it towards Mara's open hole and guided the head until the thick ridge of his glans was safe inside. 'One thrust only, for now,' she commanded. 'No more until I have managed to soothe the pain that you give.'

Jodai held still as he readied himself for the single push Ehlana demanded. Ehlana moved to stand behind him, her hands resting on his shoulders, her gaze held by the view between their thighs: between two sets of curls a white stem stretched. It seemed to belong to both bodies at once and to neither.

Ehlana whispered to Jodai and dutifully he lifted first Mara's right leg and then her left, shouldering her limbs where Ehlana placed them. He felt the axis of the flesh shift around him and knew his aim would now be true. He thrust and held. Mara screamed and twisted on his shaft. Ehlana's nails dug deep into his shoulders before he would move.

Ehlana commanded Jodai to step aside. He did so, reluctantly. Ehlana sank to her knees before her wounded friend and leant forward to kiss the pain away. Her tongue pried apart the assaulted flesh. Her tongue licked its way through swollen lips to find the small spot she knew would reconcile Mara to the pain she felt. As Ehlana licked at the little mound of Mara's hardened flesh, she felt hands on her buttocks and then soft stabbings, as Jodai tried to find his way inside her from an unknown angle. Ehlana pushed back against him, angling herself to better receive him. At last Jodai found the orifice he sought and slid deep within her. Ehlana gasped at his easy penetration and her tongue ceased its attention. Mara's hand reached down to press Ehlana's face hard against her groin, in determined reminder of an earlier promise.

Jodai grasped Ehlana's hips and slowly began to move in and out. Ehlana tried to mirror his movements with her finger in Mara's punctured opening, her tongue stroking the same rhythm on Mara's rampant bud. Jodai's speed began to increase and Ehlana strove to match it.

Mara raised her long legs and wrapped them tight together across Ehlana's back. Her knees locked Ehlana's mouth tight against her bony pubis.

Jodai's hands gripped Ehlana now, holding her hips still while he slammed into her, and then a second, gentle slap against her labia as his heavy sac continued moving once his prick could go no further in. Ehlana could no longer compete with his speed. Instead, she let Mara move on her fingers while her tongue worked slavishly at the source of Mara's pleasure. She could hear Jodai shouting, but knew not what he said, for Mara's soft thighs muffled his words. Jodai held her tight against him, his prick throbbing deep inside her; Mara convulsed around her fingers and under her tongue. For a moment they held still, and then broke apart.

'Sunfire!' said Mara, as she stretched herself out on the pallet. 'How long have the two of you known of this thing without telling? Or have you left it long merely before telling me?'

'Not more than a month,' explained Jodai, as he moved to sit beside her, his hand moving down to caress the tight place he had so recently breached. 'Ehlana taught me after her first returning. None know of it but we three,' he added in appeasement, in case she felt left out, his hand reinforcing her inclusion to their select group. Ehlana laughed as she saw he was already eager for more.

'I must leave you now, hatchlings,' she said, 'for there is much I must do before I travel again. But stay here as long as you wish and spare a thought, if you are able, for me. If you are still here when I return, you can entertain me by showing all you have learnt.' She left them to play.

Ehlana went to the Library to see if she could further her researches. The Magister Librarian, Lora, was sitting at a lectern, reading the book that Ehlana had brought back from her first journey. She stood in front of the woman and waited to be noticed. After what felt like a considerable time, her patience was rewarded and Lora looked up from the book.

'Yes?' she asked.

'Magister,' Ehlana began. 'Forgive my intrusion, but I have a favour to ask of you.' Lora raised an eyebrow, but said nothing. Ehlana continued. 'In the course of my recent excursion, it became obvious that my knowledge of known events immediately before and after the Sunfire was far too shallow. I hoped that you might allow me sight of some of the early documents in order that I might have a better understanding of those events.'

'Petra's Journals are on the third shelf to the left of the door,' was the terse reply.

'I had hoped to study something a little more contemporary to the period: Petra wrote almost two thousand years after Professor McGregor's death.'

'My esteemed predecessor has not been bettered in all the time since then,' the Magister replied stiffly. 'She had access to more source material than we have now and provides the ideal basis for all scholarly endeavours into the early days. I suggest you re-read them before making such an uninformed judgement.' She immediately buried her head again in the book before her.

Decidedly put out, Ehlana strode over to the relevant section and pulled out the first volume of Petra's writings. She found an empty lectern in front of a window, sat down and began to read.

Four days later, her work interrupted only briefly for meals and sleep, and thirteen volumes on, she loathed the 'esteemed' Petra with a vengeance. Without doubt, the woman was one of the most arrogant ever to succeed to magistership! The style was effusive and inelegant and the content was not the wisdom of the ancients, but Petra's own. The words were steeped in self-congratulation. An exercise in egotism! The only interesting piece of information in thousands of sheets of paper was a footnote which referred to a letter McGregor received 'across the seas of time' and which was, apparently, the reason why he had first started his crusade. Apart from that, there was little else. Even the section dealing with the Sleepers gave less detail than Ehlana recalled from her archival primer.

In all the days she had spent in the Library, Magister Lora had not acknowledged her further and Ehlana decided the time was right to re-approach her.

The stern, grey woman sat at her lectern, Lulu's gift still open in front of her.

'Magister, forgive this interruption. But might I ask if there are any books which make reference to a letter received by Professor McGregor? It is noted in Petra VII, but I am interested to learn more,' Ehlana asked politely.

'I should imagine the Professor received a great many letters before the Sunfire. I cannot recall anything specific,' was the off-hand reply. Ehlana tried again.

'Are there documents from which Petra might have sourced this information, then?' Ehlana was becoming as vexed by this librarian as by the late and, by her at least, extremely unlamented Magister Petra and she heard it echo in her voice.

'All sources are listed in the bibliography, volume XIV,' was the cold response.

'I could find no listing of such a letter and, with

so many listed, I had hoped for a little assistance,' continued Ehlana.

'I am not here to assist! Young woman, you know as well as any that if you wish to study archive material you must either be Magister or take apprenticeship as an archivist. I have already granted you more than you deserve,' Magister Lora stated. 'You are familiar with the protocols involved and I have neither time nor inclination to waste further on this matter.' At this the woman slammed her book shut, stood up, turned on her heels and walked towards the far end of the Library.

Ehlana stood there, glaring at her back for some minutes while she tried to work out a way around this unmovable obstacle. Then she retraced her steps to the History Laboratory. When she reached the lab, Magister Tolai was in deep discussion with two of his students. Again, she found herself waiting patiently to be noticed. It struck her as more than a little ironic that, having travelled thousands of years through time, she was then forced to waste so much of it.

'Magister,' Ehlana asked, 'I need your assistance and wondered if you could spare me some time.'

'For you, child, any time. But not, I fear, until later. If you come to my rooms in the Magistratum around sunset, we can discuss what I can do to help. For now, I must endeavour to instruct these two idiots.' He pointed out the taller of the two young men, who blushed quite red at this unwanted attention, 'Horai set Pulai upon a three minute loop it took me six hours to break, and he still cannot see what it was he did wrong. I think that Pulai only attends us fuelled by his desire to repeat his colleague's idiocy and exact revenge!'

'Later, then, Magister,' replied Ehlana, and took her leave. She decided to return to her room and further consider her current predicament. She was still angry that Lora had denied her request. After all, the latest volume in the Library would never have been added, if not for her. The thought that Lora could stop her from studying even that incensed her. Damn the woman, she thought. If she could not persuade Magister Tolai to do what she needed, that route was lost.

Almost idly, she wondered if the Magister could be swayed by her body. What was it Lulu had said? *That there had never been a man created that wouldn't be led by his prick if one tried hard enough.* She smiled, remembering her friend so long away. What would Lulu do for Tolai?

She stood up and walked towards her wardrobe. The clothes within were either the ochre robes that all wore, or the few treasured gifts she had brought with her: Lulu's jeans, blouse and long, green dress. She took the latter out and laid it on the bed, stripping off her robe so that she might wash before she dressed again. She pinned her hair up and began to sponge, recalling the first time she had worn Lulu's green gown.

She could almost feel Clem's warm breath at her neck. A shiver ran along her spine and her nipples hardened in the cool of the afternoon. She pressed the sponge hard against her collar-bone and felt the chill trickle of water over her swollen flesh. Between her legs a small, but insistent, bump ached for attention. It seemed to Ehlana that the more notice she paid it, the more frequently it called. Seeking to cool its ardour, she pressed the damp sponge against her groin, discovering too late that it only served to further inflame her passion. Realising that there was now no escape, she lay down on her pallet, spread her legs wide apart and let her mind wander as she slowly rubbed. She shut her eyes tight and remembered other hands that had laboured there, other mouths.

So strong were her recollections that she could almost feel the weight of a body above her, almost smell the strong, sweet scent of warm male flesh. She heard again in her mind a deep-throated laugh, saw a dark head thrown back and the memory of that first, lancing pain echoed in her loins as pleasure.

She stayed still for some time afterwards, recalling all she could of the man who had laughed.

Eventually, she slipped into the cool, green silk and, after taking one last look at her reflection in the window, she covered herself with the ochre robe and headed towards the Magister's rooms. Aware of the satisfied smile she wore, she reflected that she could think of few finer ways to kill time!

The route to the Magistratum was empty. At moments like this it felt as if she must have travelled through space rather than time. Even in the dead of night, the London of her visits thronged with people; so many to so few and her life encompassed both.

Confronted by the long, low building she hesitated, unsure of herself for a moment. Would Tolai aid her, as she hoped, or merely stop her from travelling again? She did not truly know the old man and realised the repercussions could affect the rest of her life. If she misjudged ... But no, there was no other way. Boldly, she knocked at his door and waited.

'Come in, come in,' said the Magister by way of greeting. 'I have only just returned myself and thought I might have missed you.' The room he led her into was nearly twice the size of her own and two doorways in addition to the one she entered through guaranteed more space beyond.

'Sit, child,' he said, 'and I shall fetch us a drink.' While he turned away, Ehlana slid the ochre robe from her shoulder and sat down as he had instructed. She accepted the glass that he returned with, taking it out of his hand as he seemed no longer able to pass it to her. Looking away from his staring eyes, she sipped and began to speak.

'It seems unreal that only twelve weeks have passed since I learnt there was more to drink than water.' She crossed her legs the same way she had seen Lulu do countless times, the dress outlining her long thighs. Tolai was spellbound. 'Do sit, Magister, or I shall have to wrench my neck to speak with you.'

Mumbling apologies Tolai sat opposite her, trying hard to look only at her face, but failing absolutely. Inhaling deeply, and noticing the effect that her heaving breasts had upon her host, she continued. 'Magister, I have a problem. I need access to archive materials from the time Underground. Magister Lora insists that I cannot. I will not spend six years as apprentice, so that route is closed. But I know that, should you choose to, you could find what I need to know.'

'Everything you need is documented, child. Petra's Journals chart history Underground and the

Sleepers' Agreement is common knowledge. Anything else is surplus to need: it merely gives unclearly and inconcisely everything that Petra included,' he explained.

'So Lora said. But I have to confess I am heartily sick of Petra and her writings.' She glanced up at Tolai, aware that her attitude might anger the Magister. She received a conspiratorial wink in reply.

'For my own part, I always found Petra a mighty tedious read. But there is little else that deals with the early days in such detail,' he replied.

'It is not details I seek – more a confirmation that Petra has missed nothing. It is arrogant, I know, but I need to be sure. Possibly, with my small knowledge, I might see something that Petra deemed unworthy of note. Particularly in the McGregor papers. Petra VII makes some mention of a letter received many years after it had been written and it is that which truly interests me.' She leant forward, trying to recapture his attention with her body. 'Magister, may I speak frankly with you?' He nodded his assent. 'I am sure that the History Machine is the key to solving our age-old problem. But I do not know what it will unlock. I am sure you have considered this yourself since I first travelled so far, but do you think it possible that History might be undone, be changed, by any action I might take in the past?'

'We have debated this long and hard in the Magistratum since you first returned to us and we currently have no reason to suppose that it could. It was agreed that any action you might have taken when you journeyed would already be manifest now: therefore you cannot manipulate the future,' he replied.

'But what if I had done nothing yet, but did so on one of my future journeys?' she asked.

'This proved a contentious point in our debate, but many insist that even if you were to do so on a journey you have not yet taken, it has no value for there is no evident manifestation of any such future action in our present time,' he replied. 'Did you have any specific plan in mind?'

'I had thought to leave something for Professor McGregor, that he could use to dissuade the politicians of his time from their folly,' she explained.

'Try, by all means, but if it had been successful we could not now be here. You see the logic?'

'Yes, but it might at least be worth the attempt!' Ehlana felt as if she were losing the battle of words and decided to change tack. 'Magister, I have noticed in my journeying that much study and devotion is given to the procreative act; however, conception is often deliberately avoided. I am assured by all then to whom I have spoken that they are merely fulfilling bodily appetites and pleasures. How is it that we have foregone such hungers?'

'Ehlana, you forget the fundamental law governing civilised beings! Those desires mesh most closely with aggression. In a truly civilised society, there is no aggression. The physical needs of the past dissipated at the same time as hostility,' he explained. He looked her directly in the face. 'Are you troubled by such hungers, child?'

'Oh, Magister Tolai,' she cried. 'What am I to do?' With this imploration, she slid to her knees before him and pushed her head into his lap. Immediately, the old man's rod began to stiffen beneath his robe. As she pretended to sob, he patted her gently on the shoulders, mumbling his consolations, while, she imagined, he tried to find a solution to his predicament. She pressed little, warm airy kisses against the fabric of his robe where it strained against the forces within it, willing him desperately to give in to her. Slowly her hand crept up beneath the hem of his robe, along his calf, his thigh and then cupped gently around his scrotum, massaging gently to the same beat she pressed against his prick. By now, the Magister's hands were no longer patting: one pushed down against the back of her head whilst the other fumbled for her breast. She pulled away from him and stood, her hands moving to the fastenings at the back of her dress. With one movement the zip was undone and the green gown slipped down to the ground. The Magister's breathing was heavy now, and she stretched one hand towards him.

'Take me to your bed, Tolai, and let me show you other things that I have learnt while I journeyed.' She took his hand and pulled him to his feet. In turn he led her to a door at the far end of the room which, once opened, revealed his sleeping quarters. 'Remove your robe and lie down. Tonight is my gift to you: your pleasure is my only requisite.'

The old man unfastened his robe at the neck and undid the complicated, ceremonial knot at his waist, then shrugged his robe to the floor. Ehlana moved to stand in front of him, her hands rising to touch his shoulders. From there, they slid down his chest. Her fingers tangled in a blanket of curly, white hair that covered most of the upper part of his torso. Beneath, his skin felt warm and slightly flaccid, for the years had robbed it of its suppleness. From the join of his ribs to his groin a thick, white rope stretched, interrupted only by his navel. As her hands passed, she could feel his deep inhalation, his chest swelled and his belly drew in. Tolai struggled for a long time to maintain his pose, but suddenly exhaled with a great gasp. Ehlana laughed and Tolai looked away. She lifted her hands and placed one either side of his head, forcing him to look at her.

'I only laugh because you try for me to be someone you cannot be. I am here because I wish to share with you – not with some younger man! Come, lie down on your stomach and let me rub you.' He lay down, she knelt astride his buttocks and stretched herself forward to knead his shoulders. 'I believe this is best done with the aid of aromatic oils obtained by crushing certain plants – it would reduce the friction and mean that my hands glide over your skin rather than have your skin try to follow my hands. As it is, I shall try to use only the lightest touch and hope that your imagination can bridge the disparity.' Closing her thighs tight against his hips, she began a gentle stroking that covered every inch of flesh before her. Even now, beneath his skin, she could still see evidence of the strong young man he must once have been. Ehlana ran her hands around the sides of Tolai's rib cage and along the curve of his waist, down to his hips. Raising herself slightly, she commanded, 'Turn over.' He turned round beneath her, his hip bone grazing gently against her tender place. Once he was settled, she dropped back atop him and pinned his stiff member between their bodies; she wriggled until it fitted comfortably into the groove of her labia and pressed satisfactorily against her prominent bud. Then her hands moved up from his hips. His white-haired chest held her mesmerised. Richard and Tom were blond and Clem had just a small triangle of dark hair; Jodai had none at all. Hiding underneath it were two large brown nipples, which hardened just a little as her fingers brushed lightly across their peaks. Encouraged, she began to tug gently on the stiffening flesh and, as she did so, she pressed her groin down and forward against his prick.

They groaned together.

Then his hands rose to cup her breasts and repeat the caress she had given his. She glanced down to where they joined and saw his swollen head peeking from between her lips. One hand left his chest and trailed slowly along his body until it found the angry, red tip. One finger stroked across its fine hole to carry away the tear that formed there, moving on to smear the little droplet over her own tiny shaft. A wave of pleasure rolled over her body as she caressed the sensitive bulb, so intense that she could not break what she had intended as just a brief contact. Tolai, who had followed her hand's progress down his body with increasing interest, watched with fascination as she played with herself.

'They are the same, then, or very similar, those two strange pieces of flesh?' Tolai asked, his question more of a statement than anything else. Ehlana, surprised by the image, looked down.

'I have never heard them described as such, but yes, they must be. My earliest thoughts on discovering what they did left me never knowing whether I should feel jealous that mine is so small, or ecstatic that it functions far more efficiently than the cumbersome thing you men must carry around. If nothing else, there are the times that it stiffens when you wish it would not – my own state of arousal is known only by those with whom I choose to share it.'

'But why choose to share it with me? There are plenty of men here more able, I am sure, for my body tells me already that it is a thing which requires stamina. My question stands: why me?'

Ehlana sat back on her heels, all fingerings forgotten, and thought how she should best answer. 'Initially, there were many reasons. But now that I am here, astride you, I discover that above all it is because I desire this sharing. Others I could have, but at this moment I want you most.' She knelt upright, seeming to tower over his prone form. 'Will that suffice, or would you rather that I left?'

'No, never that,' he said, his eyes fixed on her face. 'That first moment your face pressed into my lap, it was as though this thing sprung into life. Many have rested there innocently over the years and never before did it stir. The difference, I believe, was your intent, your desire. But now I am the pupil in need of instruction, sure only that there is much that I must learn.' She laughed softly.

'I think your first lesson begins here.' She angled his still hard staff at her target and sank slowly down on it; his fingers gouged her thighs, shocked by the novel sensation of his engulfment. When she could slide no further, she rocked gently on the axis of his prick, feeling its head rub softly deep inside her. Unbidden, his fingers crept swiftly towards the hidden place he had watched her toy with earlier and fought in turn for possession of her trophy.

Her moan proclaimed the winner.

94

The victorious digit continued its devoted and subservient caress while, slowly, Ehlana began to rise and fall along his shaft. His vanquished hand climbed again and parted the soft red curls that fell to cover her breasts, then played with each of her hard peaks in turn.

'See,' she said quietly, 'there is little for you to learn, now, just its culmination remains unknown. I shall take you up to a high place and for the longest moment our bodies shall soar together. For that brief time, it feels as if mankind's every effort since our ancestors crawled out of the ocean has worked towards this one, simple consummation. Nothing else in history merits comparison.' Her voice was husky as she spoke, breathless but only through exertion of will-power as she struggled to keep her rhythm slow. This was her gift, and she intended that he should have time to enjoy it.

Despite her efforts, he strove to meet each of her thrusts with one of his own and began to force her speed. No matter how she tried, she could not resist matching his faster pace.

For a while, their bodies ran together, his finger beating time against her tiny bulge. Then she overtook him as her body craved more and quicker. He lay back and let her run, her warm tight sleeve gripping and pulling at his excited flesh. The intense friction grew at last unbearable and Ehlana shuddered to her climax, her strong inner muscles rippled along the length of his imprisoned cock and proved to be all that he needed to join her. He inhaled deeply and his mouth flew open, but not a sound emerged. She feared for his life, but his large hands gripped her thighs tight to stop her moving. Inside, she felt the great pulse of his prick and closed tight around it, her tunnel flexing in encouragement.

Eventually, he breathed out, a sigh so profound it touched her heart. He patted the bed beside him and spoke, his voice cracking.

'Come, lay still beside me and let me hold you until my heartbeat quietens and slows. Had you told me before how fine the line would be between exquisite pleasure and death by rapture, I might have refused. I am glad I did not.' She moved to his side, her head rested on his outstretched arm. Even from here she could feel the pounding of his heart inside his rib-cage. She said nothing, content just to be there. At last his breathing slowed and Ehlana turned her head only to discover that he slept.

She half-raised herself on one elbow and looked down at the stranger beside her. How curious it is, she thought, that a face you know so well can change so profoundly after one small interaction. She bent her head and bit gently on one of his nipples. His eyes flew open, instantly aware.

'Sleeping so soon?' she asked, archly, and then continued, 'Can this truly be a product of aggression, Magister? How can anything this wonderful be forgotten and locked away from us entirely?'

'I do not know,' was his candid reply. 'I had thought it a mere extravagance of lesser men, pure hedonism from a time when the planet provided whatever was asked of it. But now, I do not know.' He looked sad, now, and older. She bent her head again and kissed him full on the lips.

'So, will you try and see if that letter still exists?' she asked.

'If you wish it, but I do not believe that it will aid

you: nothing in the past can be undone. But if it pleases you, I shall entreat Lora to surrender it to me.' He smiled up at her. 'But now you must leave: it would not do for anyone to guess how we might have spent the evening.' The simple statement acted as a souvenir and his staff began to rise again. 'If you would have me do any research at all, you must go, else I shall be a corpse before sunrise!' He laughed, pushing her away from him as she moved to start anew.

'I bow reluctantly to your wisdom, Magister,' she replied. 'Although I would have relished another opportunity to share with you.' She stepped into her gown and turned her back towards him, indicating that he should fasten it for her.

'Until the next time, Tolai.' She leant forward and kissed his cheek. Drawing on her ochre robe, she held it tight around her and stepped out into the dark street.

Ten days passed uneventfully and at last the time had come again for Ehlana to travel. Arriving early at the Laboratory, she found it deserted apart from the young man, Horai, who sat studying the Mother Crystal. She recalled that he had graduated some three years before her. He looked up and saw her, blushed for some reason, and looked away. He said nothing and Ehlana could think of nothing to say. After a long silence, he nervously cleared his throat and began to speak.

'This time your crystal is a full three carats. The Magister spent the whole past week working on it – I saw him at his desk well into the night, as if he strived to make it his best work.' He paused for breath and handed her the large crystal that he held. 'I begged him to let me finish it, or at least to rest a little, but he would have none of it. He gets so tired nowadays – I fear for his health.'

Before Ehlana had a chance to reply, Tolai walked into the Laboratory. Try as she might, Ehlana could detect nothing to confirm Horai's concern. Indeed, it seemed to her that she had never seen the Magister in better spirits.

'I am sorry, my dear,' he said to Ehlana. 'But I slept right through the bells. I do hope you have not been waiting too long.'

'No time at all,' she replied. 'Horai has told me how hard you have laboured with my new crystal.' She touched the stone at her throat. 'It is beautiful and I thank you for your efforts. Now all I need is your promise that you will rest well while I journey, for I am sure I shall have need of your sage advice when I return.' She took his hand and walked towards the dais. Tied around her waist was a pouch containing the soil sample Jodai had brought to her from the Field. He had no hope that a solution might be found – pedologists in plenty had studied the hardened crust and found nothing they could do with it, but she took it anyway. Tolai seemed intrigued by her quest and wished her every success.

By now, another four of her Guild brothers had arrived, but at the platform Tolai could not resist showing off: he placed his hands either side of her waist and swung her up, as if he had lost thirty years over night. She bent forward and kissed him, unconcerned by whoever might see it. Someone, Horai she thought, had initiated the translation, for her crystal began to vibrate. Tolai stepped back out of danger and walked to his place by the Mother Crystal.

'Farewell, sweet girl, and return home soon. I shall not be happy until you are safely back with us,' he said.

'Fear not,' she replied. 'For I leave friends to find friends and shall come when you call.' The familiar song grew louder and she embraced the pain.

Chapter Six

London, October 1987AD

*I*t was dark where she travelled to and one step
brought collision with a hard, low object. Ehlana
stretched out to touch it: a table, the one in front of
the sofa. From the next room she heard a moan.
Softly, in order to avoid startling Lulu, she walked
towards the open door. Before she reached it, she
heard another groan, and realised Lulu was not
alone. For a long while she stood still, unsure
whether she should call out to let them know they
had an audience. But she had a second motive for
her silence. The instant she had recognised what
she heard, she experienced a thrill of vicarious
pleasure. To know what they were doing, to imagine the caresses that produced those sounds. Her
hand rose to cup a breast beneath the rough fabric
of her robe. Its tip was already hard. She could hear
Lulu muttering encouraging syllables, but could
distinguish no words. A dull ache filled the space
between her legs now and she was torn between
declaring her presence and finding somewhere she

could sit and listen further. Lulu's voice rose, little moans becoming longer, her breathing rapid and broken. Ehlana found a chair where she expected one and sat down, then her hand moved to lift the hem of her robe. She had barely found the mark when Lulu yelled out once, and then silence. Shuddering with disappointment, Ehlana readied herself to call out. But before she caught her breath, she heard a man's voice.

'Roll over,' he said, huskily. 'It's my turn now.' The rustle of bedding and bodies moving reached Ehlana. Then silence. Then a loud, drawn-out sigh.

'God, but it's good to be inside you.'

'Bet you say that to all the girls,' was Lulu's slightly muffled reply.

'Not all the girls are quite as accommodating, though. No, seriously, there's no place I'd rather be right now,' said the man.

'You lie, but I'll forgive you as long as you carry on doing what you're doing. Oh, yes, just there. Ahh.' Lulu's conversation was punctuated by another long groan.

Ehlana could hear flesh slapping lightly against flesh. Her eyes tight shut, she imagined Clem's hand where her own played. It was no good. She had to see. Quiet as she could, she moved back to the doorway. Her eyes had grown accustomed somewhat to the darkness and she could see a figure, silhouetted by the pale moonlight, kneeling upright at the edge of the bed, his legs spread slightly apart. It appeared his hands rested on the hips of the woman who crouched on all fours in front of him. The scent in the room was potent and intoxicating. Ehlana leant against the door jamb for support. She could see his hips sway as he moved slowly in and out of Lulu's tight orifice. Noiselessly she moved towards him. She feared that her breathing might give her away, it sounded so loud in her ears, but eventually she stood just behind him. One hand sneaked round to cover his mouth, at the same time another dropped between his legs and reached forward to gently caress his balls. His reaction was not what she expected. Sharp teeth sunk into the palm of her hand and he moved backwards at such a speed she was knocked over. He followed, landing so heavily on her chest it completely winded her.

'What the hell are you doing, Clem?' asked Lulu.

'Get the light, quick. I've got an intruder.' Lulu reached for the light and for a moment all three were blinded. Lulu was the first to see the funny side. Clem, stark naked, sat across Ehlana's chest. Ehlana was turning a strange shade of blue beneath him and was quite incapable of doing anything.

'Hello, Ehlana,' said Lulu. 'We were only just talking about you, and here you are.' Clem shot up as if he was sitting on something hot and stood there staring down at Ehlana's prostrate form. 'Give the poor thing a hand, Clem. She looks like she needs one.' He stretched forward to comply and Ehlana weakly raised an arm. He pulled her up so forcefully that, in standing, she stumbled. For an instant he held her tight, but then thrust her away from him and clasped his hands over his genitals and backed away. The bed hindered his progress and he sat there uncomfortably. Behind him, Lulu was laughing uproariously.

'God, if I only had a camera, or better still a video, I'm sure I could win prizes!' she said.

'Well, how the hell was I to know it was Ehlana?

I think I deserve a medal at least for trying to protect you.' Clem tried to regather his shredded dignity. Ehlana stood, still a little dazed.

'Come and sit down,' said Lulu, patting the bed beside her. She did, as Clem slunk off to the bathroom. 'Welcome to 1987. How long can you stay?' Ehlana opened her mouth to speak, but nothing came out. Clem returned in Lulu's loose robe that hung behind the bathroom door. 'Go and get us a drink will you, darling?' Lulu asked him. He appeared happy to have something to do.

'How long since you arrived?' she asked Ehlana, her expression quizzical.

'Not long,' she said. She shifted, her embarrassment evident.

'There's no need to blush,' said Lulu. 'Not after your first visit! Did we sound good?' Ehlana nodded. 'Why don't you get into bed, then? There's more than enough room for three. It just means that Clem's going to have to work harder tonight than he thought!'

By the time Clem returned with three mugs of coffee, Ehlana was sitting close beside Lulu and both of them were naked. He dropped the tray.

'What the fuck's going on, Lulu?' he demanded.

'I thought we might as well all have some fun. What did you want me to do: make her sleep on the sofa?' she replied. 'It's not as though we haven't done it before.'

'Is that all you think I am – a prick on a stick? "Don't worry about him – he'll do anything I tell him." Doesn't it occur to you that I might like to be consulted? Or aren't I allowed any feelings on the matter?' he retorted, grumpily.

'If you think about it, you've never admitted any

feelings on that particular subject, in fact you've always strenuously denied them!' replied Lulu, quite angrily. 'All I was doing was suggesting something that I thought all three of us could enjoy – we did before. The fact that you now decide to be shocked and appalled at the very idea is hardly my fault.' She shrugged. 'Oh, get off your high horse and come to bed. We won't eat you – much!'

'You won't eat me at all!' he replied. He began to dress. 'I don't want to play your silly games. You can do what you like, but I'm going home.'

At last, Ehlana found her voice. 'I am so sorry. I had not intended any of this,' she gushed. 'I should hate it if you argue on my account. If it were not for me, you would both be content now and close to sleep. If you quarrel, it must be my fault. Please do not leave because of me.'

'No, it's my fault,' said Lulu. 'As usual, I just didn't think it through. Don't go,' she said to Clem.

'Oh, all right. But only because you both asked so prettily! I'll go and make more coffee, you two can come and join me once you're decent.' He bent to lift the mugs from the floor. 'But any more suggestions like that and I won't give you the opportunity to change my mind a second time.' He left the room.

'Oh, Lulu,' said Ehlana. 'A thousand apologies. I never intended to cause such trouble. I had thought to surprise you both, not shock you.'

'Don't worry. God only knows why he's so touchy. It's him, not you. We better get dressed, or he'll shout at us again.' Lulu peeled herself out of the bedclothes and picked her bathrobe up from the floor where Clem had dropped it. 'Are you happy in your dress, or do you want something of mine?'

'No, it is fine,' Ehlana replied, carefully lifting her pouch of soil from where she had left it atop her robe. She put it on the dressing-table.

'The soil sample?' asked Lulu, picking the pouch up. 'Christ, it weighs a ton. How did you manage to carry it?'

'Tied around my waist. It was not that heavy and I thought to bring as much as I was able. The one thing I forgot to ask was how much would be needed. Jodai was sure this would be enough, but he does not believe I shall learn anything new from it,' Ehlana explained, as she struggled to dress.

'Oh, well, it's worth a try,' replied Lulu. 'It is good to see you, no matter what Mr Grumpy might say. And I know really he's as pleased as I am.' The kettle's shrill whistle called from the kitchen. 'Let's go and get that coffee.'

They talked and drank, and Lulu smoked. A loud noise outside caught their attention. In the square below, violent winds tore through the trees and a large branch lay in the middle of the road, one half of it buried deep in a dark-coloured car. Clem tried to open the window, but the sheer elemental force held it shut.

'Did we miss something on the weather forecast this evening?' he asked.

'Certainly nothing like this. Maybe it's just cutting the wrong way across the square? Try the one in the bedroom,' suggested Lulu.

He came back shaking his head. 'I'm just going to have a look downstairs. I won't be long.'

When he did come back, it was to request assistance in shutting the front door against the wind. It took all three of them to do it. They climbed the stairs back to the flat in silence, the noise of the wind echoing through the building.

'That's it,' said Clem once they got back. 'I'm shattered. You two can talk all night, if you want to, but I've got to get some sleep. Though I don't know if I'm going to be flying anywhere tomorrow afternoon if this storm keeps up.' He left the two women and walked into the bedroom.

'You look pretty tired too,' Lulu said to Ehlana. 'If you want to sleep, I can fix you a bed out here.'

'That would be good, but I am happy just to sit here and listen to the wind. I must commit its song to my memory, so that I can properly describe it when I return. Anything that powerful is a force to be recognised and deserves to be honoured long after it has ceased to blow.'

'That's fine, but you can at least do it in comfort and warmth. I'll go and get some bedding.' Ehlana stood in front of the broad window, watching the storm outside. The trees bent at incredible angles, as if tugged this way and that by some giant hand. How any still stood, she could not understand. Across the road she saw a car with amber warning lights flashing. Occasionally the sound of a high-pitched siren reached her, only to be swept away by the wind. She helped Lulu to convert the sofa into a bed.

'Sleep well, if you can with all that going on outside. We'll talk later,' said Lulu, her arms around Ehlana's shoulders. 'It's good to have you back.' She walked away to join Clem. Ehlana undressed, switched off the light and clambered into her makeshift bed. Above the wind's howl she distinctly heard Clem's voice from the bedroom.

'I said no, not tonight. Just leave it alone will

106

you, Lulu, and for God's sake go to sleep. It's late and I'm too bloody tired.'

The morning, when it finally came, revealed the extent of the wind's depredations. Ehlana sat for hours, listening to the various accounts of the storm on both radio and television. Lulu left for work as normal but soon returned as she, like so many others, had no means of getting there. Clem, however, drove to Heathrow, sure that whatever the damage was there, they would soon have the airport open and running. All Ehlana received from him in parting was a swift kiss on her cheek. This distressed her more than she expected and the promise that she would see him when he returned was small consolation.

When Lulu suggested that she try and find Malcolm in order to deliver the soil sample, she recalled why she was truly here and her mood lifted. A long phone conversation with Richard, followed by a much shorter one with Malcolm, resulted in an appointment for that afternoon, so long as she was able to get to Islington. Lulu insisted on going with her. It took them three hours and four buses to get there. On the way there, they had agreed that Ehlana's true origins should remain hidden.

Twenty-seven Canal Bridge Street was much like its immediate neighbours. A textbook example of Victorian architecture was how Lulu described it: three storeys high, a large bay window either side of the front door and large amounts of ornamental plaster-work to the frontage. She also explained that most of the adjoining houses would probably now be split into flats.

'We are an hour late,' said Ehlana. 'Do you think he will still see us?'

'There's only one way to find out – ring the bell. At worst all he can do is tell us to go away and it'll take us another three hours to get home!' replied Lulu. Ehlana did as she was told. Above them a window opened and a head popped out.

'Hello,' said the head. 'You're late! Don't worry though – I can imagine how hard it's been getting anywhere today. Here, I'll throw the keys out. Let yourselves in – sitting-room's the first door on the left. I'll be down in a couple of minutes, but there's something I must finish before I join you.' A set of keys emerged through the window and plummeted down to land at Ehlana's feet. It took them a while to find the right one, but when they did, the lock opened with a satisfying click, and they walked in.

The entire hall, ceiling, floors and walls were intricately panelled in wood, smooth and warm to the touch. The door on the left they found only by virtue of the brass door handle – its outline was cut to match the grain in the wood, not the standard oblong one would expect. It opened into a vivid blue and green parlour, carpet and sofas emerald in colour, two walls and curtains azure. A third wall held a large bay window which looked out towards the canal. The fourth contained a glass panel, some five foot square, that looked as though it was tinted red. Behind the glass was a strange picture depicting a complicated series of lines, which ran maze-like across the whole image. It was painted in shades of brown: from nearly black to the palest beige. It was the strangest thing Ehlana had ever seen, and from her expression it seemed peculiar even to Lulu. Lulu stepped back towards the window as if hoping to see more from a distance, whilst Ehlana moved forwards. Staring hard, she concentrated on one of the pale streaks which she was convinced had moved.

'Jesus,' gasped Lulu. 'It's alive.'

'I see you've met my pet worms. The soil's little helpers,' said the tall man as he walked into the room. 'I'm Malcolm Travis.'

Lulu walked towards him, introducing herself and Ehlana. She added that Ehlana was her cousin.

'So, which of you is the one that wants a sample tested?' he asked. Lulu pointed to Ehlana. 'I have to admit it's something I don't do very often, at least not any more, but Tom insisted that I see you. What can you tell me about it?'

'If you do not object, I would rather not tell you precisely where it comes from. Not out of need to make you guess, but rather that I think it might cloud your judgement if you knew from the start,' began Ehlana. 'I live in a small, closed community of some two thousand people. We have sufficient soil to produce foodstuffs for that number, but no more. The rest of the land is covered with stuff such as this.' She brought out the heavily wrapped parcel and placed it on the table in front of him. 'I hope, or at least we all do, that you might know some way that we could use it. So far, despite many experiments with both soil and crops, we have enjoyed not even the smallest success. More than that, I cannot really tell, for my expertise lies in other fields. I am sent as emissary for I am the only one who could get here.'

He looked at her, his face puzzled. He began to unwind the layers of cloth that bound the sample.

Once it was free, he picked up the largest piece and held it up to his face.

'When was this piece dug up?' he asked.

'A considerable number of years ago,' she replied. 'Is it important?'

'Only in that there's very little weathering. I would have expected you to say just a few days ago,' he explained.

'Ah, then accept that it would have had very little opportunity to weather. Does that answer that question?' she asked.

He did not reply, but moved towards a shelf and picked up a glass lens which he held between his face and the sample.

'Can you tell me that it doesn't come from Herculaneum?' he asked.

'Definitely not,' Ehlana replied. 'Where is Herculaneum?'

'It is a Roman city in Italy which died much the same time as its neighbour, Pompeii. But where Pompeii just got covered in ash and pumice, Herculaneum was engulfed by lava, then topped off with a tidal wave of such proportions that the lava was cooled really fast. Among other things, it resulted in a layer of soil that wasn't quite lava but wasn't quite soil any more. It reminded me a little of that. Anyway, you'll have to leave it with me and I'll get back to you once I've had a serious look at it. For now, as you've come all this way, can I offer you a drink and a look around the house. I don't get that many visitors here, and spend so little time in it myself, it's a great treat to be able to show it off.'

'If you're sure we're not intruding,' said Lulu. 'I've never seen any of the twins' work – only their

110

own house – and would love to see what they've done here.'

They started in the kitchen, where Malcolm made tea in earthenware mugs, then began their tour of his home. The whole thing, he explained, was designed with trees in mind and each of the rooms related somewhat to a tree's-eye view. The hall, all wooden and internal, the sitting-room the space beside the tree: sky and grass. He explained that originally he had wanted the worm farm they had seen to be underfoot. Tom had convinced him it would be much more interesting built through the wall adjoining the dining-room. He was, he said, very glad that he had listened, although his sister had steadfastly refused to eat where the worms could watch her! He had hoped, he continued, that it might deter her from visiting entirely, but unfortunately it had not.

Ehlana asked Malcolm to explain his work, which he did. Mainly it seemed to consist of persuading soil that wanted to grow little or nothing that it could be super-productive. Ehlana asked what crops he was working with and how far those had been genetically improved. Lulu slept through most of the conversation. Ehlana listened intently, though it was far beyond her ability to comprehend much of Malcolm's explanations. She thought how much more Jodai would gain from this conversation than she. Indeed, how much more he could give, for it appeared that plant technology in their time was superior to the time Ehlana found herself in.

Eventually, Lulu stirred.

'Oh, god. I'm so sorry,' she gushed. 'I'm not normally this rude, it's just that I had a very late night ...'

'Really, don't worry,' interrupted Malcolm. 'It's flattering that you feel comfortable enough to sleep. I'm not at all offended, so don't give it a second thought. How had you intended getting back home?'

'By bus, again. Though I dare say the tube's running okay now,' replied Lulu.

'It's only Earls Court you've got to get to, isn't it?' he asked.

Lulu nodded.

'Fine, then, I'll run you back. It's not that far and, call me a chauvinist if you have to, but I really don't like the idea of just sending you out into the dark.'

Throughout this exchange, Ehlana was unavailable for comment, being lost in a deep study of the worm farm. In and out of striated layers of soil and sand and humus, the worms cut their trails, unlocking nutrients and spreading them throughout their dark domain. What had Malcolm called them? The producers of the best slow-release fertiliser in the world. But fertilisers had done nothing to improve the harvest – they only managed to maintain it. She heard her name and turned away from the wall.

'Come on then,' said Lulu. 'If Malcolm's going to give us a lift, we ought to go before he changes his mind!'

'My apologies,' said Ehlana. 'I was years away. It is a most remarkable wall that you have.'

'I have to confess that it was started more as a joke. My sister, the bossy one, kept insisting that I should have a fish tank. She thought it would be a "nice"addition, something for me to take an interest in. The worms were a wind-up and a pun at the same time. She's not really that bad, though, I just get a kick out of baiting her. Having said that, I do enjoy watching them and the cost of the tank was entirely tax deductible as I managed to convince the taxman it was a necessary piece of equipment!'

He drove them home in a large, comfortable car. Lulu sat beside him in the front and Ehlana lounged in the back, surveying the evidence that still remained of the wind's violent passage. At one point her hand reached up to touch the crystal that hung at her neck. She remembered other journeys she had made and the fact that so often they seemed to be accompanied by unseasonal weather. This time she had travelled with the largest piece of crystal ever recorded and within a short time the country had been hit by the large, entirely unexpected, storm. Was it possible that she could have been its cause? She determined to make some study into the matter but, if she was correct, it would knock serious holes in the Displacement Theory currently held as valid by the Guild. They arrived at Nevern Square without incident, Malcolm taking Lulu's phone number for a promise that he would call as soon as he had anything to report.

Two messages had been left on Lulu's answering machine: the first from Clem to let them know that he would be flying only one hour later than expected and that he would see them on Thursday. The second was from Tom: a reminder about the twins' fancy dress birthday party on Friday night and an insistent plea that Ehlana join them.

Lulu had difficulty explaining the concept of fancy dress to Ehlana, who could see nothing exciting about pretending to be anyone other than herself. But she finally accepted that it might be entertaining if she threw herself into her role. Lulu explained how she and Clem were going as Josephine and Napoleon. Very appropriate, she said, but would not be drawn further. She then had to explain European history of the late-eighteenth and early-nineteenth centuries!

Trying to find a suitable character for Ehlana to masquerade as was something even more complicated. After many hours with both their heads buried deep in the heavy tomes that Lulu had dragged back from the library, Ehlana had still only found Marco Polo to identify with, despite Lulu's insistence that she could not go as a man. In the end, Ehlana gave in to Lulu's persuasive argument and agreed to dress as Persephone. Lulu's link was tenuous, but the woman did spend part of each year in a place to which she did not belong.

Having spent two days deciding who Ehlana should go as, it took less than an hour to find an appropriate gown because Lulu had a friend in the Wardrobe Department of the BBC.

When they returned from White City, it was to find that Clem had called. He was going straight home from the airport, said his tired voice from the mechanical heart of Lulu's answerphone. He would meet them at the flat around six the following evening. The excitement building for the party was just enough to offset Ehlana's disappointment at Clem's absence – she had been looking forward to testing his reaction to her costume.

Ehlana lay awake much of the night, her thoughts on tomorrow's party. The hours soon passed. In the morning more debris from the storm was cleared and soon it was time to dress for the party. She was glad that Clem did not arrive until Lulu had finished preparing her. Her face painted; her hair so cleverly pinned that it appeared to be caught in the very act of cascading down her back; her gown, a simple white robe that stretched from shoulders to floor, a mass of tiny pleats, the stark purity of its lines broken only by two golden cords that encompassed her rib-cage just below her breasts and held the diaphanous fabric close around her; her shoes, more soles with long leather thongs that crisscrossed her legs from foot to knee. She stood at the open door to greet Clem when he arrived at Lulu's flat. She was well aware of the way that the light travelled through her costume, and found that his expression more than compensated for the disappointment she had earlier felt. Once he was changed, she had to admit that he and Lulu made an extremely attractive couple.

There seemed to be hundreds of people crammed inside Richard and Tom's house when they got there and the overspill filled the marquee that had been erected in the garden. The enormous canopy was of black silk, cut through with glistening bands of gold and the entire structure swayed gently in the evening breeze. Vast urns filled with all manner of flowers were placed about the garden and the temporary structure was lit with tall candles. She took a glass of champagne from the tray that was offered.

She lost sight of Lulu not long after they arrived and quickly discovered she had been following the wrong Bonaparte. Richard greeted her effusively but then was swept away by an enormously tall woman with a bare midriff and the exotic fruit section of her local supermarket on her head.

Ehlana took another glass of the bubbling liquid

and conversed with a six-foot tall Emperor Penguin, who offered to let her hold his egg. She declined and went to find another drink.

She was pursued ardently by a man named Rudolph Valentino, insistently by one of the two Giovanni Casanovas she was introduced to, both of whom fetched her more alcohol, and successfully by one called Mephistopheles, whose dark and brooding features she found quite irresistible. His costume was elegant: black and red with a silken cape that seemed to shimmer as he moved.

This stranger left her side only once all the evening after he had met her and that was at the beginning of their acquaintance. When she named herself Persephone and could not give him the seed that he asked for, he accosted the woman with the fruit and stole the pomegranate from her head-dress. With a small blade he drew from a sheath at his hip he peeled the greeny-orange skin away to reveal the tight-packed jewels beneath.

'Eat,' he said to her.

Ehlana marvelled at the succulence of the tiny seeds as they exploded in her mouth. The stranger lifted the fruit to his mouth and bit deep into it. She reached up to wipe away a trickle of pale red juice that seeped out from the join of his lips. He turned his head to kiss the tips of her fingers. Then he explained that, if one cut across mythologies, he was just another incarnation of Persephone's husband, who held her only because she had eaten a few pomegranate seeds while she stayed with him in Hades. He, Mephistopheles, intended to honour these marriage vows by taking her up to a high place and offering her the kingdoms of the world in exchange for her soul. Or at least offering his body, if she would return the compliment and offer hers.

He took her hand and drew her towards the staircase. His arm stole around her waist as they began to climb the stairs. She leant against him, liking the feel of his body close beside her. He opened the door at the top of the stairs and closed it tight behind them. Ehlana giggled as she recalled the strange three-headed beast that Richard and Tom had helped her create in this room. He stopped her laughter with his mouth, his lips full and hard against her own. His tongue darted out to meet hers and the electricity generated by their first contact coursed through her body.

'You were going to offer me the kingdoms of the world,' she said, and he wordlessly led her to the door which opened onto the terrace. The tumultuous noise from the crowd below assailed them and he pulled her towards the parapet. The music drifted up over the voices: he held her and they danced on the cool, damp grass. He unpinned her hair, untied the cords that defined her breasts, then slipped the fine straps from her shoulders. The fine cotton slithered down to pool around her ankles, shining whitely against the green.

'Now you are Eve,' he said, and kissed the smooth globes of her breasts before bending down to pick up her costume and hang it half over the parapet. He had no apple to tempt her with, instead he used soft caresses and honeyed words.

She shivered, but not with the chill of the air, rather with the fire that slowly grew inside her as his hands moved over her body, touching everywhere but that one small spot that longed for the attention of his cool long fingers. He read her body like a blind man and with such practised ease, his mouth and fingers tracing fiery lines across her skin. She sank to her knees in the grass, overwhelmed by her need of him. He took off his trousers and knelt before her, his stiff rod standing proud of his long white shirt-tails. His caresses continued, stealing closer and closer to her own small shaft. She trembled at his nearness, anticipating that first, sweet touch.

He laughed, a chilling, thrilling sound. 'I'll not offer you the kingdoms of the world until you pledge me your soul,' he told her. He pushed her gently back into the soft grass and at last his finger found her swollen bud. She thought she must come then, but a prick as solid as steel burned its way through her labia and from there travelled up into the slick velvet darkness of her deep well, tearing her mind away from her climax to concentrate on the flesh buried inside her. He moved, slowly at first, but increasing the force with each thrust. Her hand moved down to find and finger the nub of her pleasure while he rode above her. This time, her need would not be ignored and she led him, her hips moving to meet him, driving him harder each time, until she could fight it no more and shuddered beneath him as her orgasm ripped through her entire body. She triggered his: he pushed hard down, filling her tight hole with his flesh as he strained and quivered.

'Ehlana?' A familiar voice cut through her rapture. She turned her face to the house. The door opened and a dark shape in pale trousers walked onto the terrace. 'Ehlana, are you there?'

She froze. She heard the newcomer's sharp intake of breath as he took in what he saw. Then he spun about and retraced his steps. The door shut, loud and hard behind him.

'Ehlana?' her lover said, seeking recognition of the name that he guessed must be hers. She looked up. 'I'd really like to see you again.' She reached up to stop his mouth with her hand. He fought against her, but she silenced him.

'Tonight we have shared fantasies from the beginnings of mankind,' she said. 'Let that be enough. You are Mephistopheles and I, Persephone. Let us slip gently back into the dreams that we came from, not break them by letting the mundane world in.'

Silently, they dressed. Then they returned to the party. Half-way down the stairs she saw a Napoleon leaving, the front door slamming shut behind him. Lulu stood in the hallway, an exasperated expression on her face.

'Clem?' Ehlana asked her, glancing to the door.

'Yes, Clem. He suddenly developed a headache and insisted that we leave. I only asked if he couldn't wait half an hour and he just blew up and stormed off. Fine, he can go back and play the invalid – you and I can get a cab when we're ready!' She linked her arm through Ehlana's and moved towards the garden.

The sun was up before they finally left and, when they reached it, the flat at Nevern Square was empty. There was a message for Lulu from Clem on the answerphone. He said he was sorry, but he just needed to get away from the noise and, once he was in the car, home seemed the best place to go. He promised that he would call her later and hoped that they had both enjoyed the party.

119

In fact, Clem did not return to London before Ehlana left: first, he was unwell and although Lulu went to stay with him for a few days, Ehlana stayed in Lulu's flat. Then he returned to work and did not have time to visit. Ehlana was disappointed she had had no opportunity to try and explain, or apologise for, what he had seen. His hurt had been almost tangible. But she knew to keep it to herself and not burden her friend.

Instead, Ehlana immersed herself in research, building up a collection of books that she would insist on delivering to the arrogant Lora. See if she can just brush me aside again then, she thought.

As it was, she had only just stepped out of the shower when the first stirrings in her crystal reminded her that she belonged elsewhere. She had time enough only to pull a robe from the back of the door before the pain-filled blackness gathered her into its heart. Then she had no room for thoughts of the books left behind.

Chapter Seven

Nucassel, October 3550PS

The Laboratory was teeming with people: the low buzz of their voices was the first thing her returning senses brought to her. Liranai passed her from the podium to hands she did not recognise. Tolai bustled forwards, his pleasure at her safe return apparent on his face. Aware of eyes other than his upon her, she gathered the blue silk of the robe tight around her and wished, not for the last time, for a little more warning before she travelled. She was not allowed long for self-pity, as her colleagues gathered swiftly around her and took notes as she answered their many questions about her visit.

She was relieved when she was finally permitted to leave: it felt as if days had passed since her return and she longed for the quiet of her room. The corridors were empty and silent as she walked – so different to the constant bustle of London.

As she reached her door, she was surprised at the sound of laughter that filtered through. Unsure quite what to expect, she threw it open and went in. Seven, no eight, naked people were moving around her room in a frenzy of activity. One of them, a tall black man she thought she recognised as Divornai, had a piece of material covering his eyes and it appeared that he was chasing the others. Suddenly the group noticed her standing in the doorway and froze, but Divornai carried on running, his face finding, and his mouth fastening on the shoulder of the man beside him. The man he sucked on reached up and pulled the binding from his eyes, then nodded towards Ehlana.

'It appears my invitation must have got lost in the post!' quipped Ehlana before she remembered that her audience would not have the slightest idea what she meant. 'Oh, hell. Never mind, it's not important. But I do think I deserve some introductions, nevertheless.'

Mara shuffled forwards, her face red, but whether with embarrassment or exertion Ehlana could not decide. 'Please forgive us,' she implored. 'We did not expect you back so soon. I must confess that, since you left, we have occasionally met here. Not usually so many, but among our friends it is not a close-guarded secret that we come here. I know we should have asked,' she gushed, 'but you were away and, well, it seemed the ideal location: you are the only one of us who does not share rooms!' Ehlana stepped fully in to the room and shut the door behind her.

'It is no fault of Mara's,' said Jodai. 'It was my suggestion. If you must be angry, be so with me.'

'I am not angry, just intrigued by what you were doing when I came in. Tell me that and I shall forgive you all!' Ehlana replied.

'Just a little diversion we enjoy. The rules to our game are very simple,' Jodai explained. 'But far better demonstrated than described.' He took something from Divornai and moved to stand beside her. 'If you would allow, I suggest that you be the hunter this time in order to discover how the game is played.'

Ehlana readily agreed, her earlier tiredness already forgotten. Jodai tied the blindfold tight around her eyes while Mara first slid the silk robe from her shoulders and then bound her wrists.

'We turn you round three times and then let you free,' Jodai continued. 'You walk around the room hunting for a victim, while your potential victims try to avoid you. Until they are found they must move constantly – an early amendment to the rules! However, once you have touched one, they must stand still until you identify them. If you guess wrong, they are free to move again and you must hunt another.'

'But how am I to name them with my hands tied behind my back?' Ehlana asked.

'Ah,' said Mara, 'that is the best part! You can use nothing but the three senses left to you. Only smell, taste and hearing remain unencumbered. If you can force a response from them, their voices often help. Sulana, for one, has a tendency to giggle if you nuzzle her neck. You are at a disadvantage, though, for this is not the first time we have played. If by your third guess you are still wrong, we will release your hands to help you in your search. You are agreeable?'

Ehlana nodded and felt hands on her shoulders that spun her round and round until she no longer knew where even her door was. All of a sudden, the comforting hands that had turned her withdrew and she found she was alone. She stood, wavering slightly, and listened. Over to her left, not far away, she could hear someone moving: a gentle patter of naked feet against the floor. She went towards the sound and felt the breeze the body made as it rushed past her. A giggle to her right made her turn and swoop. Again she closed on nothing but air. She stood motionless, hearing them weave around her. Footfalls and breathing was most of what she heard. One pair of feet came towards her, only a gentle squeak giving away their advance.

Would they pass left or right? she wondered.

She dodged right and her face grazed against the passing body. At the first contact, her victim halted. Running her nose along the piece of flesh in front of her she discovered that the skin travelled further than her nose could reach, even standing on tiptoes. None of the women in the room had been that much taller than her, so she reasoned it must be one of the men. Four men she had seen: Jodai and Lomai she knew well; Divornai had been the hunter before; the fourth she had seen often working in the Refectory but had never known his name. She stood back on the soles of her feet and pressed her face against the skin that rested beside it. What felt like a shoulder-blade angled into her temple, so she walked around him until she would have been staring him in the face were it not for her blindfold. She leant forward until her nose touched his chest. Long soft hair curled there and a warm, sweet smell lingered. The scent seemed out of place, as if it did not belong here, but she could not recognise it. Her discovery removed one from her list – it could not be Jodai. Her head moved a little way to the side and could not resist a little nip at the soft teat that it found there. She was rewarded with a groan from her victim, but it gave her no further clues. She moved further down his body, unsure of what extra information she might gather, but greatly enjoying the game.

Remembering other games, she recalled that Lomai, as a child, had responded with almost hysterical glee to a gentle tickle just above his left ankle, which had so entertained his hatchlings that they took every opportunity to exploit it. She wondered if the response would remain in the adult, assuming it was him she had found. Hampered slightly by the lack of support her hands would have given, she dropped gently to her knees. She put her face forward to ascertain where she found herself on his body, only to encounter an interested party which must have been staring her in the face. A roar of laughter behind her only reinforced the certainty that she had not found Jodai. She brushed the plaintiff prick aside with her cheek and moved her face to his thigh. Slowly, she slid her lips down his leg, which seemed incredibly long. Soft hairs stroked her face as she moved and again the familiar smell that seemed so alien here. At last she found his ankle and licked gently at the little dent behind the bony protrusion. She thought she felt a tension beneath her tongue and licked again. There was definitely some resistance there, but she was unsure if it meant it was Lomai trying hard to resist or some other who must think her an utter madwoman for attempting to name him by tasting his ankle. She lifted her face towards his and asked for assistance in regaining her feet. Around her voices whispered, too quiet for her to hear. Strong hands slid into her armpits and raised her entirely from the floor until she had stretched her legs straight out to stand. That gave her a measure of his strength. Divornai and Lomai both were strong, but the one that laboured in the Refectory had never particularly impressed her with his strength.

So, two now to choose from. Divornai she had seen when she first entered the room, but she could not recall how much hair he bore on his chest; of Lomai she had seen only his face before the blindfold cut off her vision. They had left shared rooms long before a single hair would have grown on his chest, so she had no way of telling if it could be him. She was left then only with the smell. Divornai was an archivist, she thought, and Lomai worked in agriculture. No, the fragrance certainly did not come from the Library. Then it must be Lomai. Or could it be that she had underestimated the strength of the cook? What was it she smelt? She pressed her face hard against his chest and breathed in deeply. It reminded her of somewhere she had walked not so long ago, somewhere dark and strange. She inhaled again, her eyes tight shut beneath the folds that blinded her, struggling to remember. Then she spoke.

'I name you Lomai,' she said. The reward for her success was his removal of the blindfold and the smile on his face.

'What gave me away?' he asked. 'I thought I had you totally confused.'

'I am new to the game,' she replied. 'It took me too long to tie your smell to who you are. Of all the men, you are the only one who works in the Field. Your odour brought back a walk I took late one evening on damp grass under a sky very different from here. Once I remembered what it reminded me of, I knew it could only be you.' Behind her back, someone worked at the knot that tied her wrists.

'Now it is Lomai's turn to hunt,' said Mara. 'You bind his eyes while I attend to his wrists.'

'Beware, Ehlana,' he whispered as she moved to wrap the cloth around his head. 'If I catch you, I shall teach you how seriously we play. Then you will realise how gentle was your treatment of me.' He leant forwards, she thought to aid her bandaging, but instead his lips found hers and stole a kiss, his tongue darting forth to effect the softest of penetrations. 'You cannot say I have not warned you!' She checked that the binding around his eyes was neither too tight nor too loose, then she stepped back and watched as Mara deftly turned him.

As soon as she released him, the others began to move around the room, dodging him as best they could. Twice he almost had her, but she managed to slip away before he touched her. When he finally caught the tall blonde colleague of Mara's, she felt a little disappointed. She watched as he pressed his body fully against that of his captive, as if he hoped to imprint her form upon himself. He dropped his head to feel the hidden face with his. He pushed his head down until he located his quarry's neck, but no signs did he find there. He moved to stand behind his prey then knelt. He pushed his face into the round soft skin at the top of her buttocks, then with exquisite precision traced his tongue down the line between the two. When he could go no further, he named her.

'Elia, you are taken!' The blonde swung round and pulled the blindfold from his face.

'Sunfire! But you are a rogue to name me by one small contact,' his victim replied, as she looked over her shoulder, straining to see the flesh that had given her away. 'It must be truly vast to be so easily identified!'

'Not so. A sweet rump,' he replied, 'but recognisably yours.'

After she was tied, Lomai moved to Ehlana's side whilst another spun Elia.

'I hunted for you,' he whispered quietly in her ear.

'I know,' Ehlana replied. 'Twice you nearly caught me. But I do not think you would have named me so easily.'

'I would have known you because you are new to me: I have never had the chance to taste or touch you. The very strangeness of you would have told me which you were. But I would have taken time before I named you.' Elia had started moving now, so Lomai took Ehlana's arm and pulled her into the far corner of her room behind the single chair it held.

'Is this allowed?' asked Ehlana.

'Oh, the occasional breach of the rules is permissible. In fact, Jodai had great difficulty the first time we played for he had to identify a joined couple! But if anyone's conduct is deemed unbecoming, a forfeit must be paid. I am sure our talking will be tolerated, but we must keep our voices low, else Elia will surely find us.' He shut his eyes and buried his face in her neck. She could feel his breath upon her skin. He breathed in deep, inhaling her scent. 'Thus I would recognise you,' he said. 'One breath would be all that I needed. But then I would take my time to make sure.' He held her face solid between his hands. He bent forward, his tongue sneaked out between his lips and traced the softest of lines along her eyebrow: her eyes closed involuntarily 'I would possibly start here. Then perhaps here.' His tongue set forth again, this time its pressure even lighter as it ran along the fold of her upper eyelid. The sensation was strange to Ehlana, but exciting. 'Then here,' he said, his mouth dropping to hers, his tongue this time hard and insistent as it fought briefly with her own. 'By now, I would definitely know it was you. But I would not name you, yet. Next, I would move down a little more. His lips brushed against her collar-bone and his descent continued. 'Until I reached here.' His mouth stopped at her erect nipple, his tongue flicking out to caress it, then he swallowed it between his soft, warm lips.

Ehlana sighed gently at his insistent sucking and Lomai brusquely moved his head away.

'That too would have proved your name, but still I would not name you.' He knelt at her feet and then pushed her gently back against the wall. His hands slipped between her slightly parted legs and forced them wider open. 'Then I would move to taste you, here.' His head dropped forward and his tongue darted out to touch the apex of the split that hid her bud. She slid down the wall, her legs weakened by the unexpected contact, only to find his hands at her buttocks. They dragged her a fraction closer to his waiting mouth. His tongue trailed from her bud to her aching hole and when it got there, it slid within, tasting her core. 'Ah,' he sighed, as he moved back from her. 'From that I would know you best of all, but alas I would have to name you then, else risk a forfeit.'

'Forfeit?' asked Ehlana. 'I do not know this word!'

'Divornai found it in his readings: it is a penalty to be paid for a perceived wrongdoing. There are many actions that result in forfeits when we play,' Lomai explained, 'and nearly as many different types of forfeit.'

Ehlana was still a little bemused, but when his hand dropped to stroke her labia, she put her confusion away and concentrated on the effect his fingers were having on the prominent nub of flesh they had found. Slowly, he teased it. Harder and larger it grew. Behind and below it, Ehlana craved something more solid than the finger he slid in and then brought back for them both to taste. She wished the others gone, in order that she might better enjoy her first encounter with this hatchling. As if reading her mind, he quietly laughed and sent both hands to forage at her groin. With two fingers he pushed back the hood which tried to cover her most sensitive spot. Then another joined them, its purpose purely to stimulate the exposed bud. Faster and faster it flicked across the tiny place, until Ehlana forgot everything apart from his hands. She groaned out loud, afraid that he might stop before she was ready. His efforts increased and she pitched headlong into a shuddering climax, still pinned against the wall. When she finally opened her eyes, it was to find the two of them surrounded by the others. The game, it appeared, was over.

'Forfeit, forfeit,' they chanted together. Ehlana raised one eyebrow and looked quizzically at Lomai.

'Did I not tell you that the greatest forfeit goes always to the first person to achieve their goal?' said Lomai. She glared at him. 'How foolish of me,' he said shrugging his shoulders. 'I regret that rules are made to be kept and even if I wished to intercede on your behalf I would not, because I know what follows.'

'This is ridiculous,' she retorted. 'How can I be asked to pay something when I had not even realised there was a price?'

'But you must,' said Sulana. 'If you do not, our game is ruined. I will not permit otherwise.'

'Nor I,' said Divornai, and his words were chorused by the others.

'If you refuse to obey, it will go harder for you,' said Mara, her severity mocking, but her knowing smile confident.

Ehlana gave in and, as she was ordered, she sat upon the bottom of the bed and lay back. Mara came to stand at her right shoulder and took her wrist, then moved back until Ehlana's arm was at full stretch. Sulana repeated the process with her other wrist. She felt her feet being lifted from the ground and looked along her body: Elia and Almira held an ankle each and together lifted her legs high and wide apart. She tried to struggle against them, but they held her solid. All she could move were her hips, and those only a little. She saw Lomai kneel at the foot of the bed and she felt his stiff prick at her portal. Momentarily, she resisted his pushings, her hole clenched tight to bar his entry, until his finger found the key and rubbed softly until all her resistance was gone. Then he slid his massive head inside her. Ehlana grunted, so little had she expected its girth, but it did not travel far before she felt the pressure of his hips against her buttocks. Relieved that she would not be split in two by an unanticipated giant, she began to enjoy the sensation of his head as it probed her. From time to time he would almost withdraw, but not quite, stopping to feel the pulse that throbbed at her widespread doorway, but when he began his battering in earnest, one of his fingers moved to rub against her bud while another found its way inside the tight dryness of her arse. Ehlana found herself incapable of movement as he drove inside her, the intensity and fury of his thrusts increasing as he moved inexorably towards his orgasm. She fought to meet him, but her efforts only spurred him on and he came before her. As soon as his spasms had finished, he moved away: it seemed involuntarily. His place was taken by her other hatchling, his familiar prick seeming smaller inside her than she recalled.

'So, do you approve your penalty, sister-lover? It seems appropriate that we should all enjoy our benefactress for, without your intervention, we would all be hard at study now. Instead I ride hard inside you – a much more delightful prospect.' As he spoke, he moved himself in and out of her slick hole.

Held as she was, Ehlana wriggled as Jodai spitted her, desperate for a little more friction on her swollen clit. He guessed what she sought and moved a hand to aid her. 'In some ways it is a design fault,' he said as he rubbed her. 'If a man had designed you, it would be just inside the entrance, ready to be stroked by each thrust of the prick that moved inside you. As it is, a little manual assistance is so often required. There again, for your part, you would probably design a man who wore his mouth just above his member, so that he could eat you and take you at the same time.'

Behind her head someone called for him to cut short his conversation and not forget that others still had a turn to take. 'Your pardon, friends.' To Ehlana he said, 'I am sorry, but it appears our little chat will have to wait. I had sought merely to prolong our pleasure, not to keep desperate men from theirs.' Ehlana, distracted by his conversation, now returned her attention to the more important things. His finger still played with her bud, rubbing rings around her distended bulb. In time with his rubbing, she flexed her inner muscles along the length of his prick. He moaned and increased both friction and pressure in each place that he touched. The speed of his breathing increased and a second finger joined the first to drum an insistent rhythm on her clitoris. Ehlana changed her own inner flexings to a wave that drew him ever deeper until, at last, neither could resist the orgasm that engulfed them both.

Her breathing had not yet returned to even a semblance of normal before Jodai moved and the stranger took his place, his slender tool encountering no difficulty as he stabbed into her.

After no more than three thrusts, he withdrew, but only to insert his thumbs in Ehlana's wet hole for moisture before he moved them down to the tight ring of her arse. He pushed them in slowly, prising her apart at the same time as he burrowed deeper in. When she felt she could take little more there was one, final pull before he slipped her close shut around the head of his prick. Haltingly, he introduced his length inch by inch until he was buried inside her tight, dark hole. As he moved, he brought a large hand down to stretch her labia wide apart. One finger he pushed deep inside her empty tunnel, and for a while stroked his length through the fine membrane that separated them. Then he drew it out and, with it, began to caress her exposed clitoris. The tightness of her hole and the dry friction therein made him come before Ehlana was more than half-way there.

His place was taken by Divornai, whose skin reminded her of her first taste of chocolate. 'Let us see if my friends have attended properly to their task. It would not do if you were still too tight to take me.' Ehlana thought he boasted but, when he spread her hole wide open with his fingers in order to admit a head at least a match in size to Lomai's, she thought again. This one did not stop short, but continued in until she thought she would die.

'Still constricted,' he said, 'but all the better for me. Just once, I should like to go first, but they always insist that I wait.' He put the tip of his index finger in his open mouth and licked its underside slowly with his pink tongue. His hand dropped down and pushed her hard down on the bed, his damp digit finding and fingering her bud. She felt her legs being placed on his shoulders and the sudden release of tension as gripping fingers freed their hold. Her arms too were laid on the bed above her head and the vice-like pressure left her wrists. Although her limbs were now her own, she was incapable of any kind of movement, so full she was of Divornai's monster. At first he could hardly move: her hole held him as tight as she had been held by the others. But slowly, almost imperceptibly, he began to shift inside her, fractionally, as her tight walls struggled to provide the oils essential for the task. It seemed ages before he began to move more easily, but the more he stroked her, the more leeway the tight stretch of her tunnel allowed him. Against her other hole, his two heavy sacks swung: their slap an erotic reminder of the much slenderer weapon that had recently sheathed itself there. She hung with her ankles locked behind his thick neck, her legs tight against his torso, as he began to thrust hard. The hand that held her open dropped outside her thighs and from the movements she felt there, she knew he massaged his pendulous balls. The strong spasms that Ehlana felt detonate along his massive length as he came triggered her own, and she screamed out as it ripped through her body.

Some time passed before she entirely regained her senses: smell was the first. All around she could scent warm bodies and sex. She looked and found couples joined all around her room, some still in satiation, others yet seeking release. Lomai and Mara were the last to stop moving, Mara dropping down to collapse on Lomai's broad chest. Eventually, and silently, each one rose almost in turn to dress and then depart.

At last, all had left save Jodai, who came to sit beside her. He seemed a little awkward and said nothing, so Ehlana hunted for something to say. It took her a while before she could find any subject which did not appear mundane after their earlier experience.

'So,' Ehlana asked him, 'do you still see much of Emora?'

'It is partly due to her that these entertainments began in your room. I met with her again not long before you left, but this time she came prepared. Once we were alone, she donned a magister's black robe – you know how they open from the neck?'

135

She nodded and he continued. 'Well, she put on the robe but did not fasten it: I could see a pale band of flesh stretching from her neck to her feet, the curve of her breasts nearly to their peaks before the black fabric claimed them, the dark patch of fur at the juncture of her legs. I moved towards her, eager for contact, but she produced a wicked-looking switch and beat me off. She forced me to face away from her and to remove my gown. Then she whipped me – eighteen strokes across my back and buttocks. She beat me so hard I could feel trickles running down my skin and knew they were not sweat trails. Her breathing was so loud and fast behind me it sounded as if she ran a race. To this day I do not know if she finished my beating or merely fainted before she was through, but when I turned to face her once the pain allowed me, I found her crumpled in a heap of black cloth and white flesh upon the floor. I lifted her up and carried her to the pallet, then arranged her limbs as best I could. Throughout my agony, my staff had remained rigidly hard and seeing her prone, I just could not ignore its presence. I moved her legs apart on the bed and bent forward to taste her. On that matter, I have made an interesting discovery, or I at least am fascinated by it: each woman has her own, personal flavour. My current goal is to taste all! But I digress. I allowed myself a sip from Emora's lips and found her to be wetter than any I have encountered before or since. I could not resist further investigation and, as I played, she woke. The first indication I had that she had regained herself was when her thighs wrapped so tight around my head I could not move. She locked them tight behind my neck and trapped me there. My only escape was to lick her and suck

136

her until she achieved her summit. Three times I felt her writhe beneath me before she finally let me go! I do not know how long a time had passed, but my poor tongue ached for days. Since then she has repeated the procedure many times, but will never allow even the very gentlest of penetrations. Naturally, this was becoming somewhat uncomfortable for me, though Mara and I shared frequently. Over a short while, both Mara and I introduced others to our conspiracy – if nothing else it meant I could often find the kind of companionship I craved, no matter what time Emora was finished with me. So, you see, you could just as easily blame Emora for the activities in your room as you blame Mara or I!'

'And there are but the eight of you?' she asked.

'Oh, no,' he replied. 'That was all who were free and willing for games this afternoon. In all, there are nearly forty conspirators.'

'Jodai, I have only been gone two weeks! You cannot have done anything else in all the time I have been gone!' she cried, surprised by both his calm acceptance of the figures and the meagre total of his discretion. 'I thought we were trying to discover why only we knew of this thing, not introducing it to all the populace!' He sat there, his face twisted as if he sucked on something sour.

'I meant no harm, it just sort of grew: I showed one, Mara showed another, they each showed someone else, and so on. In no time at all we were a group rather than a few. I am sorry you are angry.' He looked so woebegone that Ehlana could not chastise him long. Apart from which, his tale of Emora had strangely excited her and she dare not antagonise him if she required his assistance.

'Oh, well, I shall be here but one night and then

you can continue your activities unhindered by my need to use my room. I am not truly angry, but would caution you: we still do not know who we might offend with these activities. There must be enough of you now to keep each other entertained – leave it there and make all swear that they will not name others if pressed. You cannot tell what may happen if too many know.' He promised her that he would do as she asked. Then he enquired whether there might be some little service he could offer in atonement.

'A little of what Emora craves could do no harm,' she replied as she slid the blue silk of Lulu's robe from her shoulders and lay down on her bed. 'And it might soothe the bruises that I fear grow there. But do it because you want to please, not appease, me.'

Jodai lay down between her legs, his arms under her thighs and drove his mouth straight to the heart of her. The immediacy of the contact with no preamble left her breathless. With strong licks he brushed aside the folds of her labia until her erect clit was exposed entirely to the mercies of his tongue.

'Sunfire! But you do this well,' Ehlana exclaimed. 'How many hours have you practised since the last time with me? No, do not answer. I do not think that I could bear it if you stopped.'

His rhythm continued, insistent, as his tongue beat a new pulse into the tiny bead of flesh it tormented. He paid no attention to any other part of her body. The room was warm and nothing stirred the air, just the softest breeze of his breath at her groin. She felt an overwhelming ache, a quiet desperation that wanted both Jodai's oral contact and his hard prick simultaneously. She let her mind wander, trying to find in her head what she desired in her body. Memories washed over her as, in turn, her imagination placed each man she had shared with deep inside her. Lomai, with his short, thick implement: how tight she would stretch around his distended head. She thought of Tom and the reality of Jodai slipped easily to an imaginary Richard: the twins would take turns to fuck her and suck her. She groaned as the image threatened to achieve her climax before she was ready, before she had finished her list. She turned her mind swiftly to Tolai: try as she might, she could not see him sharing this task gladly with Jodai – for some reason it made him seem undignified.

She concentrated again on what Jodai was doing. The beat continued, unchanged, but he varied the pressures of his tongue and she knew not what to expect – a short, staccato burst or a leisurely licking that made Ehlana's hips rise from the bed in order to maintain the sweet contact for as long as she could. It felt as if her tiny bud had grown enormous under his tongue and she thought again of her lovers. Only Clem remained and as her memory slipped him inside her, she knew that his was the best fit.

'If you really want to please me,' she said through lips far drier than she had realised, 'slide up the bed and roll over. I want to try something different – more of the same for you, but something else altogether for me.' She moved off the bed and waited until he lay still. With her knees either side of his rib-cage and her hands by his thighs, she crouched on all fours above him. Slowly, she lowered herself down to his face and, once his tongue regained its goal, concentrated again on her earlier vision. Swiftly it came: she could almost feel his hands upon her hips as he readied himself to take her; the pressure of his great head as it touched the swollen entrance to her warm darkness; the gentle stretchings as her walls moved to accommodate him; the soft tickle of his hairs against her labia; the hard edge of his pubis as it crushed against the taut flesh between her two holes.

Beneath her, while Clem fucked her mind, Jodai sucked her body. With her mind so occupied it felt as if all her physical senses were now concentrated in the one, small place. Jodai increased the tempo of his lickings and the phantom poised above her matched his speed. Her vision expanded to include what Jodai would see if he looked up from his vantage point: the small tight sacks swinging just below the slim white thing that slid in and out of her, glistening with her dew; the movement of her tight lips as they tried to follow after his withdrawing prick, their happy return as he thrust back inside her. She collapsed her shoulders across Jodai, her face nestling against his groin, as she struggled to give the ghost in her vision even deeper access to her core. The changed angle pressed her pubis down against Jodai's soft mouth and he increased the friction of his lickings. The imaginary fingers gripping her hips dug their nails into her skin and the invisible prick moved so hard and so deep she thought it would pierce her. Jodai's tongue maintained its frenzied attack: licking and sucking and rubbing until Ehlana had no option but to let her vision explode with her climax. She rolled to one side of him and lay there panting. The image had been so strong that she was surprised to find that they were alone, but when Jodai made to mount her, she pushed him away.

'Ah, no. If you recall, I was playing Emora, so you shall have to find someone else to play that game with,' she admonished. 'Apart from the fact that I leave in the morning and must sleep before I travel, I have taken such a battering tonight that I could not face another!'

'But we would have nowhere to go!' he complained.

'Try the Field, then!' she replied, exasperated by his petulance. 'It is your own fault. You have become so good at that particular game that I do not need another. Kiss me, first, before you go. Tomorrow you can use my room to your heart's content.' He bent to embrace her, gathered his robe around him and walked to the door. Just before he opened it, he turned towards her, a hopeful expression on his face.

'If I beg, would you change your mind?' he asked.

'No,' she replied and pulled the cushion from beneath her head to throw it where he stood. By the time it hit the door he was already gone. His parting, fraught expression made her laugh – in so many ways the discovery of what his adult body could do had made him a child again, so eager and inquisitive.

She slept well, though, that night and awoke early. Before she left her room, she debated hard whether she should return Lulu's blue gown: the red and gold beast embroidered on its back stared at her from the chair, willing her to decide. There was nothing she could hope to take in exchange so, reluctantly, she folded it carefully and carried it with her when she left.

Magister Tolai was alone in the Laboratory and embraced her tightly in greeting. As they moved apart, she raised his hand to her breast and pressed it there for a long moment. His smile rewarded her gesture. Before they had a chance to speak, the door burst open and Horai rushed in, abject apologies on his lips.

'Never mind, never mind,' said the Magister genially. 'You are here now, so we may begin. Come here, Ehlana, and remove your crystal. While you journeyed last, I gave some consideration to when you might like to return to. Your hopes for the soil analysis would require time, so I thought to circumnavigate your wait, by sending you some years further on.' From his work-bench he lifted a crystal on a chain. 'This one is three and a half carats and, if my calculations are correct, should take you at least seven years after your last visit. It is my hope that in that time your scientist will have made all of his tests.' He stood up and fastened the new crystal around her neck. In return, she bent forward and kissed him deeply.

'You are too thoughtful, Tolai,' she said. 'Simpleton that I am, it had not occurred to me to even consider it.'

'The premise and cutting were mine, but the calculations were Horai's – if you do not arrive when we expect, you must blame him!' His smile to Horai denied the criticism inferred by his words. 'Now, the sooner you leave, the quicker you will find your results.' As she turned, he slapped her gently on a rounded globe. 'Step lively, child!'

She moved onto the podium and waited. The

142

new crystal hung heavily on its golden chain. When the pain started, she was surprised to find it was no longer alarming: it had become instead a reassurance that she travelled.

Chapter Eight

London, May 1995AD

She found herself in the bedroom of an unfamiliar house. The light was just beginning to seep through the curtains and she saw that Lulu, her face lined even in sleep, was lying next to an equally unfamiliar man. Ehlana stretched forward and shook her gently awake.

'It's me,' she whispered, as her friend struggled to surface from slumber. 'It's Ehlana.'

'Ehlana? Here? Give me a couple of minutes and we'll go back to my place,' Lulu replied, as she slipped out between the sheets, picked up some clothes from the floor and began to dress. Once she was ready, she shook her companion, saying 'Rob, I've got to go. I'll call you later.'

He mumbled something in response and Lulu led Ehlana through a doorway and down some stairs. Pausing at the front door, Lulu swore and turned back, motioning Ehlana to stay. She returned no more than a minute later, this time with a bag in her hand. 'Come on, it won't take us more than an hour to drive back to London.'

It seemed to Ehlana that Lulu handled the car extremely well. She had never understood the need they all had to travel at such incredible speeds. Planes were one thing: they needed the speed to stay up, but she couldn't fathom why, when the traffic so often moved at a snail's pace, cars should also need to go so fast. As they travelled, they talked.

'Who is Rob?' asked Ehlana.

'Just the latest model in a long line,' explained Lulu.

'What about Clem? Does he not object?' Ehlana felt she still did not entirely understand 'relationships'.

'We split up about five years ago. It just wasn't working out. Neither of us was really where we wanted to be, nor with whom we wanted to be with. Clem even tried marriage afterwards, but that didn't work either,' continued Lulu. 'Oh, I still see him from time to time. We've been friends for so long that we've stayed friends; we still even sleep with each other occasionally, but we're just lovers, not in love,' explained Lulu. 'I'll call him, or at least leave a message, when we get back to town. He'd hate to miss you.'

'It would be good to see him again,' replied Ehlana.

'You caused quite a stir after the last time you were here. Malcolm nearly badgered us to death with his questions about your soil sample. We ended up having to tell him the truth. I don't know for sure if he ever believed it, but it did at least shut him up. I'll give Richard and Tom a call and

145

get them to track him down. I don't recall the results, but Malcolm was definitely very excited.'

The journey was soon completed. The roads were empty, almost as far as Lulu's flat. It was already very warm by the time they got inside.

'I wonder if there's a storm brewing,' said Lulu. 'It's either that, or you've brought the summer with you! You can get some breakfast together while I make some phone calls.'

From the kitchen, Ehlana heard one half of Lulu's conversations.

'Come on, answer the damn thing.' A pause. 'Shit!' said Lulu and began to dial another number. 'Hi, Ruthie. It's Lulu. Any idea where Clem is now? Hell. Listen, will you get a message to him for me – it's really important. Tell him Ehlana's back. She's staying with me, but I don't know how long for. Okay? Great. Thanks a lot. Send my love to the boys. Bye.' She hung up and dialled a third number.

'Hello, Tom and Richard, Lulu here. I've got a visitor who'd like to see you and more importantly, though I know you'll be green with envy, needs to see Malcolm. Give me a call as soon as you get this. Cheers, bye.' She hung up and walked into the kitchen.

'Well, for the moment, that's the best I can do. Give it a couple of hours and I'll wake some people up if I haven't heard anything by then. Clem's *en route* to Hong Kong and I've sent a message; Tom and Richard aren't answering their phone yet, but I don't know if it's because they're asleep or away.'

Richard rang three hours later and Malcolm fifteen minutes after that, adamant that Ehlana must come to Islington and hear his findings face to face. His only concession was that she could come as soon as she could get there. Lulu took her part-way on the Underground and left her at Piccadilly Circus with instructions and a map. The Victoria Line train was packed so tight with commuters that although she could reach nothing to hold on to, the sheer volume of the crowd held her upright on the uncomfortable journey.

Whenever she left the security of Lulu's flat and moved among London's crowded streets, she felt sure that someone would point her out as alien – a concept she had encountered during various news bulletins, but she had no idea quite where the authorities might try to extradite her to. However, none of her travelling companions paid the slightest attention to either her or anyone else. Ehlana supposed that, if she fell to the floor that instant, dead, not one of them would even glance up and they would merely step over her as they reached their destination. She was glad when, at King's Cross, she finally found a seat.

Malcolm met her at the ticket barrier and she was glad of an amiable face in the sea of disinterest that had carried her there. However, he refused to be drawn on the sample before they reached his house. When they finally arrived, he sent Ehlana into the sitting-room while he went to make tea. Very little appeared to have changed in the few days and seven and a half years since she had last been there, except for the worm wall, which was far darker than she remembered. Malcolm came in then, laden with cups and files.

'Sit down,' he said, 'and take this.' He passed her a large china vessel filled to the brim with the pale brown, steaming liquid that seemed to be an intrin-

147

sic part of contemporary life. He sat beside her on the long, green sofa and opened the first of his files. He passed her a sheet of paper and continued. 'These were my preliminary findings. You caused me quite a few sleepless nights, I can tell you. Until Lulu finally explained, or at least I accepted that the line she was feeding me was as plausible as anything that I could come up with. My closest guess was that it came from a meteor crater, though not one I could find any reference to. Did she really tell me the truth?'

'That I come from an Earth seared by the heat of an angry sun some four thousand years in the future?'

He nodded.

'It is true. I journeyed the first time to Lulu by accident and now do not seem to travel anywhere else. Tell me, is there anything we can do to reclaim the land? I do not know what has been tried there already: if there is other, more technical information you need, I am possibly the least able to provide it, but I am sure I could find much if I knew the questions to ask.'

'That probably isn't necessary,' Malcolm replied. 'You were looking at the solution when I came in.'

'The worms?' asked Ehlana, incredulous. Malcolm nodded again, vigorously. She moved back to the wall, and studied it more carefully. For a long time she saw nothing, then a pinkish-grey head poked out to touch the red glass of the wall and slide down it for a hand's span, before returning to the warm embrace of the soil. It was as thick as her finger and as long as her forearm. 'They are much larger now, and the soil is much darker, but I cannot see much else to indicate success.'

'The worms should only have increased in numbers, not size – those you saw before were fully grown adults: these are something else altogether. I can't even claim it as a conscious experiment. It was Christmas five, maybe six, years ago. I got drunk and I got maudlin – sat about crying how the planet was going to die. Stupid, I know, it'll happen one way or another and it's not as if I'll be about then anyway, but that's alcohol for you. Anyway, I'd still got a heap of fragments left from the tests I'd carried out, and I dropped half a dozen small pieces into the tank. I seem to remember wondering whether there could be any nutritional value in eating something now that wouldn't be created for millennia. Anyway, I did it and then I didn't think very much about it again for a couple of years. It took me that long to notice how much they'd grown. So, unfortunately, my records only start from then.' He passed a weighty, battered file across to Ehlana. He continued his discourse, quoting ratios and quotients. Ehlana flicked through the papers, hoping to find something in the charts and notes that might better explain to her what he was trying to say. She was unsuccessful. 'The really interesting research began when I started using some of the soil from the tank. The yield increased one thousand-fold in undiluted soil and by three hundred per cent in a mix with ordinary earth. Two years ago I took three hundred grams of the tank's soil and a dozen worms out to a project I was working on in the southern Sahara. There's now a square metre of viable soil in one of the planet's most inhospitable deserts, and it's growing!'

'In laymen's terms, what does it mean for us?'

'If you carry a worm farm back – nothing as big

149

as this one – given time and sufficient care, the worms will change your exhausted soil into that.' He pointed at the rich brown earth of the tank.

'How long?' she asked hoarsely, her tongue stuck to the roof of a mouth gone suddenly dry.

'Difficult to estimate, really. It would depend on how much soil you have and how many worms you take. Say a couple of thousand years. What's the atmosphere like?' Ehlana looked at him blankly. 'The air?' Still blank. 'Oxygen, nitrogen, carbon dioxide?' he continued, hoping to prompt some recognition on her part.

'Breathable within the Dome, where it is produced. Negligible outside. No one ever ventures out without breathing apparatus,' she finally replied.

'Once the surface area has increased beyond a certain level and the plants grown to fill this, there's no reason why careful management should not eventually change that.' Ehlana's expression prompted further explanation. 'I mean that sufficient arboreal growth would, over time, produce a breathable atmosphere. It's not markedly different from the way it started in the first place.'

'All that, from these small things?' she said. 'Can you tell me where I might find a tank?'

'No, but I shall help you build one. If nothing else, you should have a better understanding of the inhabitants once you've created their environment. Once they've grown large enough, they'll be better off split up into smaller units and you'll be there to show your colleagues how. All we need to do is work out how large a tank you can take. Any information you can give me on that?'

She stood and thought for some time. 'I think

'that I shall need to be able to hold it: when we travel with another, the guide must maintain physical contact throughout the journey. I must also be unable to drop it – the travelling is both arduous and painful. If I lose contact, the tank is gone forever.'

'Okay. I'll get to work on that basis. How long are you here for?'

'A month,' she replied. 'Will that be long enough?'

'It'll have to be! No, really, a couple of weeks would do. I'll drop you back at Lulu's and then go and organise a tank. Until I've got all the constituents together, there's not a lot for you to see or do. It's Monday today: I'll see you back here on Thursday morning, nice and early.'

'So long?' she asked.

'Yes. I'll go to a friend in Northumberland for the worms – he's seriously into organic farming and it's where mine originally came from, so I can be fairly sure they'll survive the metamorphosis. I can't guarantee they'll survive the journey, though. Have you ever taken anything living with you before?'

'From here, only seed stock, but we travel "locally" in pairs with no ill effects,' she replied.

'What about animals? Any early time-travel research to give you some indication of how well they travel.' Ehlana shook her head. 'Were no experiments made with them?'

'The only animals available for anything are human.'

Malcolm looked horrified at her response.

'The only survivors were the two thousand who went underground before the Sunfire. Nothing remained when they finally came Skyside,' explained Ehlana.

'What caused the Sunfire?' he asked.

'Humans! It was a misguided attempt to solve the nuclear problem,' she said, simply.

'My god! All gone!' Malcolm sank back into his seat and remained there for a long time, silent. Then, at last, he continued. 'I hadn't realised. I hadn't thought it through. Current thinking expects the insects to inherit the Earth! Christ, what a pitiful set of planetary tenants we turned out to be.' He drifted again into silence and Ehlana did not intrude. Eventually he spoke again. 'Tell me about the Dome.'

'There is little to describe,' she replied. 'It covers an area of some ten hectares and at its centre is forty feet in height. It is constructed from panels of semi-translucent epoxy polymers, tinted to refract the Sun's harmful rays. Apart from the Field, all available space is given over to two- and three-storey buildings which provide accommodation, work space and the various laboratories. If you stand on the roof of the buildings nearby the Dome's perimeter, you can reach up to touch its warm surface. Unlike here, it is a place of few colours: white, brown and dark grey predominate. From the Dome's edge the view is broken only by the planet's curve on the horizon.'

'How did they manage to build anything at all?' he interjected.

'Those who went originally under the ground were mainly scientists, convinced that McGregor's warnings should be heeded. Beneath the stone sky of their sanctuary they built an environment that would sustain them for as long as they needed.

Almost all of the materials used to build the Dome were salvaged from there. Eventually they acquired the skills of engineers and architects and forced the planet to grant them a living space upon its surface. I do not know how they purify the air or reclaim the water, I know only that everything we have is reused or recycled.' She paused for a moment before continuing. 'It is strange, really, that I never appreciated whilst I was there quite what a peculiar creature the Historian is. We contribute very little to the running of society – remove us and there would be no noticeable difference. In fact it would seem that we have no true function there. The others call us Dreamers, wrapped as we are in a vocation that is as productive as sleep.' Her voice trailed off and Malcolm left her to the silence.

Eventually, he stood up and offered her his hand. 'Come on, we'd better get started.' He drove her back to Nevern Square and left her there. Throughout the journey he had not said a word, apart from reminding her to be early on Thursday morning.

Lulu returned a few hours later, laden with bags full of provisions. Richard and Tom would be joining them for dinner and, no, she had not heard anything from Clem. The second piece of news disappointed Ehlana more than she expected, but it would be good to see the twins again, if only to thank them for introducing her to Malcolm.

She helped Lulu to prepare the meal, which consisted mainly of a strange, tiered construction of stiff sheets of green board interleaving alternate layers of vegetables, sliced inexpertly by her own hand, which were suspended in a thick red juice and an even thicker white sauce that Lulu had seemed to stir for hours. When it was finally assembled, Lulu placed it in the square hot box that figured predominantly in the food preparations Ehlana had witnessed on her earlier visits. She counted nine different types of leaf in the salad Lulu mixed – only two were familiar – and the spicy, acidic oil that was sprinkled liberally over them brought out flavours that she had not even known existed in the normally dull, green leaves.

Lulu showered and changed while Ehlana watched the television news. When her friend finally emerged from the bedroom clad only in the thick blue denim trousers and T-shirt that she so often wore, Ehlana was a little disappointed that no 'dressing-up' was required for the evening. The immense variety of clothes that could be found in Lulu's wardrobe was one of the things that she most enjoyed – a frivolous attitude to time-travel, she knew, but it did enhance her journeys, more so when she thought of the ubiquitous robes of her own time.

In the end, almost as a penance for her vanity, she selected an ankle-length cotton robe, dark blue in colour, with rich patterns worked in fine blue and gold cords at the neck and wrist – it was the closest thing that Lulu possessed to the ochre robes of Ehlana's own time. She felt supremely comfortable wearing it and, when she stood in front of the mirror to examine how it looked, she was pleased with the result. The deep narrow slit ran from the base of her throat to well below the visible curve of her breasts. Her hair she plaited into a long, auburn rope that hung heavily down her back. She debated applying some of Lulu's paints to her face, but in the end, having experimented with a little red powder to her cheeks, she decided that she did not have the requisite skills.

By the time Ehlana emerged from the bedroom Lulu had just opened a bottle of wine and poured a glass of the rich red liquid for each of them. They sat down and Ehlana sipped slowly at the intoxicating contents of her glass.

'About Clem,' said Lulu. 'I ought to tell you – ' She was interrupted by the door bell and never did finish what it was that she had wanted to say. She answered the door phone and announced the arrival of the twins.

When they finally reached the door of the flat, Tom staggered in and collapsed into an armchair while Richard hung grimly on to the lintel of the door.

'I hope you've got the oxygen ready – my lungs are in danger of imminent collapse!' gasped Richard.

'Why on earth you insist living this high up in a building with no lift, we just cannot imagine!' said Tom from where he sat, sprawling.

'It keeps me fit!' replied Lulu. 'Though I know what you're getting at. Some days I feel every cigarette I've ever smoked exacting its revenge. Wine?' she asked. 'Or something stronger?'

'Mm, wine please, but only as long as it cost more than £1.99 a bottle! Your taste in liquor is sometimes as incomprehensible as your choice of dwelling,' replied Tom.

'Me too,' said Richard, 'but subject to the same proviso as my sibling.' He closed the door behind him and walked over to embrace first Lulu and then Ehlana. 'It's good to see you,' he said to her. 'It's been far too long.' He dropped onto the sofa beside her and asked her what she had been doing with her life since they last met. It seemed that he expected a recounting of seven and a half years' activities and was surprised when she spoke only of a couple of weeks. She did, however, tell him of the entertainment she had been introduced to on her return to her own time and he was astounded.

'They've reinvented Blind Man's Buff!' he called out to Tom and Lulu, who were deep in quiet conversation in the kitchen, and then retold Ehlana's story. They all seemed very amused. 'It's a game we play as children, but never truly in the buff!' he clarified. She must have looked a little confused, for he continued. 'Buff means naked. It certainly sounds like a much more exciting variation on a very old theme!'

The conversation continued on the subject of games on and off throughout the meal, as each of them remembered other games. It was Lulu, though, who suggested that they play one of her favourites after they had eaten.

'It doesn't have a name, at least not one I know, and it's very simple,' she explained. 'It's also good fun and can be extremely dirty! All it needs is a couple of sheets of paper, some pens and a penchant for depravity.'

'What does one have to do?' asked Richard.

'It varies slightly, depending on how many people are playing. As there are four of us, we each have four strips of paper and on each one we write our own name and then the name of some part of the body: hand, mouth, leg, anything. You don't have to possess one in order to name it. When that's done they all go into a hat and we each take turns to draw one out. Whatever piece of anatomy is named on the slip that you pick has to be used to touch the person who wrote it. There are only two exceptions to the rule: the first one is if you pick your own strip of paper, then you can use that part of your body to touch anyone you want; and the other is when you are asked to touch with an anatomical feature that you don't possess, in which case you can touch, with any part of your body, the requisite piece of the author's flesh. The tricky bit is the fact that once you've made the contact, you cannot break it until all the slips of paper have been used. If you enjoy the first round, I'll explain the second. If not, we can do a jigsaw puzzle or cut our throats!'

'It sounds like fun,' said Richard. 'I'm game.'

'So what's new?' said his brother. 'No, seriously, it does sound diverting and I am certainly keen.' All three turned to look at Ehlana.

'I enjoyed the last game I learnt – I cannot see that this one will be less pleasurable, although I am not entirely sure that I understand it any better. Does this one have any hidden forfeits I should be aware of?'

Lulu laughed. 'Not unless you want it to! I'll go and grab some paper.' She walked across to her bureau and returned with paper and pencils which she handed out. 'Okay. Tear your sheet of paper into four strips and write your name and a part of the body on each one.'

Ehlana wrote mouth, foot, hand and, after a small pause, breast, then folded them as she saw Lulu was doing. When the little scraps of paper were piled together in the middle of the table, Lulu suddenly remembered the missing piece of equipment.

'I'll get the hat while you lot clear everything out of the middle of the room. With four of us we're going to need quite a bit of space!' She went into the bedroom and Ehlana and the twins shifted furniture. By the time she returned, they had piled things high in corners and had exposed some very clean areas of carpet. 'Good grief,' said Lulu. 'My mother always told me I was lazy, but I really should make a little more effort when I vacuum!'

She picked up their slips of paper and put them into the battered straw hat she had found. 'Well, as it's my game, I suppose I had better draw first.' She reached in and pulled out the first strip of paper. 'Okay. It's Richard and finger.' She went over to him and placed her index finger against his chest. 'Ah. There's one rule I forgot to mention. The contact has to be direct – skin to skin. So, Richard, if you'd just like to unbutton your shirt, we can continue. As I pulled your name out, it's your turn to draw next.' He tugged his shirt out of his trousers and unbuttoned it down to his waist. Lulu waited until he had finished, then replaced her finger and passed him the hat.

'I've got Ehlana's breast!' he exclaimed. 'At least, I think I have. I can't touch her with one of my own, for I don't really have any. It says breast, not nipple. So I must have to touch hers, right?' he asked Lulu. She nodded in agreement. 'Come and stand here, beside me,' he told Ehlana, who moved towards him. His hand sneaked into the low-cut narrow channel of material that covered her fleshy mounds and rested gently on her left breast. 'Your turn now.' Ehlana took a folded strip from the hat as Lulu passed it to her.

'Tom, it is your knee,' Ehlana said. Tom moved

to stand beside her and pressed his left knee against her right thigh.

'No, no,' said Lulu. 'You've got to touch Tom with your knee, Ehlana. You'll need to lift your dress above your knee and Tom will have to be bare where you touch him! I think it's time you took your trousers off, Thomas!'

'God, I only put "knee" because I thought it would be a nice, safe part of the anatomy!' he said.

'If you wanted to kneel, she could rest it against your chest or your back, but it would make life very hard if you needed to touch someone's shoulder! It's either that or you make Ehlana stand on one leg until we've finished!' replied Lulu.

'I see what you mean. Oh well, I suppose it's going to have to be the trousers!' He took them off and hung them over the back of a chair before going to stand beside Ehlana. Her knee bent to rest against his calf. Tom pulled another scrap of paper from the hat. 'It's Richard and tongue. Lean over my way, brother.' Richard obliged and Tom pressed his tongue to the lobe of his sibling's left ear. 'Your turn now,' he mumbled.

Richard picked Lulu's strip that stated navel. He undid the belt of his trousers and slid the zip down until his navel was exposed. 'I think you're going to have to drop your jeans, Lulu, or I'll never find bare flesh!' With one finger still attached to Richard's chest, she wriggled herself out of the dark blue material and Richard pressed his belly tight against hers.

'My turn,' said Lulu, as she picked another slip out of the hat. 'Ehlana and foot.' She spread her legs apart and covered Ehlana's left foot with her right.

Ehlana drew Tom and hand: she rested her hand on his hip.

Tom pulled out Lulu and nipple: his shirt joined his trousers and he pressed his chest against her side.

Lulu drew Richard and penis. They both struggled out of the items of clothing that they still wore below the waist, hampered by Richard's need to maintain the navel contact he had already established. Tom, his tongue still glued to Richard's ear, helped Lulu to slide down the scanty black lace that impeded Richard's contact. The conjunction of limbs was becoming very complicated.

Lulu drew Ehlana and mouth. She turned her face towards her friend and kissed her, her lips warm and open. For a short while, Ehlana forgot that she needed to draw another slip of paper. She drew, and Tom read for her, Richard and buttock. She raised her gown to her waist, but no matter how hard she tried, she could not touch Richard with her buttock without breaking contact with Tom's calf. One final, manic effort succeeded only in toppling the unbalanced bodies to the floor. Richard and Lulu were still joined from the navel down and her wrigglings as she fought to get up were having a strange effect on their respiration. At first Ehlana thought to help her friend, but then she realised that the gentle rocking motion of Lulu's hips was not only familiar, but one that did not require any assistance. Curiosity moved her gaze down their bodies to where they were most closely joined and then, filled with a desire to see better, she moved her head until it was level with the smooth, soft flesh of Lulu's arse. She was not entirely surprised to find Tom's face there also.

'Don't they make a pretty picture?' he asked her

160

quietly. Lulu's legs shifted a little further up Richard's body, allowing Ehlana to better see the stiff white stem as it was drawn in and out of Lulu's slick passage. She moved her hand to stroke first the hard prick and then the fleshy mouth that swallowed it. Tom moved his hand until his finger rested against the tight, wrinkled hole of Lulu's arse, then pressed gently against it.

'Would you like to just watch?' he asked Ehlana. 'Or would you rather play too?'

'Can you think of a way in which I might do both?' she replied. He laughed at her candour.

'I think I can!' He stood up and removed the clothes that he still wore. Ehlana knelt up and he helped her to pull the blue gown over her head. 'Now, if you crouch on all fours and crawl until you have the best view...'

She did as he told her, eventually stopping when her forehead neatly rested against the soft clefted flesh of Lulu's buttocks. Tom moved to kneel between her legs, his fingers stroking gently at the lush curls they found there, parting them softly until he found the warm flesh that they concealed. A long cool finger slid into her warm damp hole and mimicked the movement they both watched.

Ehlana bent a little further forward and flicked the tip of her tongue against Lulu's tight, dark hole. In the distance she heard Lulu's replying groan and felt the other squirm beneath her probing tongue. Tom's finger slid forward to find the tiny nub of flesh that hid between her other lips. Ehlana echoed his caresses with her tongue. His hand withdrew and its place was taken by the more solid presence of his shaft. Gently he rubbed its large head against her little bud.

To Ehlana it seemed as if an age passed before he moved far enough back to find the entrance to her waiting hole and then another age before he finally had her impaled upon his strong hard prick. This time it was Ehlana's turn to groan. Slowly he began to slip in and out of her, his palms pressed down on the curve of her buttocks. She slid her right hand down to touch the small piece of flesh that begged for her attention and, once she had found it, traced little circles there with her finger. All the time she watched intently as Lulu rose and fell upon the stiff shaft of Richard's manhood. She dropped her head and, starting at the tight sac of his balls, ran her tongue along its surface as it lost its fleshy sheath: Lulu, guessing what she did, held herself for a long moment at his apex, granting Ehlana the time to taste the entire length of his uncovered sweetmeat. Once her tongue encountered the taut ridge of skin that gripped Richard's swollen head, Lulu dropped back down and swallowed his prick entirely with her rapacious hole so that no part of it remained outside her body. She lay there, pressed tight against his groin, while Ehlana recommenced the gentle probings of Lulu's tight, dark hole with her tongue. Behind her, she could feel Tom's excitement mounting and he began to thrust harder and deeper, his hands no longer resting on her buttocks but gripping at her hips, holding her steady as he moved in and out of her.

Her finger worked to match his rhythm, her little shaft growing painfully hard with her touch. A sudden fantasy imagined it a thousand times larger and buried deep within Lulu's tight arsehole: the four of them bonded together with the fleshy spears linking to form a delicious, human chain. Her tongue probed deeper still, and Lulu pressed hard against her face. The image was enough to send her cascading over the wall of her climax and as she pulsed and flexed around him, she drew Tom with her. Lulu surrendered herself to the sensation of Ehlana's probing tongue and came as she rode hard on Richard's flesh. Guessing that he might be left out, Richard reached down to cup the heavy sac of his testes and gently massaged them. It did not take much contact for him to join the others. Ehlana collapsed against Lulu's cushioning buttocks and Tom fell against her. All four lay there for some time: the only things that moved were heaving chests as they struggled to regain their breath.

'If that was only the first round, what on earth happens in the second?' Tom asked Lulu when he had finally recovered enough to speak.

'I don't know,' she replied honestly. 'I hadn't got round to making that bit up yet. I was hoping you might have forgotten.'

'You mean that all that just came straight out of your head?' asked Richard. She nodded. 'My god, but you're a wonderfully depraved woman! I am seriously impressed. Where have you been all our lives?'

'Around,' she answered cryptically. 'And if it's any consolation, the older I get, the more debauched I seem to become!'

Eventually, once Lulu had regained the use of her legs, she fetched bedding and they slept together in a comfortable heap on the floor.

When Ehlana eventually awoke, the morning was almost over and the flat was empty. She had no way of knowing whether the others had been extremely quiet when they left or whether she had slept so soundly that it had not mattered what noise they made. Lulu had left a note by the kettle and in it insisted that Ehlana should not try to tidy the flat before she returned. But with nothing better to do, Ehlana fell to it with a vengeance.

By the time she had finished, Lulu still wasn't due back for a couple of hours, so Ehlana decided to take a bath, as both a luxury and a way to pass the time. The abundance of fluid available at the twist of a tap still amazed her – it was one of the everyday things that she so envied them. Once it was full, she stepped in, then realised she had left the bathroom door open. Not wanting to wet the floor, she shrugged her shoulders and sat down. The warm water enveloped her so sweetly that she lay back and eventually she dozed.

How long she had lain there she couldn't tell, but a noise startled her awake. Guessing it to be Lulu's key in the lock, she called out. 'I'm in the bathroom, I won't be long.' A lot of her hair was already wet, so she decided to wash it before she got out. She dunked her head under the water, then poured a little shampoo into her hand. Her eyes tight shut against the foam, she completed her task and stood up beneath the shower to rinse herself clean.

At last, stretching out for the towel she had placed close at hand and not finding it there, she opened her eyes. It was in the mirror that she saw him first, standing close by with the towel in his hands. It was Clem. She turned to face him, rivers of water running down her body from her long, wet hair. Without saying a word he passed her the towel, she wound it around her head and then stepped out of the tub. He took another towel from the rail and knelt before her, then proceeded to dry each of her feet.

Digit by digit he dried them, gently patting at her skin with the soft fabric, progressing to her ankles, her calves and then her thighs. Once he had passed her knees, Ehlana planted her feet wide apart, granting him an easier access to the inside of her thighs. His ministrations came to within a hair's breadth of Ehlana's now quite desperate labia when he suddenly stood upright and moved behind her. Involuntarily, the towel slipped from her head and her hair cascaded down the long sinuous line of her bare back, a dark red rope along her spine. She heard his breath catch – a half sob – but then he continued with his task.

Throughout the whole operation neither of them exchanged a word. Wrapping her finally in a great, loose gown, he opened the door and let her pass. As she drew level, she turned and snaked a hand behind his head, drawing his lips towards hers for a kiss. The immediacy of his response overwhelmed her – he wrapped his arms around her waist and pressed her hard against the door jamb: she could feel the straight edges of the wood imprinting themselves upon her flesh much as his lips did on her own. Then just as suddenly, he pulled away and would not look at her.

'If I have done something to offend, then I apologise,' she said stiffly. 'If you would rather just leave, then do so!'

'Christ, Ehlana, you just walk back into my life like it's some kind of holiday,' said Clem. 'I never know when you'll come again, or even if you will. And every time you do, I'm older and you screw someone else! I was twenty-seven when we met:

you were about twenty-three then. You're still twenty-three and I'm bloody well nearly forty-five! How do you expect me to cope? Oh, shit. It's not your fault, it's just me. Every time I see you, I want you more and I can't even say so. I don't know if I love you, but I don't really know if you even like me. You're always the polite guest, never overstepping the bounds. Everything I feel for you is tied up in two fucks sixteen years ago. I don't know whether you even remember it. Can you wonder that I'm confused? About the only thing I've really known in all that time was that I didn't want Lulu, I wanted you.'

'I would have shared bodies with you many times,' she replied. 'I could not then, because of Lulu. There is no such hindrance now. For me, only four months have passed – but I think I shall always clearly remember that first sharing. It saddens me still that it was cut so short.'

'I want to share more than just bodies,' he said. 'I want to wake with you beside me in the mornings; I want to turn and find you there in the dark of the night. I want to make love with you, not just fuck you, though I want to do that as well. I want to be everything and nothing to you...' She brought a hand up to cover his mouth and still him.

'Then show me,' she said. 'Share everything with me and see if it is still what you want; let me see if it is what I want.'

'How can I? I never know when you're going to vanish again,' replied Clem.

'If I knew that I wanted to stay I need only to take this off.' She tugged the crystal at her throat. 'But we would need to be sure it was what we both desired. Until then, until we are sure, I shall

166

promise you always to come back. I cannot offer more.'

'It's enough, at least for now.' He drew her close to him and held her.

'Do you remember the first time?' she asked, coquettishly.

'God, it's imprinted on my brain. Every line of you, every curve...' he replied.

'No one else but you has bound me and I have often waked from dreams hoping to find you there again.' She pressed herself against him, aching to feel his skin close to hers. Her hand snaked up and began to unbutton his shirt.

'Wait,' he said. 'Not here – it's too caught up in all the things that confuse me. Get dressed and we'll go.' She considered challenging him, but quickly understood his logic. In all the short time she had known him, he had always been inextricably linked with Lulu. If they shared here, it would be no more than a repeat and it needed to be something new. Clem sat and watched her while she dressed, his eyes never straying, their look as tangible as a caress. Waves of anticipated pleasure swept over her.

Eventually – it felt to Ehlana as though hours had passed – she was ready. They left Lulu's flat and walked down to the street. She realised then that she had no idea where he lived or how they would get there. Almost in answer to her silent question, he said, 'It's too far to go to my place – at this time of day it'd take us over an hour and I can't trust myself that long. I want you so badly that I could end up ravishing you on the hard shoulder.'

Ehlana looked at him a little confusedly: she understood his urgency, for it matched her own, but she had no knowledge of motorway driving and did not think his shoulders particularly hard. 'If you don't mind, I'd rather we went to a hotel now and then drive down there tomorrow.'

'You decide,' she replied. 'But make it soon.'

He raised an arm and hailed a passing cab. 'The Criterion, Chelsea Wharf,' he told the driver. He opened the door for Ehlana and climbed in behind her. Initially they sat each in one corner of the wide back seat, unable to think of anything to say. Ehlana felt the tension between their bodies mount even without contact, she was sure that if he touched her she would ignite. The cab solved their problem: cornering too tight and too fast, Ehlana was slung from her remote and lonely side to tight close against him. His arms wound around her and his lips pressed warm against hers. A hand moved down the length of her body, only to creep up beneath the hem of the long skirt she wore, and work its way slowly from her ankle to her hip. In order to facilitate its progress she brought her leg up over his, her knee applying a gentle pressure to the hard flesh at his groin. His hand moved up and round, stroking the soft, rounded curves that it found. A loud cough reminded them that they were not yet alone. They separated, reluctantly, but remained apart only by virtue of clothing.

'Hot for May, isn't it?' said the cabbie, obviously desperate for something to say. 'Listen, it won't be long before we make the Embankment. If you can both hang on a little bit longer, I'd appreciate it. I've only just got started and won't finish for another seven hours at least. If you carry on like that, I'll have to pack it in and go home early, otherwise people will think I'm driving around with a night-stick down my trousers.'

Clem laughed and apologised. Ehlana did not understand the joke, but he explained it and she blushed. At last they reached their destination and got out. As Clem paid, Ehlana heard him tell the man to go home anyway – it was a day for celebrations – and guessed that he gave him far more than the fare had been.

The man was still calling back his thanks as they walked in through the large glass doors. The sumptuousness of the place momentarily overwhelmed her: high ceilings, intricate decorations and sofas huge enough to swallow her. Clem led her over to one of these and left her to idly flick through a magazine filled with images of exotic clothes, cars and faraway beaches. She still had little idea of the true value of money, but knew enough to realise that both the hotel and the magazine were for the seriously rich. At long last, he finally returned.

'Everything's sorted, but I suspect they think I'm a dirty old man who's picked up some young thing for an afternoon's fun,' he said. 'I suppose it's not far from the truth!'

'No,' she replied. 'If that was all we had wanted, we would already be bedded at Lulu's and it would have cost you considerably less. The cab fare, at least. And I have some understanding of the value of money from all my outings with the twins. This is something else entirely.'

A very young, uniformed man approached them and asked that they follow him. He led them into an elevator, pressed a button high on the panel and Ehlana felt her stomach stay behind as the lift flew rapidly upwards. The metal doors separated and in front of them, across a short hallway, was a wooden door. The young man opened it and ushered them in. An enormous window spread across the whole room and Ehlana moved towards it, entranced by what she saw. The city sprawled around them and just below the broad black ribbon of a river trailed east and west. A door shut behind her and almost instantly Clem was there, his arms around her waist, a hard presence against her buttocks.

'The same river runs at the end of my garden, but you'd be hard pressed to recognise it. I brought you here for that reason and because I love the view from above. It's nowhere near as high as flying, but when you're grounded it's the next best thing.' He turned her round to face him and this time there was no denial when she again began to unbutton his shirt. That done, she slid her hands over his strong shoulders and with the aid of his shrug, pushed the shirt down from his arms and onto the floor. Then she knelt at his feet, like a supplicant and lifted her hands to unfasten his belt. As she worked, she felt him rigid underneath restraining fabric. Her hands trembled as she searched for, and managed to find, the awkward little tab that kept him confined. His trousers fell to his ankles and he deftly kicked them off. She picked up first one foot and then the other, sliding black socks from pale skin. A final obstacle remained before she reached her goal – the fine dark cotton that restrained his hard flesh.

She leant forward and kissed the beast's angry red head, softly at first, then pressed her lips hard against it. Her tongue snaked out to taste the tiny hole at the tip and then teased its way down to the base before returning to engulf his hot flesh. Once

170

she had taken him deep inside her mouth, his hands
came down and rested around the base of her head,
his fingers entwined in her hair. But he brought no
pressure to bear, it was more as if he held her there
for balance. Slowly, her mouth moved down along
his shaft, closer and closer to its juncture with his
body. Dark hairs brushed against her lips and her
tongue beat a slow insistent rhythm against his
captive prick.

'No,' he said again. 'Not this way, not yet. Stand
up.' She obeyed. 'Take off your clothes.' Her fingers, awkward in their urgency, fumbled with the
fastenings of her own clothes far more than they
had with his. All the time she worked she could
feel his gaze on her body. She had never before felt
as naked as she did then. By the time she had
finished undressing, her need of his body had
rendered her incapable of speech: her desire overwhelmed her.

'Christ, you're so beautiful.' Gentler now, he
picked her up: one arm across her back, the other
beneath her legs, and carried her over to the large
bed. He put her softly down and fell smoothly
beside her. 'Oh, lady, you've made me wait so long
for this that I don't intend rushing anything.' His
hand reached out and stroked a firm, full breast. 'I
want to learn everything about your body: what it
likes and what it cries for.' His fingers gently
pinched at a hardened nipple. 'The first time you
fooled me – I thought you were somebody else.'
His hand moved down to her inner thigh and with
one finger he traced a fine line from her knee to her
groin. 'The second time was something else entirely
– Lulu's game, not yours or mine. And then, when
Lulu tried to offer you to me again.' Ehlana's

breathing began to quicken as his fingers toyed with the soft curls on her fleshy mound. 'But this time, it's just us.' A finger sneaked down and rubbed the tiny bud between her swollen lips – Ehlana gasped. His hand returned to playing in the mossy tendrils of her pubic hair. 'Did I hurt you badly, that first time?' he asked.

'No, you set me free,' she stretched up a hand to touch his cheek. Two fingers then moved to stroke his soft lips – the dark hairs of his moustache tickled at her fingertips and a sudden memory of how it felt against the tender flesh around her bud flooded through her. As though he read her mind, he moved to crouch between her legs, his tongue finding the root of her pleasure. She gasped as he slowly licked at its tiny shaft, at the ripples of expectation that the gentle contact spread throughout her body. He broke away for a moment, to tell her how good she tasted, how he wanted to spend his life between her legs, licking and sucking at the tender sweetness of her hole. He lifted her legs to his shoulders and then returned to devour her, his hands under her buttocks to lift her closer to his waiting mouth. She tried to find a foothold against the wave that threatened to envelop her, but the surge of electric ecstasy that his tongue stirred up in her was inescapable and she came, pressed tight against his mouth.

He did not move a muscle until she lay quiet again, then he lifted his head from her groin and leant forward to kiss her. Eagerly, she licked at his lips to taste what he had wrought. As they shared the essence of her coming, he lifted her hips to meet his. Then, with no sight of its own to aid it, his prick slid surely to the home it craved deep inside her. Ehlana sighed, her mouth suddenly slack against his invading tongue.

Clem threw back his head and laughed at her frailty, its golden sound vibrating down the slender stem that joined them. He raised her higher still and straightened his back, then began the slow acceleration of his thrusting. He slid outside her body and she gasped against the loss of him. He returned immediately, but this time pushing his way through the tight ring of muscle at her arse. She had time enough only to acknowledge his presence, before he escaped, returning to the warm wet deepness of her cunt; she gripped hard against his elusive flesh, but he withdrew to find again the dry tightness.

Stroke after stroke he repeated this faultless rhythm, until Ehlana could hardly breathe with the tension. Each tiny moment when he broke contact with her body, she feared that he would not find the mark: each time he did. The hole left empty mourned his passing and was greedy for his return. She slid her hand along her body, until a finger found the little bud that complained of its neglect. She stroked it, placating its anguish but stoking the fire deep inside her. He looked down to where she played, the slow tempo of his movements increasing as he watched her gentle ministrations. When her pressures increased unbearably, he took two strokes, then three, between each change. When her breathing changed, he stayed in her smooth, silken tunnel, hammering his passion home as her finger flew against the swollen bulb of her clitoris. They came, explosively, together, her strong walls flexing around his pulsing flesh. Afterwards, he placed her gently back down upon the bed, slipping finally free of her still trembling body, then slid around to lie beside her. A deep sigh, a dry sound as his mouth tried to work, then he spoke.

'Hell, I am now completely shattered! I was in the air for twenty hours non-stop – I broke god knows how many rules and regulations to get back to you so fast!'

'Was it fast?' she asked. 'It seems like an age since I arrived.'

'I got the message in Delhi and arranged to swap duties when I reached Bangkok. I had to pull in every favour I was owed! I could only have been faster if I was piloting Concorde!' He wrapped his arms around her and drew her close to him, nestling spoon-like behind her warm body. He breathed into her hair. 'Oh, god, you smell so wonderful,' he murmured.

His breathing slowed and changed: she knew he slept. She lay there, alert and thinking. Was it a wise promise to make? she asked herself. His arms felt good around her: strong and sheltering in a way that she had not known before. Was that love, or its beginning, or just something she had not recognised in the other men who had held her? The sharing was sublime: no tangible reason why it should be so, but she thought it in some manner generated by his desire for her, as if the measure of his yearning demanded reciprocity from her. In the end, all that her analysis revealed was contentment with her present situation, so she put the matter aside and joined him in slumber.

A tingling sensation roused her just as the dawn began to creep over the sleeping city. At first, she thought she dreamt again, but when she put her hand to her crystal she knew at once that it called her home. She knew also if she woke him he would try to stop her going, hold her close to prevent her leaving. She had only heard once the tale of that Guild-brother who had tried to travel in tandem without a crystal of his own. It was one of the early lessons, designed to frighten off all but those truly committed to the Guild. She dared not wake him, but crept from his side in the dark. She tried to find something to write with, to leave him a note, but the Mother Crystal drew her away before she had time.

Chapter Nine

Nucassel, November 3550PS

'Catch her, you fool, before she falls,' shouted Tolai. Someone, jolted out of his reverie, moved forward and Ehlana felt strong arms around her. She leant against her rescuer: it was a little while before she remembered she was naked.

'A pretty picture the two of you make, to be sure,' said the Magister. 'Horai, put the poor child down and go and find her a robe.' The arms around her stiffened and dropped away. Horai sped off, more, thought Ehlana, through embarrassment than the need to do his master's bidding. 'I do hope I have not brought you back from anything too exciting, my dear,' he continued.

'More awkward than exciting, I am afraid, Magister. I shall have to think long and hard about how I can mend what I left behind,' she replied.

'Time is not a thing you have in plenty here, Ehlana. I have brought you back because there is a problem. Or two problems in fact, if Horai's deductions are correct. If he is, I do not know that I could choose which is the most serious. The first is your hatchling, Jodai. He has been taken by the Evaluators.'

'Why?' asked Ehlana.

'It seems he had "corrupted" one of their number and the Magister Prime learnt of it. I might not hear a great deal any more, but I hear enough. Child, there is much that I have not told you: much that I am forbidden to tell. The Evaluators know more than most and old lore is passed to all their graduates. They feared what he had learnt from Emora more than what they did together. To their minds, they had no choice but to take him,' he explained.

At this point Horai returned with a robe for Ehlana. She put it on. Horai made to leave but the Magister waved him back. 'Sit down, both of you. We need assistance to do what we must and it seems that you are best suited for the task, Horai. There is also the matter of the Mother Crystal: it is your diagnosis, so you will have to explain. But anything you learn here must never be divulged, lest you choose the same fate as that ordained for young Jodai.'

Horai sat and stared intently at the old man.

'I still do not know exactly what they intend for Jodai, though there are certainly provisions for all exigencies contained within the List,' Tolai continued.

'What list is this you speak of?' Ehlana asked.

'Ah, the List. It names the conditions the Sleepers imposed in return for their sacrifice,' replied Tolai.

'I know only of the Sleepers' Agreement,' Ehlana interrupted.

'That is as it should be. The Magisters all learn the List, though, it is a requisite of their appoint-

177

ment and they vow to honour it. It contains all manner of things that the Sleepers specified as both reward and recompense for their actions! The first item on the List was the compulsory sterilisation of all male hatchlings. This guaranteed that the children of other men could not rule the planet and blithely forget their fathers' promises, as all ova must be fertilised with the Sleepers' banked sperm.'

'You mean that all hatchlings are fathered by the Sleepers?' asked Horai.

'Pay attention, boy. The second – ' he was interrupted by Ehlana this time.

'But what then of the Eugenics Laboratory? I have seen the chamber where the male gametes are kept until required for fertilisation,' she said.

'They are not used – they are there purely for display. The semen was supplied by the Sleepers and frozen until required. That is why only the Magister is qualified to make the cross-fertilisation. The glass jars you have seen contain mere pieces of infantile tissue, kept solely to sustain the myth the Sleepers engineered. It is one reason why the Magister Eugenics, Lamora, looks more haggard than the rest of us, when you consider that hers is the responsibility to produce healthy stock when the gene pool is maintained by the seed of just two thousand! I digress, though. The second condition on the List, as I have only recently begun to understand, was a rather more selfish demand, in that the whole populace must join them in celibacy for the duration of their sleep. For this, I can see no good reason now. I had always thought that greater wisdom than mine had taken the decision – perhaps they were just more desperate than I.' Horai had done nothing throughout this explanation but stare at the ground by his feet. At last he looked up.

'Then I sire no child when I am gone?' he asked.

'No, nor I,' said Tolai. 'Ehlana shall, for her gametes are viable and will be used. For us, we can hope only for half-brethren to inherit the world that we leave,' the Magister explained.

'And what of other conditions on the List?' asked Ehlana.

'The rest, I believe, little concern our present trouble and would take a great deal of time in the telling,' replied Tolai. 'But once the List was drawn and the Agreement signed, everything was put into place. The entire populace – bar of course those admirable men who had volunteered to suspend their lives until a solution to the problem could be found – suddenly found that their libidos were going in to a rapid decline. Questions were asked and the Magister Prime at that time, Enorai, commissioned a report across the Guilds. In the end, it was agreed that the libido was merely a creative function of man's pre-solar flare behaviour and without the stimulus of warfare and aggression it had atrophied. In short, sexual intercourse was barbaric. The ultra-civilised populace gave it up with no hesitation. Within a generation it was almost entirely forgotten, apart from a recidivist few who were taken in hand by the Evaluators and re-educated. The reality was that over a very long period of years a complex manipulation of their hormones eradicated any physical need and, without the sense of urgency that need impressed, they did not even try to fight.'

'But why should they want such control?' asked Horai.

'I do not know for a certainty,' replied Tolai. 'It may have been at the time truly considered to be a wise course, for reasons that I have never discovered. But in my heart, I am now angry that they thought to treat all those who must die without knowing in so harsh a fashion.' Ehlana could understand his ire and, looking at the old man, could not help but share it. 'I am fortunate, for I found early on an object for my devotions, although they could not be returned.' Ehlana did not understand the old man's comment, but she did not interrupt. 'Nevertheless,' he continued, 'this does not help your friend who now guests with the Evaluators. The second problem I shall leave Horai to explain.'

The young man swallowed hard and then began to speak. 'I was in the Laboratory the first time you returned. On learning how far you had travelled, I decided to monitor the Mother Crystal carefully to see if the distances it sent you caused any physical changes that the other, shorter journeys did not. I hoped to use it for my paper. The next time you journeyed I watched closely. Near the heart of the Crystal I could see a strange blurring. Initially I thought it was my eyes, for the Crystal has always been perfectly clear. I looked again, and harder, and there was a definite opacity deep within. Perhaps foolishly, I did not tell the Magister at once, wanting to see how it developed. When you returned, another flake appeared, though somewhat closer to the Crystal's edge.'

'At least that time you told me about it,' cut in Tolai.

'I know, Magister, and I have apologised more times than I care to remember since then, all to no avail. If I may continue – ' He looked at Tolai, expecting more interruptions but finding none. ' – it seems that it is only your journeys that materially affect the interior of the Crystal. Six others have journeyed in the past five months but new opacities appear only when you travel. Whether it is the distance or your gender that acts as the catalyst, I have no idea. But in my heart, I fear it bodes ill. I have no facts to prove it, but I believe that when the Crystal is fully opaque there will be no further journeys.'

The implications of his conclusion hit Ehlana hard. She would as soon cut off her right hand as cease to travel. She stood and walked over to the core of the History Machine. The lights gathered around the Mother Crystal generated a warmth, but it seemed to emanate from deep inside it. She wanted to place a hand on either side of the gem and gaze deep inside, but could not as touching it was forbidden to all but the Magister. Peering hard, she could not at first see the reason for Horai's concern. But then she understood that what she had assumed were odd reflections or refractions were shimmering patches of the palest blue which stained the Crystal's core. Horai came to stand beside her and joined her contemplation of the gem.

'They are still quite isolated, but just there – ' He pointed at a large splash of bluish opalescence. ' – are three conjoined. And that one I have not seen before tonight.' He pointed towards the other side of the Crystal.

'So, you appreciate our dilemma?' said Tolai, who sat watching the two of them together in their studies.

'How much does Jodai risk?' she asked.

'At the least, serious re-education and possible induction into the Guild of Evaluators. They could not leave him unbonded and in possession of their Lore. At worst, they would send him to join the Sleepers,' Tolai replied.

'They can do that?' asked Horai.

'Oh, yes, indeed have already done so. When the Sleepers finally awake they will find that their number includes some they do not know. Only five or six that I am aware of, but there could be more,' the Magister answered.

'It might not be that great a sleep,' said Ehlana. 'For I learnt not long before you called me that we travellers might hold the key.'

'How?' asked both Magister and acolyte together.

'As you know, two sendings past I carried with me a pouch containing a quantity of the planet's crust, excavated from the Field at the time of the first plantings. I gave it to a pedologist I met there. Seven years and eight months elapsed between that journey and the next. It appears that in those few short years he has found the solution to a problem we could not unravel in two thousand.' The Magister sat down, disbelief written across his face.

'But how? There is nothing we did not try, no possibility unexplored. Can you be sure that he does not lie?' Tolai said.

'There are beasts we know of only as legends that live in those times. The zoological gardens I learnt about from my first visit contained many such animals, some rare even then. A lot of the population kept small animals in their dwellings as companions. All animals were classified in the first place as belonging to one of two main groups: vertebrates and invertebrates, those with and those without spines. Once this simple division was made, more complicated ones followed: species to sub-species. One group of invertebrates was the annelids, which contained over eight and a half thousand different species of red-blooded worms whose bodies were made up of ringed segments. Some, but not all, of these acted as tillers of the soil, eating and breaking down organic matter which they then passed back into the ground. Almost by chance, a small portion of the crust sample I exported found its way into a display chamber colonised by a species of this group. After five years there remained no discernible trace of the sample: the worms had assimilated it completely. But that was the least of it. On an arid area project with which he was involved, Malcolm, the soil scientist, introduced worms from the display chamber together with just a handful of their soil. The results were apparently astounding. The end result is that the worms thrive: they break down the crust and with it produce, in time, viable soil. In less than one hundred months the worms I saw had trebled their expected adult size and their life-span had increased in proportion with their size. Their labours are long, but it appears that if we can transport some here, we could in time transform the planet. In the long-term Malcolm believes, and I have no reason to doubt him, that given sufficient arboreal growth, we could even reinstate a breathable atmosphere.'

'Sunfire!' whispered Tolai. 'A world without domes? Is it possible?'

'Not for you or I to see, for certain. But it could

mean a waking for the Sleepers. Then all would be free to follow their desires.' Ehlana glanced over at the Magister, who looked older and more exhausted than she had appreciated. 'Gentlemen, it is late and we are all, I fear, too tired to make any clear decisions this night. If you do not object, I should like to return to my room and sleep. Tomorrow we can decide what should be done.'

'Alas, child, it must be done now!' said Tolai. 'It had not occurred to you that you might be suspect. I fear that if you went now to your room we might never see you again. I know of your involvement with Jodai. It is likely that the Evaluators also know. But the decision is mine, as Magister, and I have already made it. Your news of the worms just further complicates the situation. None of us shall sleep before both you and your hatchling have travelled far away. You may rest here though, Ehlana, while Horai and I seek to release your friend.'

'But Magister, what of the risk that you run?' she asked, concerned for his welfare.

'I doubt they have done much more than turned the key in the lock outside his cell in the Magistratum. Unless we are very unfortunate, they will suppose he succeeded in freeing himself and vanished, never to be seen again. But we shall take care, I promise.'

Ehlana did not think Horai was as confident as his master, but then neither seemed cast in the heroic mould. 'I shall lock the door behind me as we leave here. You will be undisturbed until we return. Use the time as you will and do not fret for us.' Turning to the pale-faced young man, he continued. 'Come, Horai. It seems as if we may have a larger part to play in this history than we might have hoped for.' They left her then in the silence of the empty room.

Softly, she walked barefoot across the floor to stand again by the Mother Crystal. Reaching behind her head, she unfastened the chain that held her crystal, holding the glittering thing just above the Mother Crystal's polished surface. Tolai had indeed worked hard – it replicated exactly the Mother stone from which it had been cut. Ehlana laid it down gently atop its source. Offering no disrespect to either Magister or Crystal, she placed a hand either side of where her gem lay. It was cool beneath her palms and it seemed as if she felt a gentle pulse. Could the Crystal be failing because its energies were depleted, or because its task was nearly done, she wondered? Whatever, her own travels were almost finished. She must journey back with Jodai and remain there, exiled. A lump formed in her throat as she considered her dilemma. She shut her eyes and rested her forehead against the cool, glassy surface of the stone. In her mind's eye she saw a young man clad in black lift a fine chisel and a hammer from a bench across the room. It seemed as if he walked towards her. His empty hand stretched out to touch her face, gently stroking it while he muttered soft words of endearment that she could not understand. At last, he moved back a pace, raised both hammer and chisel and brought them down towards her face. Expecting pain, Ehlana pulled away, to find herself standing alone by the Crystal.

It was a few moments before she realised that the vision was not hers. Eagerly she placed her hands and forehead back against the Mother Crystal. She shut her eyes again and found herself looking at the same young man. His dark hair, though, was now streaked with grey. Again the sweet sounds and gentle touchings, followed by the hammer and chisel. Ehlana braced herself for pain but did not move from where she stood. The blow came but the expected pain did not. It was a strange sensation, though, a sort of separation she could neither describe nor comprehend. Again the man returned, greyer still, and round featured now, but this time he was someone Ehlana could recognise. This time, she did retreat from the Crystal. Suddenly, she understood Tolai's earlier comment: he had loved the Crystal, and, in some incomprehensible fashion, it had shown her what it knew of him. Eager for deeper understanding, she made to reconnect. This time she saw another, older man. This one had no time for words, merely advanced with his tools and took what he wanted. Then another face, another cold reaving of her substance. And on and on it went. Of all those faces, only one had shown concern and care.

A noise outside the door drew her from the Crystal. Quickly, she picked up her gem and hurried towards the door. Tolai and Horai came in, half carrying Jodai between them. Ehlana moved to help them, taking Tolai's share while he in turn locked the door behind them.

'Tolai, the Crystal – ' she began.

'Hush, child,' Tolai broke in. 'Get up on the platform. We have not a moment to lose. It seems his disappearance was discovered a little too soon after it was effected. I do not believe we were seen, but the sooner you leave the safer we all shall be.' He looked down and noticed her crystal in her hand. 'Do you wish to go elsewhere than when you left, child?'

'I had not thought it, but yes, no more than five years before. Is that possible?' she asked.

'Carrying this one certainly,' said Tolai as he glanced towards Jodai. 'Horai, fetch the three and a half carat stone used on the earlier journey. Oh, and a graduate's stone for the boy. Hurry, man, hurry. They must be gone before anyone gets here.' Horai rushed towards the ante-room that contained all the fragments not currently in use. Tolai passed one arm under Jodai's shoulder and pulled him to his feet. 'Come now,' he muttered encouragingly, 'it is not far to walk and I am too old to carry you. Just a few steps are all it will take.'

Haltingly, Jodai shuffled forward with the Magister's assistance. He could not, however, find energy enough to join Ehlana on the dais.

Horai returned then with the crystals his master had requested. Handing the larger one to Ehlana, he bent and fastened the other around Jodai's neck. Between the three of them, they managed to push, lift and drag Jodai onto the platform beside her.

'Hold him tight as you journey,' warned the Magister. 'He can do nothing to aid your passage, and if you lose hold, he will be gone. The pain he will bear, I hope, as the Evaluators have so recently increased the threshold of his tolerance.'

Horai moved towards the control panel and Tolai went to stand by the Mother Crystal. The resonances had already begun to fill the room before Ehlana remembered the last thing she must do.

'Tolai,' she cried, her voice ringing hollow in the already fading room. 'Magister, give me two weeks, then call me back. Just two weeks. I must bring you the worms.' She knew she shouted, but she saw no sign on his face that he heard her call above the Crystal's song. Then the pain took her.

Chapter Ten

London, April 1991AD

*S*he collapsed on the floor, Jodai a forgotten bundle at her side. Before, the pain had been bad but, with her additional burden, this journey had taken her to new limits. Eventually, the throb inside her skull abated enough for her to sit up. Lulu's bed stood two feet from where she had fallen. The sound of running water came from behind her. She turned her attention then to Jodai, who lay unmoving and silent where she had dropped him. Panic seized her before she noticed the slow rise and fall of his chest. Unsteadily, she rose to her feet and staggered into the bathroom where a figure stood obscured behind the frosted glass of the shower door. 'Lulu,' she called, her voice hoarse and rasping. The water's noise cut off. She called again, the glass door opened and Lulu poured out.

'Hell, you look done in. What's happened?' asked her friend. In reply, Ehlana could do no more than stumble against her naked form for support. Much

189

as Tolai had so recently carried Jodai, Lulu helped Ehlana back into the bedroom and on to the bed. Lulu wrapped her in the quilt before going to fetch her a drink. Returning, she helped Ehlana to sit up and passed her the glass she had brought. Ehlana sipped slowly at the cool juice. Her tongue felt swollen and dry: the sweet fluid acted as a balm. When she had finally emptied the glass, she turned to her worried friend and smiled.

'It is nothing. Just an arduous journey,' she explained. A groan from the floor reminded her she had more to divulge. 'For this time I did not travel alone. Need forced me to bring the closest thing that I have to a brother, but I fear he does not yet know quite where he is. By the sound of him, I would say that his journey has been somewhat worse than mine. He might also be in need of a little medical attention. If you would help me move him, I shall better see what needs to be done.' Together, the two women lifted Jodai on to the bed and rolled him over on to his stomach. The back of his robe was torn in several places and in others had stuck to his skin. It was obvious to both of them that it could not be easily removed.

Lulu walked across to her dressing-table. 'There's a pair of scissors here.' She moved back towards the bed. 'Do you want to do this, or shall I?'

Ehlana shook her head. 'You do it. My hands still shake from the journey.'

Carefully, Lulu began to cut the material from hem to neck. Gently she pushed it away to the side where she could. Where she could not, she cut around, leaving little islands of blood-soaked fabric on his back. Eventually she finished. 'He's taken quite a beating. I'll go and get some things to clean him up with. Get a sponge from the bathroom and see if you can work some of those scraps off. I won't be long.' Ehlana did as she had been told. By the time Lulu returned she had managed to remove only one of the pieces.

'I think you'd better go and run him a bath. Not too hot, and pour some of this in,' said Lulu, handing Ehlana a bottle of brownish liquid. 'Not too much, either – it'll sting him enough as it is! What the hell happened to him, anyway? Not only are there new wounds, but it looks like he's been whipped.' She pointed at pale lines that marked his back. 'Some of the marks are already very faded and others fresh. Is there some little aspect of life at home you forgot to mention to me?'

'In many ways, it is my fault. It began because he sought to aid me in my quest for information,' Ehlana explained from the bathroom. 'But it continued because I had woken a need in him. I do not rightly understand how they were discovered, but I suppose I am partly to blame for that. It is best if we leave him to explain. Our situation also is different this time. We are no longer visitors – this time there is no sure return.' It occurred suddenly to Ehlana that they must not outstay their welcome with Lulu: somehow they must find sufficient means to live independent of her kindness. Over the noise of the running water, Ehlana heard voices.

'Come on then,' said Lulu. 'Time for you to get in to the nice warm water, baby. Ehlana never did tell me your name – what is it?'

'Jodai,' he replied, hoarsely. 'Where am I?'

'My flat,' said Lulu. The blank expression on his face reminded her of her first conversations with

Ehlana. 'Come with me and Ehlana will tell you. For the moment all you need to know is that you're safe. Can you stand? Okay. Put your arm around my shoulder and I'll help you. It's not far. Three more steps and you're there.' Lulu walked him to the bathroom door, where Ehlana took him from her. 'You get into the bath and I'll go and get us all a drink.'

With Ehlana's assistance, Jodai stepped into the tub. He flinched a little as the water touched his wounds, but soon, at Ehlana's suggestion, he lay back and immersed himself in the warm liquid. She left him there and went to find Lulu.

'I've left him floating,' she said. 'He should be happy for some while. What year is it?'

'1991, April 4th to be exact,' replied Lulu.

'Then the last time you saw me was October 1987, the time of the great winds, yes?' asked Ehlana.

'Yes, you left towards the end of the month, if I remember it right.'

'That is right,' continued Ehlana. 'But the last time I saw you was in May 1995, yesterday by my reckoning.'

'This sounds like it's going to be complicated. Let me get a cigarette before you go any further – I think I'm going to need it,' said Lulu. She grabbed a packet and a lighter. 'Right. Take it slowly, you know how dense I can be.'

'Well, the most important thing I learnt was that worms can convert the crust sample that I brought into a viable, indeed valuable, growing medium. Do you still share with Clem?'

'Uh, no, if you mean are we still seeing each other regularly.' Ehlana nodded. 'No, we decided that it really wasn't getting either of us anywhere, so we gave up, just over three months ago now.'

'And you, are you happy with this?'

'Yes and no. It meant I finally got to play with Richard and Tom, though! On the whole, I'd say it was better without him. I miss his company, but at least I only have to please myself now.'

'Would you object if I asked to see him?' asked Ehlana.

Lulu looked directly at her, as if weighing up the implications of her request. 'You know he's always been rather hung up over you, don't you?' Ehlana nodded. 'Shit! It's nobody's fault. I was jealous as hell to start off with, but I tried not to show it. We had some bloody awful rows, though. Oh, I know he never tried anything on after that first day, but my problem was that I knew he wanted to. It could even be that I made it worse by goading him. You remember that time I invited you to join us? I tried to kid myself that I'd made the offer innocently, but I think I did it to force the issue. Hell, I don't know.' She paused and thought. 'No, in all honesty, I'd be really happy if it worked out for the two of you – but is it what you want? What about Jodai?'

'He is my hatchling and dear friend. We have shared and it was good. But I do not see that it would ever be more than that. I do not even know for sure that there can be more. But I must at least try to find out. And it is Clem that I wish to try with. But more urgently I must find Malcolm, for I have just two weeks to prepare what I must carry back,' said Ehlana.

'Back? I thought you were stuck here now?'

'No, the Magister will call me back and I must take worms. But I am outcast now, and as soon as I have delivered them I shall return here. So, before I plot my future, I must first hunt worms! As for Clem, I cannot be sure that he will even want me now,' she added.

'Oh, no, he'll want you! In the end it was about the only thing I did know for sure. Listen, I'll go and see how the invalid's doing, you call Richard and Tom. Their number's in here.' She handed Ehlana a battered, leather-bound book containing many loose sheets of paper.

Ehlana went and sat beside the phone. She knew she should ring the twins first, but instead she called Clem. Three rings and then: 'Sorry I can't get to the phone now, but if you leave a message I'll call you back. If you don't, I shan't. Speak after the tone.' Ehlana could find no words to leave, so she hung up, disappointed. The next call was more successful. Tom was home and happy to track down Malcolm for her. He promised to call back as soon as he had found him. She did not overcomplicate the conversation by mentioning her previous visit, saying merely that she needed to know the results of the soil tests before she returned. After she had put down the phone, she sat still for several minutes, trying to work out what message she should leave for Clem. At last she picked up the phone again and dialled his number.

She waited for the answerphone message. It did not come. 'Hello, is there anyone there?' said a voice.

'Clem? It's me, Ehlana,' she said.

'Where are you?' he asked, excitedly.

'At Lulu's. I need to talk to you. Can you come and see me? Now?'

'Yes. I'll be there in about an hour. See you then.'

She put the phone down and went into the bedroom. Jodai had finished bathing and was now lying face down on the bed while Lulu applied an ointment to the cuts on his back.

'Did you get through?' asked Lulu.

'Yes. Tom has promised to call me back once he finds Malcolm. And Clem is coming to see me. Would you mind if I abandon Jodai here while I speak with Clem?'

'No problem,' replied Lulu. 'I didn't have anything planned, and it's Sunday so I don't have to worry about work. Go and have a bath – there's still plenty of hot water. I'll finish off here then go and fix us some breakfast.' It was a good suggestion and one Ehlana was happy to take up. Once she was clean and dry she went back into the bedroom. Jodai was sitting up now and looking much recovered.

'How fare you, hatchling and fellow traveller?' she asked.

'Aching but alive. I do not recall though how we reached here. In fact, I do not recall much after my arrival at the Magistratum. How did you find me?'

'Tolai brought me back. He and Horai brought you to the Laboratory and sent us here. Do you know what the Evaluators intended for you?'

'I do not think that they had yet decided. But they know that I shared with you. Oh, Ehlana, I am grieved that you should suffer for my indiscretion. Can you forgive me?'

'There is nothing to forgive. True, matters are now a little complicated, but I am sure we can sort everything out, given time.' She leant forward and kissed him on the forehead. 'There are many wonders to be admired here – it will be good to have

195

someone else who can see them as I do. I must go out later – will you stay with Lulu? She will answer any questions that you may have about this time far better than I can. If you feel strong enough later, ask her to take you to the park. Be prepared for a shock. I have not spoken of it before to you, or anyone, for the enormity of what we have lost appals me. It is a beautiful world that they live in, albeit loud and large and busy.'

Lulu came back into the bedroom. 'Breakfast is nearly ready. I borrowed these from next door for you, Jodai,' she said, throwing a pair of jeans on to the bed. 'I don't know how well they'll fit, but it will be a lot better than anything I've got. Ehlana, you wear whatever you want and find Jodai a shirt while you're looking. Come and eat as soon as you're ready.' Ehlana found a skirt and blouse for herself and a jumper for Jodai.

Jodai struggled into the jeans but needed assistance when it came to fastening them. He walked around the bedroom looking decidedly uncomfortable. 'Sunfire! Ehlana, how did you ever accustom yourself to wearing these things? Is there not a gown I can have? Or something like you wear?'

Ehlana laughed. 'Here most clothing is gender-specific. But believe me, you would not merge well if you insisted on wearing a skirt. Try and enjoy it!'

'That is the problem. This strange restriction causes a hardening normally associated more with disrobing. I fear I shall not be able to sit!'

'It will die down! Come, we shall eat and you shall forget it,' she promised. Jodai followed her through to the living-room. Not long into their meal, the phone rang. It was Tom.

'No luck, I'm afraid. Malcolm's in Dubai for the next three weeks,' he said.

'Three weeks! Sunfire! But I must speak to him. Is there no way to contact him?' she asked.

'I'll see what I can do, but I don't hold out much hope. I'll try the embassy out there. Or better still, I'll speak to Lady E. Her husband's in the diplomatic service, so if anyone can find out, she'll know who to ask. I'll call you back later.' Ehlana returned to the table.

Turning to Lulu, she asked, 'If Tom rings while I am away, will you help. He will tell Malcolm just that I need the results, for that is all I explained. When I spoke with Malcolm last time, or I suppose chronologically it should be next time, he told me I should take a worm farm back with me. But I have no idea where I could obtain one, or even how much it might cost. He was going to help me construct one, but I left before learning what was required. I will also need to know what should be done with it once it reaches my own time. These are the questions I need answered. Impress upon him that I have only two weeks.' The doorbell rang.

'Don't worry. I'm sure I can manage that,' replied Lulu as she went to answer the entry phone. 'I'll try and keep Jodai entertained until you get back. Why don't you go and meet him half-way?' Ehlana was out of the door almost before Lulu had finished her question. 'We'll see you later!' she called out, not knowing whether Ehlana heard or even cared.

They met on the second floor landing. Ehlana had run as fast as she could and almost fell into him as she turned the corner. Suddenly confronted by Clem, she could not think of a word to say. He seemed just as awkward.

Eventually he spoke. 'Well, I came as requested. Where do you want to go?' he asked.

'Anywhere,' she replied. 'But somewhere we can talk uninterrupted.'

'Fine. We'll go for a drive.' He took her hand and started back down the stairs. 'Did Lulu tell you we've split up?'

'Yes, but I already knew,' she said. 'I know it sounds insane, but it is one of the reasons that I needed to see you.' They reached the street and Clem led her over to a large black car. He opened a door for her and once she was seated, shut her in. He walked around to the far side and got in to sit beside her. He turned a key and the engine roared into life.

'Okay. We're on our own, no one can bother us. What do you want to say?' he asked, as he drove out of the square.

'For you, we last met in 1987. For my part, I last saw you four years from now. We talked a lot then and you told me – ' she struggled to find the words in a vocabulary that could not express what she needed to say. ' – you asked me to share more than just bodies. You took me to a high place where we looked down upon a river that runs also past your home. And we made love. It seemed to me then both the same as other sharings and yet profoundly different. I was called home while you slept. Leaving you was almost more painful than the journey. When I was sent again, I asked the Magister to send me here, now, for Lulu had told me when it was that the two of you parted company. I still do not know whether I can feel for you in the way that you hoped then, but I sincerely desire to try, if you wish it.'

'I wish it,' he replied. 'When you called this morning, it all came rushing back. Every time I've seen you, I've wanted to touch you, to hold you, to kiss you. But every time I saw you, you were with someone else. I could have murdered the twins – not so much because they had you, but because I didn't. Lulu guessed the truth almost earlier than I did. In the end, she blew me out because she didn't deserve to be the consolation prize.'

'There is a complication, though,' she continued. 'When I left you in 1995 it was unexpected. The Magister had called me early because there was a problem with my hatchling, Jodai. The problem necessitated Jodai travelling here with me and will have resulted in both he and I being classified as fugitives in our own time. Apart from one small journey I must make two weeks from now, there will be no other leavings. For now, I have left him with Lulu, but I cannot expect her, or anyone, to support the two of us. But I am at a loss to think what we could do.'

'I don't think there's much call for thirty-sixth century historians, but what Guild did Jodai belong to?' Clem asked.

'Botanist, specialising in nursery work. Quite gifted, if my assessment is fair,' she replied. 'But his experience is limited, due to the small variety of crops we produced. I cannot see anyone hiring him for those skills.'

'Don't worry. It's not an immediate problem, anyway. He can live with us until something's sorted.'

'But how can you be sure that you want either of us living with you? At least when I saw you before we each could choose. Now, there are no options. I fear that you will feel I come to you because I have no other choice. Believe me, when I agreed to try there was no such desperation.'

'I believe you. For now, I just want to get you home.' He took a deep breath. 'I can't quite believe that I said that. I've dreamt of taking you there, even though the whole idea was unrealistic. I spent hours of my time fantasising about a woman I screwed twice and couldn't expect to have again, particularly as I didn't know quite when I might see her again.' He went quiet again, not speaking for some minutes. 'Listen, I won't hold you to anything. Quite apart from the fact that I might bore you to tears in under a week, we've got to remember the fact that you're, what, twenty-three, while I'm going to be forty in three months' time. It's a hell of a difference.'

'You have changed very little since we first met. A little greyer, that's all, and it becomes you.' She reached up to touch him at the temple. His hand met hers and pulled it towards his mouth where he kissed it. Then he returned it to her lap, but maintained the contact.

'God, there's so many things I want to show you,' he said. 'More than anything I've wanted to take you flying and now I can. But there's other things I want to do, things that I've thought of and dreamt of in the dark of the night.' His voice was warm and deep as he spoke. Just imagining his touch in the dark made Ehlana's breath catch. His hand slipped from hers and began to stroke her thigh through the thin cotton of her skirt. Ehlana leant back in her seat, little tremors of excitement building deep inside her. Inch by slow inch, he pulled her skirt up above her knees until his hand rested on the naked flesh of her thigh. His fingertips massaged the soft skin at the top of her leg. Occasionally a daring digit would stretch out to touch the folds of flesh that covered her most sensitive part. Ehlana, despairing that contact would never truly come, squirmed against his hand, emboldened by her need of him. Laughing, he gently rubbed her little bud, then took his hand away.

'Not yet,' he said. 'Not until I can have all of you. I might even have to tie you down to stop you running away.' Guessing that he would not be moved, she shifted in her seat to face him. His eyes flickered towards her briefly and then back to the road. Much as he had done to her, she reached over and began to massage his thigh. He did not resist then, nor when her hand moved up to stroke his hardening prick through the fabric that encased it. Imagining it uncomfortably imprisoned, Ehlana first loosened his belt and then slid the zip down. Her hand sneaked in through the open gap and closed around the rod it found there. She squeezed softly along its length from the base, feeling it stiffen with each gentle pressure. By the time she reached its head, she had wormed it free of his constricting garments. She stroked the smooth, silken skin then bent her head to suck where she had touched.

'Oh, god, Ehlana,' he said. He flicked a switch above her head and she heard a strange rhythmic clicking. 'I can't drive while you do that, at least not on the motorway, not without killing both of us.' In reply she slid her mouth a little further down his prick, stroking the tiny hole at its tip with her tongue. 'Ah! You've either got to stop until we get home, or I've got to stop and have you right now. It's your choice – I can't make the decision for you: it's all I can do to keep the car on the road.' She thought about it and then made up her mind. She sat back up but kept a hand in his lap.

'I'll wait, so long as I can touch you until we get there,' she replied.

'Okay.' He smiled. 'But not too much or I'll be there long before you!' She contented herself with resting her hand on his thigh, though inside his trousers, and her head on his shoulder.

'Is it far now?' she asked.

'Twenty minutes at the most. Can you wait that long?'

'I think so. But no longer. Once the twenty minutes are over, I shall begin to eat you again, no matter where we are!' He laughed and Ehlana remembered the first time she had heard the warm, distinctive sound: him standing above her, oiling her body while she lay tied to the bed. 'Could you not make it fifteen?' she asked plaintively.

In fact, seventeen minutes passed before his key unlocked the front door of his house. Once they were inside, he had enough time to shut the door before Ehlana turned on him. His trousers posed no difficulty – she had only to slip the belt out of its loop before they fell to the floor. Even as they began to drop she was unbuttoning his shirt. Soon he stood naked in front of her. While she worked, he had not been idle and her skirt was already off. He pulled her shirt up over her head and she raised her arms to assist him.

'Come,' he said, his voice hoarse and breaking. He took her hand and led her up the stairs and through a doorway. He stopped and turned to face her. 'Put your arms around my neck and hold tight. When I tell you, jump, then wrap your legs around my waist.' He placed his hands on the cheeks of her arse. 'Now!' he shouted and as she jumped he raised her up, holding her for an infinite moment in mid-air while his prick searched for her opening. Having found it, he drew her forward, the impetus forcing him deep inside her. Her legs locked behind his back and he walked the short distance to the bed. He bent forward, Ehlana cushioning his impact with her shoulders, the force pushing him even deeper inside her.

'Ah!' she breathed. He raised her hips, his hands still tight on her buttocks and began to move frantically in and out of her silken sheath. At each push Ehlana moaned. His hand moved round to seek her tiny bud and gently rub it while he continued to pump with his hips. There was no let-up in his furious pounding until at last he came. He was still for a moment and then pushed her hips down on to the bed. His prick slipped free as he forced her legs wide apart, then he leant forward to taste where he had been. Having chased a tiny rivulet that was trying to find some way into her tight dark hole, his tongue then travelled the distance to her clitoris, pausing only to probe gently into the hot recesses of that place he had so recently vacated. His tongue beat against her little hermit, trying to encourage it out from beneath its protecting hood. Ehlana sighed and pushed herself hard against his mouth, desperate for the sweet release his tongue strove to provide. She felt herself move towards the brink, nearer and nearer to the point where nothing could prevent her coming. Then he pulled away.

'Oh, no, not yet!' he told her. 'There are things I need to do before I let you come.' His hand reached up to touch the full curve of her breast. He got up from the bed and went towards a large cupboard near the window. He returned with several long, thin bands of fabric that tapered from top to bottom. He took one and wound it firmly round her wrist before tying it tight to the post at the head of the bed. He repeated his actions with her other wrist and tied it to the corresponding post. Then he moved to her feet and continued, binding her ankles and anchoring them to the foot of the bed, her legs stretched wide apart. His hand reached out to stroke the little bud where it peeked out between her swollen lips: it stopped when she began to enjoy it. He made some show of checking that the ropes held, although she knew that her shackles were tokens: she could escape the flimsy fetters if she chose to with a simple movement of her wrists, but in some strange way they seemed also symbolic of his desire for her. It seemed oddly right to begin again where they had started. He stepped back as if to admire his handiwork, moving out of her line of vision and then she heard him leave the room.

She waited for what seemed like an age for his return, but he did not come. She slid a hand free of its binding and it travelled swiftly, passing over the hard brown nut of her nipple in a gentle caress, across her rib-cage and her flat, white belly before finally finding the exposed and insistent bump that demanded her attention. He must have stood watching her from the doorway, for she heard his breathing long before he strode into the room. He pulled her hand away and retied her unresisting wrist.

'I didn't give you permission to do that. Now I shall have to punish you by making you wait even longer. Do it again, and I shall really make you suffer!' He left her again but returned sooner, his arms laden with items she could not properly see. She had not moved this time. 'I shan't hurt you,' he promised 'but I do intend to mark you, at least temporarily, so that you understand that this little thing is mine.' He ran a long slim finger over her burning bud. A cold heavy wetness fell on her groin, then he shook a strange cylinder before pointing it at her vulnerable mound. A hissing noise, then his hand rubbing against the down that covered her there. She raised her head to try and see what he did, but saw only a white frothy blanket where her red hair had been. Her head fell limply back against the pillows. A gentle pressure ironed a line across the area he had prepared, followed by a strange chill. This was repeated time and again, the coolness spreading with each stroke. Her little shaft, jealous of the attention he paid to the skin surrounding it and craving any sort of contact, was only occasionally blessed. She still did not understand what he did, until the heavy wetness returned to wipe away the residue of his work followed by the rough drying of a towel against the now naked flesh of her pubis. A splash of something slick and wet against her groin, then his hand spreading the fluid over her newly exposed skin. His finger slipped and rubbed against the swollen bud, his touch consistent but tenuous, lubricated by the oil he had anointed her with.

'There now,' he said. 'I have marked you and

now I shall claim you.' He moved to kneel between her open thighs, his hand never faltering in its slippery dance. Then his finger was changed for something thicker, broader and Ehlana recognised the smooth roundness of his swollen head as he rubbed it against her oily bud. He leant over her, his body stretched above her and gently licked at her parted lips, her tongue darting out to parry his and all the while his prick slithered against her distended clitoris. She moved beneath him, searching for a friction that the oil denied. He laughed and slid a little down her body until his stiff flesh slipped from her labia, returning at once but lower, his strong hardness pushing deep inside her burning flesh. She groaned as he started to move on her, his long slow strokes filling her entirely. Her hairless mound felt strange pressed hard against his own dark curls, but it excited her in a way she had never known before, made her feel completely naked to his touch. His tempo increased and his mouth moved down her body to fasten on an aching nipple. His tongue flicked gently at its tip while his lips sucked against its growing hardness. She imagined the same attentions to her swollen bud and bucked hard against his penetrations, seeking more and faster. The pressure on her nipple grew in proportion with his speed and her climax came, her muscles flexing uncontrollably around his imprisoned prick. He cried out as her relentless squeezing brought his own release and he buried himself in her pulsing flesh.

Afterwards he released her, then lay beside her, drawing her tight against him, their limbs intertwined. They talked and touched, kissed and caressed, oblivious to anything but the body close by. Time seemed suspended as they discovered each other.

It was not until the phone rang that she realised how much of the day had gone by. Lulu had begun by apologising for such a late call. She had just wanted to let Ehlana know that she had spoken to Malcolm. Apparently, once Lulu had filled him in on the details, he had taken little convincing that he was needed in London and agreed to catch the first available flight back, in order to help Ehlana in building a worm farm. Jodai was recovering his strength, she reported with just the barest trace of a laugh, but would benefit from several days in bed: Ehlana should not worry about him at all, for Lulu promised she would take care of all his needs. It was not until much later when Clem had made her repeat Lulu's exact words, and then explained their double meaning, that she comprehended the true extent of Lulu's undertaking and the reason for the laughter she had heard in her friend's voice.

Two days later, Clem drove her to Islington. At first he had seemed unwilling to just leave her there with Malcolm, although when pressed he would not tell her why. He had already explained that he had things to do in London and she could not understand why he could not do them while she saw Malcolm. She finally prised out the reason for his reluctance as they journeyed to the city, but it confused her almost more.

'I can't bear the thought of the two of you together,' he at last admitted.

'But what is it he has done to upset you so?' she asked. He looked surprised by her question.

'It's not just him, it's all of them: Richard, Tom,

that guy at the party. All of them had you and none of them wanted you as much as I did. I couldn't bring myself to speak to the twins for months after they...' His words tapered off and he looked pensive. Eventually he continued. 'It's not even as if I were the jealous type – at least I used to think I wasn't. But sometimes it got so bad that I could hardly breath.'

'Jealous? It is not a term I recognise,' she stated.

'It's an emotion, not a term. I don't know the best way to explain it, but I'll try. It's the anger and resentment you feel if someone has something you want and can't have; an awful possessiveness towards the things you value. It's a twisted, ugly feeling and one I very much wish I didn't have, but I have to confess that I do.'

'But those other sharings were before this: why should they torment you?'

'They shouldn't, but I'm irrational! Honestly, I will try to put it all aside. Maybe I was only jealous because they had you and I didn't. The situation's different now, so perhaps I can be, too.' She sat, quiet and thoughtful, for some time before she spoke.

'I think you are misjudging my association with Malcolm: I have met him twice, once before and once after now, but I have not shared bodies with him. Does that reassure you?' He took a while before replying, and stared fixedly at the road ahead.

'Would you like to?'

'I had not considered it, but there is always joy in the sharing.' She paused. 'Yes, in truth I should like to, but I shall not, not while you and I are lovers.'

The last word felt alien as it passed her lips. 'Is that promise enough?'

'It's more than I deserve,' he replied.

They spoke of happier things after that and agreed finally to meet at Lulu's once their separate businesses were done.

Malcolm opened the door and seemed a little surprised at the warmth of her embrace, more so when she broke free and ran to inspect the worm tank.

'Anything I can help you with?' he asked, a hint of sarcasm marking his voice. Suddenly she remembered that she had a lot of explaining to do.

'A great deal,' she began. 'But first I think you have some points that require clarification.' She walked towards the sofa and sat down. 'It may well take some time! What have you been told of me so far?'

'Not much, apart from the fact that I would have to wait until you reappeared before I could give you the results from the tests I carried out. When I couldn't source it, Tom and Lulu told me it was because it came from a distant time, where disaster had riven the planet. At first, I didn't believe them, but I haven't come up with a better answer than that. When I pressed for more information, they just said I'd have to ask you. It's the reason I came back from the Middle East – I could have told you how to build a tank by phone.'

'They did not lie. I come from a time some four thousand years in the future where the planet you know is greatly changed. There are two thousand people dwelling in an ecosphere, the Dome we call it. Outside, there is nothing but the barren surface of burnt earth like the sample I brought you. We survive, but we cannot develop or grow. There is enough sustainable land to feed two thousand, no more, and all energies are devoted towards improving the yield.'

He began to ask a thousand different questions, but Ehlana interrupted him.

'Soon I shall have much time to explain what I can, but for now it is precious. I have less than two weeks to construct a worm farm to carry back there with me and I need your help.'

'I don't understand,' said Malcolm. 'What use will that be?'

'It is one of the vagaries of time-travel,' she explained. 'You have already given me the information that I sought! I have met with you some years from now: you told me how you placed small fragments of the sample that I brought you in the tank and I saw how the worms had grown.' He looked most confused. 'At that time you told me it had taken two years before you noticed the changes, but I saw a worm as long as my forearm moving through the soil.' He got up and walked towards the wormery, then stood there silent and motionless for some time.

'I can't be sure, but I think you might be right,' he said. 'There are at least three I can see that look larger than they ought to be.'

'Believe me! You told me that a single tank of worms would, given time, free enough soil to achieve our goal and permit us to honour an ancient agreement. Will you help me?' He readily agreed and she spent the next hour answering his enquiries. Even as he walked her to the Underground station, he continued firing question after question and when she finally sat down in the empty carriage she was quite exhausted.

They had agreed that she would return in three days time to help with his constructions: until then he could work most efficiently on his own.

By the time she reached Nevern Square, Clem had already arrived. He had arranged a leave of absence from his work, at least until the tank was delivered. Lulu offered them a bed in the flat until the work was done. Ehlana was both relieved and amused when Clem replied that he'd taken the time off purely to spend time with her, not Lulu and her latest – it wasn't that far to Priors Courtenay and he intended returning home with Ehlana each evening. The atmosphere between the four of them was comfortable, though, and she was happy that Lulu and Jodai were sharing.

After a week, the tank was built and stocked: all it needed now was time. Ehlana and Clem spent the remaining days enjoying the Indian summer. Each day he planned a myriad activities but each day they ended up spending most of their time in bed, an arrangement she was more than content with.

On the fourteenth evening, Malcolm had insisted on hosting a dinner party at his house. Ehlana had hoped for a quiet departure and subsequent return, but Malcolm wanted to celebrate. At first he tried for an enormous, catered affair, but eventually agreed to invite just those few that knew the truth about Ehlana. She had spoken to no one but Lulu of her only fear: that she might be seized by the Evaluators on her arrival, but if that were to happen she wanted Clem near friends and Lulu had promised to care for him. Ehlana thought, wryly, how difficult that might be with Jodai and his demands on both Lulu's time and her body. For her own part, she was determined that the worms would safely reach their destination, no matter what the consequences were.

Clem and Ehlana reached Canal Bridge Street late in the afternoon and spent the first half-hour in the sitting-room practising with the straps and bindings that Malcolm had added to the tank, until they were confident that they would have enough time to fasten them all once Ehlana's crystal thrummed into life. Once Malcolm had explained where each of the straps went, he discretely left them alone. As the sky started to darken, Ehlana drew the heavy curtains across the window, shutting off the outside world. As she turned, she saw Clem had moved to watch the worm wall and silently she walked until she stood behind him. Her hand spanned the small distance between them and rested for a moment on his hip until it slipped round and into his pocket. Stretching her fingers as far as she was able, she could just touch the soft edge of his sleeping prick where it curled in the confines of his jeans. His response was immediate.

'Oh, no,' cried Ehlana, her voice stricken.

'What is it?' he said, turning to face her. He was torn between holding her and rushing to begin the furious fastenings required before she could safely leave.

'One of Malcolm's worms has escaped and taken up residence in your trousers! Whatever shall we do?' She leant against his chest, dissolving into streams of laughter.

'Not only was that extremely unfunny, but I

212

think it was probably highly insulting,' Clem said, looking stern and serious. She tried to control her mirth and find the breath to apologise, but he held her close and kissed her instead. Against her belly she could feel his slighted member pretending to be a snake. She wondered whether it would be 'polite' to do more than just kiss him here. One part of her decided that she did not truly care and she moved her hand to feel the strong length of him through the thick blue stuff of his jeans. He moaned, but not in complaint, so her fingers then worked at the zip that kept his flesh back from her hand. Once she had drawn it as far down as it would go, her fingers crept in through the gap and wrapped themselves around his prick. At this contact he groaned and dropped his head to her shoulder. He moved his mouth against her neck and marked out with kisses an invisible line that ran from the tiny hollow on her shoulder to the lobe of her ear. She trembled at his touch, her head stretched away from his as she tried to present as much bare skin to his mouth as she could. His hands dropped down to grip her buttocks: first, gently through the soft cotton of her dress, then, once he had hitched the fabric up until his hands found naked skin, much harder. It amused Ehlana that even after all the days they had spent together, he was still surprised and excited by her lack of underclothes. She had tried countless times to conform, but the only occasions she was comfortable in the strange undergarments they all liked to wear and have worn was when she was most likely to be taking them off. She wriggled out of his grasp and slid to her knees in front of him. As she pulled his thick shaft towards her lips, he wrapped his fingers in her long red hair, effectively tying himself in her tresses. She drew his hard, warm flesh into her mouth and his fingers tightened in her hair. Slowly, she moved back along his shaft until the ridge of his smooth head caught against her teeth. Holding him there with the softest of pressures, she ran her tongue along his little slit. He moaned and pushed her head back down towards his groin. When she had travelled as far as she could, her face buried in the dark down at the base of his prick, she swallowed, changing the tensions of her mouth around his hard stem. Now, he pulled again on her hair, drawing her away from himself entirely.

'Stand up,' he said, his voice rough as though he had forgotten to swallow whilst she ate him. He turned her so her back was towards the worm wall. Her arms wrapped around his neck and their lips met, tongues darting out to greet each other. He lifted her up from the floor and held her solid until her legs wound round his waist, then he pinned her upper body against the cool glass in the wall. His hands fought hard to free her from the confines of her dress by pushing it up to her waist. When he was finally unencumbered he slid the red swollen head of his penis between her expectant lips. The pressure that held her tight against the glass receded slightly and she slithered down its smooth surface until she was utterly impaled. Behind her, she knew, the pale pink worms laboured unperturbed by any action of the pale pink worm-like thing buried inside her, but she felt a strange affinity with the soft brown earth they moved through. She wondered if the worms took pleasure from their work, but only briefly, for Clem called her back with a sweet insistence. He began to move between her legs, a slow, sure pistoning in her tight, hot shaft. Her tiny bud was ground against his pubis. It seemed as though she were pinned entirely and the only thing that moved was his prick. He gathered strength and force, pumping in and out of her while she clawed at his back, desperate for the friction she needed for release. She felt him start to come and her hand darted down to find her small erect bud, two fingers rubbing furiously once they located it. He held her steady while she strained and then, as climax took her, held her still. Once her muscles had finished their dance around his shaft, he bent his knees until her feet touched the floor. They were still joined like Siamese twins when Lulu and Jodai came in.

'Good grief,' said Lulu, analysing their position even before they gave it away as they pulled apart. 'Can't you leave the poor thing alone for a minute? Honestly, Clem, anyone would think you'd only just discovered what you're supposed to do with that beast between your legs! Make yourself useful and go and find us all a drink. Malcolm looked as if he's far more in need of a hand than Ehlana.' Lulu looked distinctly entertained by his embarrassment and grinned at his retreating back. Turning then on Ehlana, she continued. 'And you can wipe that smug expression off your face at the same time as you remove what I presume must be your buttock print from half-way up Malcolm's wall.' Lulu rummaged through her enormous handbag and threw Ehlana the scarf she brought out. Jodai stood quiet by the fireplace, but from his expression it seemed that he was trying to work out how Ehlana's buttocks had come to be so far above the floor. Eventually he spoke.

'You are ready, then, for your journey?' he asked.

'I believe so. There are no guarantees that the worms will survive the journey, although Malcolm sees no reason why they should not,' Ehlana replied. 'All I can do is carry them there and leave them in hope.' Clem returned then with Malcolm, each of them carrying bottles, buckets and glasses. As Clem began to open the first of the bottles the doorbell rang, its sound so loud a clarion that Ehlana could not believe she had earlier missed it, and Malcolm went to open the front door. He came back accompanied by the twins and Clem peeled back the foil of a second bottle. The company quickly grew cheerful, particularly when Lulu regaled them all with the story of what Clem and Ehlana had been doing when she found them. Clem was accused of immaturity – the rest of them, Tom said, had long grown out of knee-tremblers.

'Was it good?' Richard asked Ehlana. He laughed at her positive response.

They drank, they ate, they drank more and then, as the clock had just finished striking eleven, Ehlana felt the familiar tingle begin at her throat. She stood up and took Clem's hand in hers.

'Already?' he asked.

'Yes,' she replied, moving towards the table that held the tank. His fingers, expert earlier, fumbled with some of the buckles before they were finally tight. Only seconds remained for him to move away from her before she began to truly travel.

Trying to make a last joke before she left the party, she called out, 'I might even be back before you know that I have gone!' The pain then wrapped her in its cold embrace and took her home once more.

Chapter Eleven

Nucassel, December 3550ps

Strong arms were there to catch her, which was fortunate, for the weight of the tank was unbearably heavy after her journey. Once she was safe, Tolai left his place beside the Mother Crystal and hurried over. Between Horai, who steadied her, and the Magister, she hung limply, unable to help them, but they managed to lift her down from the podium. The straps proved difficult for the two men to unfasten, but eventually she was free. They placed the tank on a work bench and stood looking at it.

'Can this one small case truly contain all our hopes?' asked Horai.

'You would not think it so small had you carried it here yourself,' replied Ehlana, indignantly. 'In answer to your question, we shall never know, but it is the first new hope we have had in a very long time.' She prised the lid from the container and peered in, searching the soil's surface for signs of annelid life, but saw nothing. She shrugged and went to find somewhere to sit and breath. 'Is there any news since I was last here?' she asked.

'Both yes and no,' replied Tolai. 'I am afraid that I have falsified my records to show that you were lost on that last journey but one. It was quite fortunate, really, that the events surrounding your return were so chaotic that I forgot to enter the two journeys that you made. I was invited to join Magister Evaluator Lovanai for breakfast about two days after you left. I say invited, but the young man who came with the invitation made it quite plain it was a summons. Whilst Lovanai was very polite, he was interested only in the operation of the History Machine: whether it could be operated without my knowledge, and could it be operated by only two who travelled or would they need assistance, and so on. I answered honestly – I should have had no reason to do otherwise – and eventually asked him why he wished to know. He trotted out the falsehoods Jodai had been called to answer, and explained that the miscreant had managed to disappear. Amusingly, he told me that the Evaluators had even resorted to sending a small team outside the Dome to seek trace of the renegade. I think they hoped to find his corpse nearby, and solve their little problem, but as you would expect they found nothing! I asked why he thought Jodai would have used the History Machine to travel, and he spun some pretty tale about the two of you having connived to ruin the Harvest. I adamantly refused to listen to his lies and then remembered that, according to the records, you were still not returned. When I told him that you could not have aided him as you were already lost, he turned a deep shade of purple and stormed about. Then he demanded to know who your friends were within the Guild and who I thought might aid the rebel. None, I told him and promised him sight of the records which list, without exception, all journeys made. I confess I did enjoy the subterfuge. He let me go then, but he still strides around with an expression on his face that would make leaves wither at forty paces! Your hatchling has been accused, and convicted in his absence, of imperilling the Harvest and his rights have been revoked. Were he to be found, he would be immediately exiled. I always thought it strange that the Law insists on naming it "exile", when it is nothing more than a sentence of death. I suppose they thought murder "barbaric" also, and sought to hide it in gentler terms. Ah, well. Horai also was questioned, but less gently, and he told them even less than I. What of you, child? Will you survive where you are?'

'Assuredly, Magister. I have dear friends to aid both Jodai and myself. In fact, they wait together even now for my return,' Ehlana replied. 'I wonder if all those truly lost on their journeys fare as well as I – it is a comforting thought and not an impossible one. But now, I must tell you of the worms and their care if you are to return me soon. Keep them for some eight weeks in their tank and let no one disturb them – they will need to settle and their biosphere is only newly constructed.' Horai looked puzzled, but she swiftly guessed the reason why. 'The language is strange, but I repeat the terms as I was told them. After that time they should be introduced to a plot of soil one hundred times the size of the tank. At various points in the soil, introduce small pieces of our planetary crust, none of them larger than a fist. And then you must wait. It will take generations to effect a change. We have no way of telling how fast, or how large, the worms might grow, but it is always possible to divide and subdivide the group once they have taken hold. My friend suggested starting with more than one plot: five would be his maximum. The only thing the worms require is water. The soil must never grow dry, for the worms would perish, but it must not be overwatered. Here,' she said, taking Tolai's hand and pressing it into the warm earth, 'this is how it should be. When you lift your hand away there should be a gentle covering of earth: too dry and your hand would come away clean, too wet and there would be great clods of soil clinging to it.' The Magister examined his hand closely, then waved Horai forward in order to repeat the process.

'Two heads are better than one!' he said. 'We can't afford to have me forget just how damp it is supposed to be. If I am not the only one who knows, then it shall not matter if I do.' Turning to Ehlana, he continued. 'Horai berates me often for requesting information more than once. I tell him that, as Magister, I can ask him what the date is a thousand times each day, if I choose. Anyway, when one has lived as many days as I have, I think I can be forgiven for forgetting which day it actually is.'

'What news of the Crystal?' she asked. 'I was concerned that transporting both Jodai and I that distance would cause it damage.' Both the Magister and his assistant replied as one, but Tolai nodded to Horai and left him to speak.

'We were more interested in how well Jodai travelled, considering that no man has ever journeyed so far. Obviously he survived, but did it cause him injury?' asked Horai.

'Nothing apparent – it is always possible that the Evaluators' meddlings did more good than harm. He was uncomfortable for the first few days, but attributed it to the beatings he had suffered. Of the journey, he has no recollection at all,' Ehlana explained. 'And the Crystal?'

'Your pardon,' said Horai. 'Your question was first and did not deserve to be ignored. Come and see for yourself.' He walked with her towards the heart of the History Machine. The Mother Crystal was more opaque than she remembered from her last inspection. 'Strangely enough,' he continued, 'this area here near the core remains untouched, but the entire left quadrant clouded after you left. Since then, it has remained stable, or at least it had. This area here has changed tonight.' He pointed to a patch as large as her hand. 'No one else has travelled since you last left – it is deliberate in that we do not wish to waste what little strength the Crystal still has in pointless journeys.'

'I remember well enough the first time I cut the Crystal,' said Tolai, who moved to stand beside them, one brown-spotted hand resting on the stone's edge. 'It was the most perfect thing I had ever seen – translucent as water and just as pure – and I was going to hack away at it. It took me the better part of a year after my appointment as Magister before I could bring myself to do it. But eventually I had no option: pieces were needed and I was the one for the task. I had practised, long and hard, for I knew that I must do it at some time, but that first blow – ah. I was so scared that I would harm it, mar it, spoil it, hurt it even. And now, when it ails, I am powerless to do anything but sit and stare at it, and remember the colours that used to dance out from it.'

'Where I journey, Magister, those colours form a thing called a rainbow: a phenomenon of nature that occurs when rain and bright sunlight occur together. It is not such a rare thing that people are amazed to see it, but it is always an enchanting one.'

'Enchanting . . .' said the Magister, almost to himself. 'Yes, that is it. From the very first moment that I saw the Crystal I knew that I wanted to serve. It was a good decision . . .' His voice trailed off and his eyes closed, but neither Ehlana nor Horai thought to break his silence. For an instant, Ehlana considered telling him of her strange experience when she had handled the Mother Crystal, but in the end she could not confess her violation.

At length, the old man shook himself out of his reverie. 'I was fortunate,' he said, 'to come to the Magistership so young. No one could have expected it, least of all I, but it gave me many years to enjoy the privilege of service. Well, Horai, it will be your turn next. No, do not shake your head. I cannot hope and do not wish to live forever, but I fear your inheritance shall be less than you might wish.'

'Magister, if you thought to name me your successor, it would be more than I could dream. But do not speak so – there are many things I must learn before you think of leaving and will take years for me to master,' Horai replied.

Ehlana felt uncomfortable listening to the two discussing such private matters and left them by the Crystal. The worm tank sat unattended on the bench and she went to sit beside it. Could it truly work? she wondered. Almost in answer to her question, a grey-pink head broke the surface, followed by the long, cylindrical body which worked its way out of the soil. The worm travelled a short, slow way across the earth and then crept back underneath. She watched its lingering progress in silence, but when a second head emerged she called the other two over to join her. At first she was concerned at the sudden activity, but when no more appeared she decided that they had only been feeding. Feeding! She had almost forgotten Malcolm's other requirement for their nurture.

'Truly, Tolai, memory is not affected only by age! I had omitted to tell you that leaves and other vegetation must be laid on the soil, not much, but enough for them to feed upon. A thin scattering, replenished when all is nearly gone.' She wracked her mind to see if there was anything more she must add. 'Their true name is *Oligochaete*, earthworm, of the genus *Annelida*'.

'Then it seems appropriate that they might indeed reclaim the Earth,' said Horai. 'We will care for them as best we can. Then hope.'

'Magister, I would return soon to my friends. My place is no longer here and the more time that I stay, the harder my parting shall be. Will you send me now?'

Tolai nodded.

'Where I go, there is another tank that I shall watch with utmost care, knowing that what happens there shall happen here. And when I watch, I shall think of you all so far away.'

Almost until this moment, she had not truly believed it could be the end. Even if Jodai had not

223

been indiscrete, there were clearly few journeys left to the Crystal and that in itself meant an end. As it was, she must leave her own life entirely and start afresh in alien climes. She embraced Tolai. 'Farewell, Magister, and think of me from time to time.'

'I could do little else,' he replied. 'We will do our best to justify your loss. But I, for one, shall truly miss you. Farewell, child.'

She turned from him and stepped up to the podium for the final time. Her face was wet with tears, but she knew not whether it was for an end to travelling or for her exile. She looked at the Laboratory – home for so many years – and her gaze fell on the tank. No matter the cost, if the worms survived and did their work, it was worth any sacrifice.

She felt the crystal at her throat begin to tremble even before the Mother Crystal's familiar song began and she gave herself up to the pain.

Chapter Twelve

Priors Courtenay,
September 1993AD

*B*ird song and the slow chug of an early boat on the river outside woke Ehlana. Half-turning, she reached out to touch the sleeping body beside her, only to find cold, empty sheets. Then she remembered that he was half the globe away. She sighed, stretched and got up. From the window she looked across the garden to the dark brown band of the river. For the first time this month the sky was free of clouds and it looked set to be a beautiful day. A fine day for flying, she thought to herself. In two years he had only been able to take her up there twice. Her non-existent status made many things difficult, but that was the hardest of all.

Once she had accepted the end to her travellings, she had determined that both she and Jodai should be independent of her friends. They were healthy and intelligent, and whilst their general knowledge was lacking in a way which might surprise potential employers, she was sure that it would not prove to be too great a handicap. She quickly discovered that not only did the lack of all formal qualifications render them almost entirely unemployable, but that even the most menial of tasks required official papers: requests for a national insurance number, whatever that was, or at least a birth certificate could not be complied with, particularly when one considered that the applicants had nearly four thousand years to wait for the happy event! In the end she accepted that they could not turn down all the offers of assistance they received.

Strangely, by the time she finally returned, Jodai had found an almost legitimate employer. While Ehlana made her last trip back to their own time, Jodai and Malcolm had discovered their mutual interest. Malcolm had invited him to visit his 'greenhouse'- a surgically-sterile laboratory where he conducted genetic experiments on various plants in an effort to engineer superior crops for the difficult areas he worked in. His passion had developed following his first meeting with Ehlana and he devoted a great deal of his scarce free time to this work. Once he had discovered the properties of the soil 'contaminated' by Ehlana's sample, the dimensions of his research expanded dramatically. Jodai had been immediately impressed: of all the things he had seen, this reminded him most of his own time. As Ehlana had done, he too had first sworn to his Guild on his seventh name-day. Since that time all his studies had been bent towards increasing productivity. Moreover, Malcolm's desire to feed the starving equated most closely with his desire to free the Sleepers and the two men were instant friends.

Jodai took to spending so much time in Islington

that Lulu got jealous and Malcolm decided to make it a formal arrangement. Following many clandestine conversations with Lulu, it was arranged that Malcolm would convert his basement into a flat – in fact a somewhat larger one than that in Nevern Square. Lulu would sell her flat and buy the one in Malcolm's basement at a heavy discount. The discount was Jodai's salary for the next ten years. There were no preconditions – if she chose to sell it later, then she was free to do so.

Jodai's relationship with Lulu was an easy one – Ehlana envied them that. Jodai's naivety aroused Lulu so intensely that she forgave his amorality. He always returned to her because that was where he felt most comfortable. She rested secure in the knowledge that whilst he was unlikely to be faithful, he would never love anyone more than he loved her. It was his nature. To her it gave the freedom to bed whoever she wanted and then return without fear of disapproval. Initially, she had confessed to Ehlana that she had been a little less discerning than she might have liked, accepting offers that would have been laughable had they been made when she was with Clem. The mere fact that she could say 'yes' had gone to her head and she had said it more often than she needed. Now, she rarely indulged unless the offer was exceedingly intriguing and when she did, it made sex with Jodai even more exciting, for he always insisted on a detailed retelling of all that she had done. So Lulu and Jodai were content: she was happy to share him and he was happy in the sharing.

For Ehlana and Clem, it was different. True, there was passion independent of the sex and the nights he spent away from her were long ones. But in him she sensed always a barrier and, what made it worse, was that it was one she had built. She had tried so very hard to find some task she could be financially rewarded for, but had no skills to sell. In the end, she accepted not only his request to live with him but had to allow him to keep her. Despite his protests that this had been the way for generation after generation of women, she always felt it to be strangely unethical. At first, she had diligently studied all those things that generations of domesticated women learned from the cradle. Clem dutifully ate all her burnt offerings without complaint, but she was secretly relieved when he suggested that they ate out more often. The equipment the average housewife was expected to wield proved no more successful: she flooded the kitchen a dozen times before Clem insisted that they use a laundry; the bag in the vacuum cleaner had exploded spectacularly and scattered its contents over the livingroom five minutes before his sister and her family arrived at the house for their first meeting.

Their first, and only, argument occurred when the lawnmower went for a swim. He had returned to find Ehlana sobbing at the end of the garden. When he had asked her what was wrong, she explained mournfully that the lawnmower had escaped. It had ploughed its way through her vegetable garden – much tended and watered and weeded, but a complete disaster from the view of productivity – decimating the few plants that had managed to survive beyond infancy, mown the hose as it passed over and accelerated down into the river where it now sat, just too far away for Ehlana to reach without getting wet. He listened to her story and began to laugh before she had even reached the end. Ehlana moved from sad to angry. How could he laugh when she had just wasted more of his money? Ever since he had rescued her from London and her ill-considered efforts to find employment she had done nothing but cost him more. All she could offer in return was sex and inedible victuals. The angrier she got, the more he laughed. He laughed so much that tears coursed down his face, which Ehlana read as a mocking imitation of her own. 'You would have been better off staying with Lulu,' she had said. 'Better an honest woman than a whore,' she cried. 'You wanted me to choose,' she shouted at him. 'But I have no choice.'

Her last words still echoed in her memory. He had stopped laughing then. As soon as they had left her mouth, she realised what she had done: that there were more ways than one in which to interpret them. But no matter how she denied what he had heard, the wall went up, one brick at a time, until it was complete and unassailable.

It was not that he loved her less, in fact the frequency and range of their couplings increased. It was more that she had entered him into a competition he could neither win nor lose and thereby robbed him of either victory or consolation. It must have seemed to him that all the things she did to try and please him, however disastrously, were her attempts to honour a mental agreement of her own, based more on honour than any emotion. He thought she stayed because she had no better place to be. Occasionally, his beliefs had made him spiteful. At first he would suggest that they repeat that first time and she, eager to recapture the memory, would agree. He thought she merely acquiesced to

229

his desire and when he bound her the ropes were taut.

At first, his violence was verbal: when he finally took her, his voice became harsh, his words laced with an obscene vehemence. It both frightened and excited her. Before long, he ceased to suggest it as a game, merely ordered her to fetch the ropes. But once the violence had been physical. He had been cold towards her all that day and their dinner at a nearby restaurant had been awkward. Almost to mask his silence, he had drunk too much and by the time they returned to the house she realised he would call for the ropes. This time he tied her cruelly, almost laced her to the bed and then he took her. No sweet murmurs or gentle caresses. He rode her hard, foul words spouting from the darkest corners of his mind. Whore, he called her, and meant it. Slut and bitch and other vile things she did not understand truly, but knew that the small part of him that uttered them truly loathed her. He loomed above her, menacing, his whole body shaking, one arm raised. Then he hit her: a vicious slap across her face. The realisation of what he had done sobered him immediately and his body crumpled against hers. Horror-struck by his violence, he begged her forgiveness and promised that it would never happen again. She, too stunned to analyse, had let him untie her and then rocked him to sleep in her arms. Since then, they had neither played with the ropes nor had he drunk more than two glasses of wine with a meal.

However, this episode provided a sort of camouflage for Ehlana's earlier mistake and after that their relationship was easier. Each gained comfort from the other as well as gratification, but she remained always aware that there should have been more. Occasionally she regretted the lost simplicity of her own time, but more she regretted that she could not have made a choice.

The first time he had taken her flying was in a Lear belonging to a client of Malcolm's. This had been some time after their argument. He had given up the commercial airline job three months after Ehlana arrived, prepared to hazard the more lucrative, but less secure, short-term contracts he could find and thereby spend more time with her. It meant mainly that he was away for longer periods but much less often. Ehlana hated it when he was gone, though she could not make him understand it. From time to time he had been invited to take a companion with him, but as she had no papers she could not fly. It had been Lulu who finally hit upon a solution. All Ehlana need do was make herself look older and then she could use Lulu's passport. Clem cursed himself for his stupidity – he above all should have remembered how alike they both looked at one time. Lulu insisted on creating Ehlana's disguise – after all it was she who was being impersonated – and declared herself quite satisfied with the result. If anyone saw beneath it, Ehlana would simply have to confess to plastic surgery! Clem had to take a charter flight out to Florida to collect the customer's plane and bring it back to London. Ehlana, travelling as Miss L Grant, would accompany him. Before she flew, she had no fears at all. But Clem had spoken only of the exhilaration of flight: he had not mentioned the excruciating noise of the engines nor the dreadful heaviness that pinned Ehlana to her seat as the plane battled with gravity, or even the strange pressure in her ears that made her think she had been deafened. If he had not been sitting beside her, Ehlana was sure she would have screamed. Once the plane levelled out her perceptions changed. Far, far below she watched a river twisting and turning, not sure if it was the same as that which flowed past his house. Tiny fields and smaller buildings fled beneath her eyes. Then the coastline and the endless blue of the sea. Ehlana had been transfixed by the curve where the sky met the sea – the two blues merging. The horizon, Clem called it. To Ehlana, it was the curve she had seen every time she neared the Dome's edge, turned blue instead of the more usual dark shade of grey. She had gazed at it for a very long time. They eschewed the in-flight movie, choosing instead to talk of the things they would see. They had just three days in which to explore before returning to London. The flight was long and the view through the small oblong window was limited. It was almost a relief when Clem told her that the descent had begun.

In some ways the landing was worse than the take-off. At least that had been rapid. The slow fall as the plane attempted to evade gravity's pull and land in its own sweet time was terrifying. Before it had been the shriek of the engines, now it was strange clicks and grinds and movement in the very substance of the wings that filled her with dread. Clem laughed at her and promised that the return would be better – a smaller plane required a lot less effort to fly, he explained, and he said that the view from the cockpit offered a much better perspective on flying. She was not so easily reassured, particularly after the landing and the engine noise which she was convinced must be abnormal and indicative of their imminent demise. Her relief when she finally stepped off the plane was almost tangible.

As soon as they had unpacked at their hotel, he made her change into the sheer bathing apparel Lulu had insisted she buy. Ehlana had fought back, convinced that such a tiny scrap of material could not possibly cost such an enormous sum of money. Clem marched her down to the beach. The few times they had been to the coast in England the sea had been uniformly grey and unwelcomingly chill. The immersion had been pleasant, but Ehlana had far preferred the bathtub. This, however, was something entirely different. Warm, golden sands sloped gently down towards the water and then continued their soft descent as far as she could see. The blue darkened suddenly just beyond the rocky outcrop that protected the little bay. No one else was in sight. He had taken her hand and walked her into the water. It was beautifully warm. At each step it claimed another bite of her body. At first it had been easy to move through, but as it advanced up her thighs, it grew heavier. At last she could hardly move at all. The water lapped at her nipples and they hardened against its caress. He had made her place one arm around his shoulders and then he lifted her feet from the sand. He moved an arm under her thighs and held her there. He took a couple of steps further down the sloping sand until the water covered both his shoulders and her arm. Then he dropped his arm from under her. She floated. She stretched her legs out, amazed that they seemed determined to rise with no assistance from her. He moved his arm to cup her chin and at the same time removed her arm from his shoulders.

Slowly, his body rose up to touch hers and he floated beneath her. Sunfire! How good it had felt! She had never doubted that she was not safe, content to let him hold her life in his hands. With little kicks from his feet and a gentle stroking through the water with his hand he had brought them back to a depth she could easily stand in.

'That's swimming,' he had said. He leant forward and kissed her mouth. 'This isn't,' he had continued. His hands moved to her shoulders and slid the thin black straps from her pale pink skin. He kissed the lines where the straps had been. He rolled the costume down over her breasts. They floated with an innate buoyancy entirely their own. He ducked his head down beneath the water and gently sucked on each of her pert, stiff teats in turn. He raised his head to breath and then dove down to her waist, sliding a hand in each side of her costume and easing it down to her groin. He emerged again for breath and a single kiss from her moist red lips before submerging to finish his task. When she was unencumbered, he surfaced and asked her to open her legs. Expecting at most the kiss that other parts of her body had received, she had been fascinated to watch him dive to the bottom of the sandy incline and propel himself just above its surface until he reached her, where he passed through the triangle that she formed with the sand. He turned behind her and returned through her legs, this time finding the surface by sliding himself along her body. Just as his head broke the surface she raised her arms and wrapped them around his neck. She jumped a little and raised her legs to wrap them tight around his waist. He kissed her hard then, his cool tongue playing

234

against her own. It required little effort from Ehlana to maintain her position and he needed to provide no assistance so his hands roved free around her body. She held him at arms' length while his hands played with her breasts and with the lightest of pressures from her knees pushed herself far enough away for one to find her hidden place. His touch was light against her and water eddied round his fingers with each movement, stroking her with a liquid caress. He struggled to enter her, but the water bore her always away from his thrusts. Still carrying her, he walked towards the rocks that sheltered the little bay from the ocean until he held her pinned against them. They were worn smooth and felt warm against her back. This time the water's inertia was powerless against his desire for penetration and once he was safely inside with her legs wrapped tight around his waist, he moved away from the rocks.

As they floated, Ehlana wished they could always be so: antagonisms washed away, replaced with a weightless union as unhurried as the waves. Slowly, the water carried them inshore, barely perceptible ripples shunting their bodies along. Clem moved forward a few paces, then dropped to his knees in the sand. The soft grains scoured gently at her buttocks while the ocean lapped around her neck. She still floated with her hands on his shoulders and her legs round his buttocks. He gripped her tightly on her hips and held her steady as he began to move in and out of her tight flesh. She moaned and threw her head back, her hair fanning out around her in the water. He bent his head to bite gently on her exposed throat. As he moved, the water undulated around her body in rhythm with his thrusts, stroking her entire form with the same caress, both inside and out. When they came, it had been together, a gentle explosion subdued by the strength of the ocean.

The high-pitched scream of a distant fighter plane winging its way through the skies brought her out of her reverie. She glanced at her wrist-watch – eight o'clock. Only a few more hours and Clem would be home. She was torn between returning to the comforting warmth of the bed or breakfast. Orange juice, coffee and toast won.

After she had eaten, she attended to the domestic matters that the passing months had finally given her mastery over. She laughed when she thought of how useless she had been. No, don't spoil it, she thought, one memory leads always to the other. Instead, she worked until all was done, the last task being immersion in the large, old-fashioned tub. One thing the years had not touched was her joy at the abundance of water here. Every incursion into its warm embrace was as wonderful as the first – she left it only when it became too cold to remain in any longer.

Once she was dry, she returned to the bedroom and began to dress. She smiled wryly as she drew each fine black mesh of stocking along her long, tanned legs and fastened them with the complicated clips that held them in place. It had taken a very long time for her to feel comfortable in the strange undergarments of the time and even now she only chose to wear them for Clem. He had a curious but exciting habit of twisting and pulling at her suspenders that made her shiver just to think of it. As she stood, the straps jerked tight and when

236

she walked towards the mirror their gentle stretchings reminded her again of his touch. Her reflection stared back at her: tall and slender in the dark green satin corset. Above each shallow cup, the small pink hemisphere of sleeping areola peeked out and she stroked each one in turn until the flesh stiffened and pressed hard against the smooth fabric. Her breasts were pushed high and tight together: black laces travelled in tight zig-zags from just below the cloven, fleshy spheres to just above the auburn fuzz of her mound. A thin line of pale flesh separated where the one green panel ended and a tiny triangle began, held at each side by the fine black thong which ran around her hips. She twisted in front of the mirror to look where it joined to a vertical line, whose source was buried in the crevice of her buttocks. Her hand ran back along the smooth curve of her bottom and down, stopping when she reached the sheer silk of her stocking. Her hand slid across the top of her thigh and moved beneath the tiny scrap of green that hid her sex. Then she heard the familiar sound of his car on the gravel outside.

Pausing only to grab her green silk bathrobe from the bed, she threw it on and dashed down the stairs to greet him. No matter how many times he came home, she was always overwhelmed with delight at his safe return. He was just shutting the front door when she reached him. He wrapped his arms around her and kissed her, long and hard.

When, at last, he broke away she found that she had forgotten all that she wanted to say to him. It did not appear to matter, for as he took her hand, her gown fell open. He stood for some time, devouring her body with his eyes, before he began to climb the stairs, pulling her behind him.

'Come with me,' he said. 'I know there's a million different things I ought to be doing now. Eating, sleeping or bathing are probably the most appropriate. But seeing you like that, I know that all I'm going to do is take you to bed and show you how much I missed you. Any objections?'

She laughed, noting that he had not paused in his climb whilst he waited for an answer. Following him happily, she replied, 'None at all. Indeed, I was thinking of very much the same thing when you arrived.'

She lay on the bed and watched him while he stripped off his clothes. He was still as lean as he had been when she first saw him, nearly fifteen of his years before. His chest was strong and bronzed, the perfect backdrop for the small triangle of long dark hairs, his nipples hardening beneath her gaze. He slid down the zip of his trousers and she stared at the deepening vee form until it revealed the first of his crisp black curls. He glanced up at her, as if he wanted to check that she still watched him. His hands, hooked into his untied belt, began to slide the dark fabric down over his hips, the fluid movement exposing his smooth pale skin. She began to laugh as his disobedient prick caught itself up in the folds of black material, but at the same time experienced a wave of fiery excitement as she imagined it caught within her own, deep folds; her laugh became instead a ragged sigh.

Finally naked, he came to lie beside her, his body stretched out against her own, but where she lay prone, he propped himself up on one elbow and looked down to her. His hand stroked where his eyes travelled. First her cheek, and he bent to kiss her gently. Then sliding down along the soft skin of her neck, pausing for a moment with his fingertips resting against the vein that pulsed strongly there. Over the high mound of a breast, his fingers closing on the hard flesh of her nipple, squeezing it harder still.

She sighed.

His hand moved over the smooth satin that encased her form. When it at last found flesh again, he slid a single finger under the taut elastic of a single suspender and continued down until his course was intercepted by the fine cord of her g-string. He followed this new route, his fingernail etching a line in her skin. As he reached the protective triangle, his hand stretched out to cup her mound, the exploring finger ventured on to slip between moist lips and rediscover her secret berry where it hid.

She moved against his hand, desperate for the contact. As she squirmed beneath his palm, he bent down again to press his lips against hers, his tongue reaching out to find hers. She raised her leg and hooked it over his thigh, with the one simple movement drawing his body closer and granting his hand greater license. She could feel the hardness of his staff against her buttocks and pressed against it. He groaned and shifted against her. His finger continued its long, slow strokings and he moved just far enough away from her to reorient his stiff prick on the soft warmth of her hole and pierce her darkness. He moved his leg up between hers, his hard shaft sliding deeper as his body twisted around to this new angle, his finger still slowly caressing her swollen bud. His lips swooped on the pink gnarled flesh of her nipple where it escaped from the soft green satin. Her hand moved to cup the other lonely breast and play with the teat that longed for the soft touch of his mouth. She rocked against his thrusts, encouraging and desperate, seeking release from the fire that burned deep inside. He strove to match her, his strong flesh forcing its way in and out of her swollen lips, his finger moving hard against her own small shaft. Slowly his speed increased, as insistent as the flowing tide. His hardness stretched her and she tensed around him, loving the sensation of his swollen head inside her body. She gasped for breath and he covered her mouth with his, his tongue probing as his prick did. She bit gently on his tongue and gripped tight around his prick. His finger increased its pressure and its speed as he moved inexorably towards his climax, determined that she must come too. His pulse pounded deep inside her and she raced to meet him, coming just as he could no longer hold back.

He sagged back against the pillows, breathing hard. 'There,' he said eventually, 'I told you I'd missed you.' He lifted an arm and she nestled close against his warm flesh, wrapped in his strong embrace. 'Would you be mortally offended if I slept now? Not for long, but I don't think I have much hope of avoiding it.' He yawned. She half rose, intending to leave him in peace while he rested, but he pulled her back. 'Don't go! I need you here when I wake up.' Her hand reached out to stroke his soft, tired prick. 'Not just for him,' he laughed. 'Sometimes when I wake on my own it feels as if I dreamt all this and, just for a moment, the loss of you overwhelms me. Please stay.' She relaxed into him and felt the soft pressure of his lips against the crown of her head. She drifted into sleep with her head pillowed on his shoulder, a peaceful dreamless slumber.

She woke to a nightmare: her crystal, still and silent for so long, vibrated strongly at her throat. She had time enough only to move away from him before she pulled him with her to insanity and worse. The painful blackness encompassed her and she fought back her scream.

Chapter Thirteen

Nucassel, January 3552PS

She found herself falling under the Laboratory
lights.

'Forgive me,' said the man who caught her as she
stumbled, 'but I could delay no longer.' Her eyes
adjusted to the brightness and she found Horai at
her side. He had changed little since she had seen
him last but now, instead of the ochre robe he wore
the Magister's black. Fleetingly she wondered how
much of his new robe he owed to others. He had
remembered her previous returns, it seemed, for
once she was steady he went to collect an ochre
bundle for her from the bench.

'Tolai?' she asked, instinctively sure of the reason
for her summons. As she pulled the robe over her
head, a tightening at the back of her thighs suddenly reminded her that she was still wearing the
satin corset and stockings. A quick glance at Horai
revealed that he had also noticed her strange
apparel: he turned his staring eyes from her and

blushed deep red. In an effort to hide his embarrassment, he answered her question.

'He deteriorates fast, almost as fast as the Mother Crystal. I sometimes wonder if it is the one that keeps the other alive, though I should not like to choose which.' Ehlana glanced towards the Mother Crystal which gleamed now with a pearly opalescence. 'I know he cannot last much longer,' said Horai. His hand gripped Ehlana's elbow and he hurried her towards the door. 'For now, he sleeps more and more and he rambles in his sleep.'

'Where does he live now?' asked Ehlana, knowing that Horai must now possess the old Magister's rooms.

'With me. He had called it home so long that I could not bear to turn him out. Apart from which there is space enough for both of us.'

Despite her earlier concerns, Ehlana found herself beginning to like the young Magister. He was barely recognisable as the shy young man she had first noticed only a few years before – the Magister's black changed all who wore it – but he clearly held the old man to his heart.

'I brought you here for two reasons: first that I know how dearly he loves you, and why. As I said, he rambles rather in his sleep and I know how much he desires to see you again before he goes. The second reason is connected to the first: he wants you to see the Field; to see what you have done.' In the distance Ehlana heard a child cry. For some reason it seemed a strange sound. 'Among us, only three know the real reasons why; for the others some strange confusion muddles their minds. As each day passes, they remember less of the truth.

Tolai and I have discussed this phenomenon late into the night.'

'I do not understand. What truth?' she asked.

'I am such a fool! Tolai always tells me I never see the obvious. The Sleepers were raised five years ago,' he said.

'Five years ago? But how? I truly do not understand.'

'Once we had sent you back, Tolai sent both worm tank and I back to the first Skyside days. Our Guild was young then and they had no real notion of what the Crystal could do – they experimented still with resonances. Tolai, however, had thought to provide me with information that proved my credentials and I was taken then to the Magister Agronomist. I left the worms there and they started working two thousand years ago. Tolai avers even now that, until he put his hands to the Crystal for your departure, it had never occurred to him that the worms should travel twice. He insists that the Crystal told him to send them, not in so many words, but that it implanted the notion in his mind. I believe it to be a delusion, but a fortuitous one.' Ehlana thought of what she had learnt from the Crystal, but let him continue. 'So I took them back and left them there. A second dome was constructed and the worms were freed beneath in what earth could be spared from the Field. Finally, fifty-three years ago, the worm keepers declared the land beneath the dome viable. A large group of agronomists left Nucassel and began to cultivate the vast area beneath the glass. Five years ago, there was at last sufficient yield to awaken the Sleepers. They walk again and only through you. But recently it seems that our fellows forget the true past – it is as if reality was to them nothing but a dream. Now only Tolai, myself and Lora, the archivist, recall what really was. Even now, I know there are things that I accept as having happened, even though I know they are untrue. For example, I enquired as to the status of your friend, Jodai, who I know full well is whenever you left him. His Guild records show him as being based in Dome Three on a four-year project. He cannot be contacted to confirm or deny this, but there are no charges raised against him. You too are assigned here, not missing as I know the Magister recorded you. Anyone asked about you merely explains that you travel. Not one of them thinks more than three or four weeks has passed since they last saw you.'

They had reached at last the doors to the Field. A woman, her head held high, passed through the doors and into the street immediately in front of them. At first, Ehlana gave her distended belly no thought: she had seen many pregnant women in the past twenty-four months. Then, she suddenly remembered where she was. Turning to Horai, she found that he had not even noticed the woman's condition.

He noted her confused expression and began to explain, 'There have been seventy-three live births since the Sleepers returned. At least forty more are imminent. As I said, things that I know are impossible even I accept as truth. But come, now, and I shall show you why I have brought you here.'

Since her first returning, Ehlana had avoided the Field. Before she travelled, it had seemed to her to be beauty preserved in a terrible place, the glimmer of hope for the future. Once she had realised how much had been lost, she had not been able to bring herself to gaze on the few resilient plants that struggled for survival.

As they walked through the doorway, she steeled herself for shock. It looked smaller even than she remembered. The air though was purer than that which she breathed in the past. They walked until they reached the Dome's edge.

'There,' said Horai, pointing to another dome some distance away to the left. 'That one was built at the same time as this, when our forebears had first returned Skyside. As you can see, it is much lower than this, only seven feet at its apex, but it was built to protect the worms while they worked and to provide sufficient growing space for crops without wastage. Over there – ' he pointed out three glistening hemispheres some miles away to the right ' – are the domes built five hundred years ago. Soil from the first was imported and worms introduced. They were allowed time to reclaim the land beneath before crops were introduced. A fifth dome is being constructed behind that group. All this because Tolai had the foresight to send me back!'

'Do not be so sure that the foresight was his!' said Ehlana. Horai looked at her questioningly. 'In order to explain, I must confess a thing forbidden. When you and Tolai went in search of Jodai, I touched the Mother Crystal. I saw Tolai as a man younger than you are and newly come to the Magister's robe. I had not realised just how young he had been at the time of his appointment. At first I was confused by what I saw and pulled away. But a second time I returned and was shown more. Tolai again, and others, all wearing the Magister's black. Of all those I saw, only one cared truly for the stone that he served. Truly, the Crystal sees his cuts as love taking, whereas the others commit acts of rape upon the stone.' Horai looked at her, incredulous. 'I know how mad it sounds. Believe me, I have reflected much upon those strange visions in the time I have been away and can only conclude that in some strange, crystalline way it loves the old man. I am no expert on matters of the heart, indeed am still coming to terms with some of love's conditions, but I think the Crystal ages with him. Tell me, have you cut any shards since coming to your mastery?'

'No, nothing new. I still practice the art and have refused to try my hand upon the Mother Crystal,' he replied.

'Then try seeing through her eyes. When I was granted this knowledge I had both hands upon the stone and rested my forehead against it,' she explained. 'I cannot tell though if it were a gift to me only or a chance vision that may not be repeated. But I am sure that it was true sight, not imaginings.'

Beyond the glass edge of the Field the sun's colour had turned to rose, its gentle light refracted into rainbows by the other domes. Ehlana watched, entranced. 'It is so very beautiful. Where I go, there are so many types of land: barren and fertile, desert and jungle. But in so many places, they offer only rape to the land. Here we try to breathe life back into the ruins of their last violent act. Back there, small groups battle to protect their planet but their voices are seldom heard. And when they manage occasionally to make a point, it is almost invariably too little, too late.' Ehlana was unaware when the first of her tears began to well in her eyes: by the time she realised she was crying, her face was already wet.

'Why do you weep?' asked Horai. 'There is now so much to be hoped for.'

'I cry for the things that cannot come again. It would take a myriad journeys to bring one of each plant, two of each creature that needed a mate. The Crystal could not permit it. But I must try. At least seed stock I could bring. Jodai and I could carry many between us on one travelling. Do you think it will survive long enough?'

'I think that matter rests almost entirely with Tolai. But you must try.' He reached up to touch her face and wipe the tears from her cheeks. 'This is no time for sorrow. Much can be achieved in one small journey. I will send you back, but it can only be for a very short while. If I delay too long there might be no way to call you.'

'What will you do if the Crystal dies?' she asked.

'Ah, I have thought long on that matter. The Guild survives only to travel and study History. If we cannot travel, we do not have a Guild. Moreover, it seems to me that in fact we existed solely to bring about the changes which you see. Once the purpose has been achieved, we are redundant. To be honest, I had considered apprenticing myself to the Agronomists, except that I am not sure they would take me. A magister whose Guild had died could easily be considered something of a Jonah! Truthfully, I do not know what I shall do if it comes to pass. I daresay I shall make my decision on the following day.' His smile was an honest one. Ehlana felt guilt at her earlier misjudgement of the man. Contrite, she stood on tiptoes and kissed his cheek.

'You are a good man, Horai, and one I am glad

to have known,' she said. He seemed embarrassed with her compliment.

'I did one further thing when I travelled back there,' he explained. 'For some reason, they considered me important because of what I bore, even though I confessed small part in its arrival, and offered me their gratitude. I asked instead for an amendment to the Sleepers List when it finally was written. Magisters from seven Guilds heard me beg for clemency on a thing they had no knowledge of, but Magisters they were and my plea became enshrined in their Guild records. Infant males have, in this adjusted present, been only sterilised, not maimed, by a procedure detailed in one of the first books you brought back with you and the operation is entirely reversible. Thus was agreement reached with the Sleepers and, now that the debt has been paid, all males who seek it can become potent.'

'And you have sought it?' she asked.

'No, not yet. It is not necessary. But I would gladly do so if...' his voice trailed off.

'But what is it you think to gain?'

'A kind of immortality; to know that others of my line would draw breath on the planet I loved long after I had gone; many things and nothing in particular. It was only because I had thought it a promised thing. If I had always known that it could not be, I presume it would not have shocked me so when Tolai spoke of it to us,' he explained.

'And what of the method for producing these offspring?' she asked. He swallowed hard, and reddened, offering no reply. She reached out to place one hand atop his shoulder. He trembled beneath her hand. Suddenly she understood why Horai seemed often awkward and gauche, whilst at

249

the same time held Tolai's confidence: he was awkward only with her. 'Look at me,' she told him. 'I have no experience in the breeding of infants, and can never promise that I should ever have the interest for it, as I never considered it a part of my life. But I know much of the sharing required to produce progeny and would teach you, if you will allow. It brings a fierce joy, but one that you must never allow to possess you. I can only share – with it I do not grant the ownership of my body, just a small part of my soul that belongs entirely to the one to whom I give it. Would you accept the sharing on that basis, and with the knowledge that it may never come again?'

He stood, quiet and thoughtful, for some minutes and then finally spoke. 'Yes, I would share with you. For many months have I dreamt of it, more fervently since that time I held you naked in my embrace. Even now, if I shut my eyes and remember, I can feel you still warm and soft in my arms.' As he spoke, he closed his eyes and lost himself in his memory. He did not open them until the contents of his arms matched his reverie and Ehlana stood close against him, her clothes cast down on the green carpet of the moss garden that they stood in. She reached a hand behind his head and, with the gentlest of pressures, drew him forward to meet her lips. His hands travelled down her back, stroking softly at the cool, smooth skin they encountered. Ehlana inhaled deeply, finding both strangeness and attraction in his scent. Her fingers worked at the cord around his waist. When it was finally untied, she let it slip to the ground. Then her hands moved to the single fastening at his neck. Once that was free, she moved the voluminous black fabric apart and stepped one half-pace closer, her body moulding to his wherever their bare flesh touched. She was surprised by how badly she wanted him. She sank to her knees and her lips found the part that they sought. His hands came to rest lightly on her shoulders as she drew him into her mouth. Slowly, she moved to engulf him, only to discover that she could not, so instead she travelled back and teased his little hole with the tip of her tongue. His hands gripped her shoulders tight in response.

After a little while, she moved her head away entirely and looked up at him as he towered over her. His hand moved forward to touch her lips then slid round to cup her cheek. He stooped to kiss her and, as they kissed, he knelt as well. Ehlana's hands moved inside his gown and stroked his hard, flat belly, then moved and came to rest one on each side of his hips. She pulled herself close and felt the stiff ridge that imprinted itself all the way from her pubis to her navel. His hand travelled to weigh the curve of one breast and she felt its nipple begin to stiffen where it pressed against his chest. He must have felt it also, for his hand moved to find it and pull softly on its hardness. She found his other hand and moved it to the juncture of her thighs. At first his fingers toyed hesitantly in the curly mass of hair that it discovered, but then worked their way towards her hidden folds. Although he knew not what he sought, he learned from her gasp when he found it. Slowly he rubbed at the tiny bud of swollen flesh and then slipped down to discover what other treasures were buried there. A long, slim finger insinuated itself into her smooth, silky hollow and she tightened herself around it. It lingered for a while, enjoying the pressures that she brought to bear then finally withdrew. Ehlana licked her lips and found, eventually, her voice.

'Lie down,' she said, huskily. He did and his gown billowed out around his form, a black blanket against the green carpet of moss. She straddled his hips and reached for his stiff rod at the same time, holding it steady as she lowered herself on to it. This time it was his turn to gasp. She slid, inch by inch, along its length until her other mouth had swallowed it entirely. When she could move no further, she paused to admire the paleness of his flesh beneath her. He raised himself up on his elbows and his eyes gazed intently on that spot where their bodies joined. Smiling, she slid a hand down to touch where he stared, two fingers spreading her labia apart and a third finding the little bump that had until then been concealed. Softly she ran her fingertip over its head, shock-waves coursing through her body. Beneath her, Horai groaned as she flexed around his prick. Her finger stroked a little harder and she ground herself against him. One of his hands found a small, tanned breast to play with and the other moved to join her own. She crouched down just above him, her hands at his shoulders, and drew her knees up level with his rib-cage. Slowly, she began to rock her hips and he matched his massage of her clitoris to her speed. His other hand clutched tightly at her breast, almost forgotten as he concentrated all his energies on the sensation at his groin. His beating finger increased its speed and now Ehlana fought to match it.

Faster now, she rode him, striving always to keep pace with his finger until finally she moved so rapidly that he could no longer keep up. His breathing now was as ragged as her own and she knew he moved inexorably to his climax. Her own was elusive and her mind scattered as it tried to find an image that would help: slowly it began to form. Behind her, as she crouched, she imagined him kneeling, imagined his hands on her back, caressing her as she fucked the man beneath her. She imagined his cool fingers trailing in the crease between her buttocks, moving down to find the small dark hole that hid there. Imagined first one, then another, pushing themselves gently into its tightness, pulling it open; then another, more solid presence – the hard, red head of his prick as he moved it where his fingers were. Slowly, slowly, the tense insertion as he softly forced it into her too-tight hole. Feeling its head rub against the other already buried deep inside her. He would not need to move, just hold himself there as she worked between them. The image grew until she could almost feel his hands upon her hips, feel his breath against her back and she came, hearing his laughter in her mind. Beneath her, victim of her frantic thrustings and all but forgotten in her fantasy, Horai screamed out at his own, first coming. She collapsed on him, no energies left to support herself. They lay still for some time, but at last she rose up and began to dress. He watched until she was done, then stood and retied his robe around him. The moss held a deep imprint of his form and they both looked down on it and laughed.

'Take me to Tolai now,' she said.

They walked, hand in hand and happy, to the doors, but once they reached the street, she dropped his hand and followed him to the Magistratum. As they went, she remembered the last time she had visited Tolai there. She suddenly wondered if the Crystal could know of it. Could it have been that the Crystal had recognised, as best it might, that each of them bore great love for the same man and for that reason alone had granted her the vision of the Magister as a youth? It may be that Horai went on a fool's errand looking for something that he could never see. But, then again, perhaps not: for it would only be the emotion that the Crystal recognised, not the act, and Horai loved the old man just as deeply.

Tolai was sleeping when they arrived. His face against the white pillows was tranquil in repose and for a fleeting moment Ehlana saw there still a trace of the young man that the Crystal first loved.

'Magister,' said Horai softly. There was no response. 'Magister,' a second time he called, louder this time. 'Ehlana has come to see you.' The old man's eyes flicked open, instantly aware of all he saw.

'Well, child, it has been a while since you were last here. Come, sit beside me and tell me what you think of it all. He did bring you here from the Field, did he not?'

'Yes, Tolai. I am confounded but at least no longer confused! You did well to think of sending the worms back. Lesser men would have made the Sleepers wait another two thousand years,' she said, smiling.

'So now you can both return and enjoy what you have wrought,' Tolai continued. 'I regret that I shall not see much more, but it is satisfying to know it for truth in my lifetime.'

'I must return for seed stock, Magister,' she said

to Tolai. 'But I feel it in my heart that once you go, the Crystal will sleep for ever more. There is so much I would spare from the Sunfire – Jodai will know what is best. But you must promise not to slip away before I can bring more. A week will be enough, just seven days. There is so much to do. Will you stay until then?'

'I promise, Ehlana, that I shall try. I am too tired to do more. But seven days does not sound like a long time to wait,' he replied. She smiled and kissed his forehead, reaching out to stroke his old, gnarled cheek. His eyes shut and he seemed to drift again into sleep.

'We had better leave him,' whispered Horai. 'I do not know how much longer we have.' She kissed Tolai again and moved to join Horai at the door.

Just before they left, Tolai called out from his bed. 'The letter, child. You remember the letter you asked about?' he said. She had entirely forgotten it. 'Why, you wrote it! The name I did not recognise, but it was definitely your hand. How many of your essays, written in that tiny, pointed script have I read over the years? I could not fail to recognise it. In all the excitement I had forgotten to tell you. The letter was yours.'

Ehlana and Horai returned to the Laboratory in silence, each lost in their own thoughts. By the time they reached there, many of their Guild brothers were already at work so there was no place for further discussion. Horai walked her to the dais and lifted her up. She bent forward to kiss him, unconcerned whether any marked her gesture.

As he walked towards the Crystal, she called out. 'A week seems like a long time. I shall try to be ready before, if you need to call. But give me the full week if you can.'

He nodded and placed his hands atop the Crystal. The familiar song began once again and Ehlana began to travel.

Chapter Fourteen

London, September 1993AD

As always, she journeyed to Lulu. Jodai and her twin were in bed, their long limbs sprawling intertwined, wrapped in sleep and little else. She called their names and instantly they awoke. 'Thank god!' said Lulu, rushing naked from the covers to embrace her. 'We've been worried sick. Clem's downstairs – he came as soon as he realised what had happened, knowing that if you could come back it would be here that you came to.'

'I will go to him. Get dressed and come down, though. We have much to do and little time in which to do it,' advised Ehlana. She left them then, and hurried downstairs.

Clem lay on the sofa, one arm thrown across his eyes, as if to shield them from the light. She knelt beside him, lifted his arm gently and kissed him.

'I am back,' she simply said.

'Ehlana?' he asked, still more asleep than awake. 'Ehlana!' He wrapped his arms tight around her and hugged her close against his chest. 'I thought you'd gone for good this time. What happened? How did you escape?' She kissed him again to stop his questioning.

'Patience, love, patience!' she said. 'I shall tell all once the others are here. Until then just hold me. We have so much to do that I would rather just enjoy the quietness of this moment with you.'

It seemed no time at all had passed when Lulu and Jodai came in. Once they were all seated, Ehlana began.

'The Sleepers awoke five years ago. I still do not know exactly how, but our plan worked: the worms thrive and the planet also. There are now five domes and the population increases. History changes daily yet few seem to realise it. Jodai, we are no longer fugitives and can return – but it must be soon, for Tolai is dying. Before the Crystal sings again, we must gather seed stock to replenish our world: trees and plants we must take back, so that all can see the marvels we have witnessed here.'

Jodai's face shone with joy at Ehlana's tidings. Grasping Lulu's hand tight, he stood and moved towards the door. 'Come, love,' he said to Lulu, 'we cannot waste a minute that the old man gifts us. We must make a beginning now and find all that we can.'

'Just let me get my bag,' replied Lulu. 'I feel sure we're going to need my cheque book!' and she followed him happily out of the room.

Clem looked over at Ehlana, a pensive expression on his face. 'She's glad now, but wait until she's thought it through,' he said. Ehlana was not sure if he spoke to her or to himself.

She went and sat beside him, taking one of his long, cool hands between her own. She lifted it to her lips and kissed it. He stroked her cheek. Neither said anything more for a very long time. At last she broke the silence.

'Come, we should not leave all the work to the others. Take me and show me those growing things you love, that they may bloom still, long after we are both gone,' she said. He stood and took her hand, pulling her up from the seat.

'You're right,' he said. 'We have things to do.'

They drove around the countryside for three days, collecting seeds and fruits. Beneath the spreading arms of an old oak tree near his childhood home, that still bore evidence of a platform he had built high in its branches, he spread a blanket across the grass and then began to remove his clothes.

'What are you doing?' she asked. 'What if someone should come?'

'Let them!' he replied. 'The first time I had sex was here and it seems like a good place for beginnings ... and endings.' Naked, he sat down and smoothed the cloth beside him. 'Join me, make love with me and let's pretend we have all the time in the world.' He lay back, his arms crossed to form a pillow for his head, and closed his eyes.

As Ehlana undressed, she watched the patches of light that fell through the oak's shade dance across his bare skin, dappling him with gold. After all the years that had passed since she first saw his body, it still exerted a strong response in Ehlana. He remained lean and fit, she remained fascinated by its soft strengths and hard weaknesses.

She dropped to her knees at his side, leant forward and kissed him. His eyes opened and his arms rose to embrace her as she crouched over him.

One hand slid along her spine, its gentle passage sending anticipatory thrills along the nerves that met there but travelled on all over her body. She slid down to lie against him, heat building wherever their forms touched. His hand ran along the curve of her hip, slipped down to her waist and then inched up along her ribs until it found a breast. He cupped it in his smooth palm, then raised his head to suck on the soft pink nipple until it hardened in his mouth. She stroked his cheek as he suckled and he turned his head momentarily to kiss her palm before returning to his chosen task. Her hand slid down to his shoulder, then over the hardness of his chest, interrupting its journey to squeeze gently at the small brown nut of his nipple. He echoed her soft pinch with his teeth against her stiffened flesh. She shuddered once, then her hand continued, reaching first the firm skin of his belly before etching a line with a fingernail just above the dark hairs. Then she continued down, along the bony edge of his hip until it curved into the seam between his thigh and his groin. Slowly, her fingers crept through the tangled forest until they found the hard cylinder of pale flesh that waited there patiently. At their first contact, Ehlana felt a jolt like an electric shock run from her hand throughout her body, earthing finally in the small core of her sexuality. He must have felt something of it, also, for he broke away from her and laughed, pushing her gently over to lie on her back beside him. He kissed her long and deep, his cool tongue probing through her lips to tease her own. One hand moved to separate her long, tanned legs and a finger sneaked through her curls to soothe the demands of a clitoris stiff with desire. Slowly he rubbed against it, slipping from time to time into her deep well in order to oil the hot, fleshy bulb. She lay still, aware only of his hand between her legs, the gentle strokings and languid probings. Then he moved away and returned, crouched between her legs, his tongue continuing and augmenting all she had felt from his finger. A ragged sigh forced its way through her dry lips. His mouth broke contact but his finger returned. Then he moved on her and in her, one continuous rolling motion. As his stiff prick slid deep inside her, the persistent digit massaged her swollen bud. He began a graceful pumping, his hard flesh pistoning slowly up and down her smooth tunnel and all the while his finger laboured, her clitoris burning beneath it.

The tempo of his movement increased and Ehlana slid over the edge of her climax, his digit never faltering as she thrashed beneath him. Once she had peaked, he moved his hand away and ground his flesh hard against the bony ridge of her pubis. He raised his chest an arm's length from her, fingers clenched tight in the soil and let his prick dictate the force of his thrusts. So fast and sure and hard he pushed against her, pinning her tiny morsel of flesh hard against the dark mound of his groin, that she had no option but to return his stabbings by rising up to meet him. Her hands on his strong shoulders could feel the tension building in him. Urgently she forced him on and answered the explosion of his orgasm with her own. They collapsed back onto the warm earth together.

'Take me with you,' he said, once their breathing had quietened.

'I cannot,' she replied. 'Your life is here. How would you feel if your wings were clipped and

261

could no longer fly? I know the joy it gives you when you soar above the clouds. It will be many ages before my brothers fly and you would then be always anchored to the earth. I could not do that to you.' She kissed him hard. After a while she continued. 'Apart from which there are but two crystals to take the travellers.'

'Couldn't you go and then come back for me?' he asked.

'It cannot be. I did not explain it earlier, but the Mother Crystal and the Magister are linked. Horai believes, and I cannot but agree, that once this journey is made, there will be no others: the Crystal's heart is all but obscured by the strange clouds that have developed inside it. When Tolai dies, the travelling finishes. I could not go and leave Jodai here: he burns with desire to return to our own time.'

She could not take him with her – he dare not ask her to stay. He ran from the confrontation and ceded the fight. 'But you will stay with me until the time comes?' he asked.

'Assuredly, there is no place that I would rather be. But when the summons comes, we must all four be together to say our final goodbyes.'

'Then take this,' he said, and gave her the small brown acorn that his hand had closed on as he came. 'It is the only child I can give you. Watch over it and care for it until it's grown and remember how much I loved you, thousands of years before.'

They drove back to London, silent but strangely content. It had long been dark by the time they arrived, but Lulu was alone: Jodai was in the 'greenhouse' with Malcolm. Ehlana, tired and

262

hoping to avoid intense discussion, begged to be allowed an early night. When Clem went in to see her not fifteen minutes later, she was already fast asleep.

She woke to hear voices from the room next door.

'... you never did answer my question,' she heard Clem say.

'Which one?' asked Lulu.

'Would you go if you had the chance?' he replied.

'What, exchange all this for a brave new world Huxley never imagined in his wildest dreams? I've got nothing to keep me here and the only man I've had more than a passing interest in since we split up is going back there. If nothing else, the complete absence of tobacco would give me an excellent excuse to finally give up smoking!' she quipped. 'I did suggest to Jodai that he took some nicotine seedlings with him, but he turned me down. Seriously though, I'd jump at the chance – wouldn't you?'

'I don't know. If Ehlana wanted me, yes. But I don't imagine I would be happy. What could I take with me that would have any value or merit in that society? She put her finger on it when she told me I wouldn't be able to fly. It's about the only thing I can do.'

'But there is so much you could learn! It would be a bit like having the slate wiped clean – no threat, no war, no real suffering. Given time, I'm sure anyone would be productive. But it's a pointless discussion, as you've already told me we can't go.'

'I'm sorry,' he replied. 'But I just wanted to know what you'd do if you had the choice. In some ways it makes it easier to let her go, just knowing that you, who don't even belong there, would seize the opportunity to go.' A noise outside the door cut short their conversation and Jodai let himself in.

Clem said his goodnights and moved into the bedroom. Ehlana lay still, feigning sleep. He clambered into bed and wrapped himself tight around her. She half-turned to him and considered 'waking', but a gentle splash of water on her shoulder persuaded her to silence. When she was at last sure his tears had stopped, she found he was deeply asleep.

The following morning Clem was awake before Ehlana and busy with the others by the time she emerged from their room. Still, there was plenty of time to consider the problem, she thought, so she put it to one side.

It was just before noon that she felt the first telltale vibration at her neck. Quickly, she reached up and unfastened the chain. Shouting loud, she hailed them all. Clem burst through the door first, Lulu and Jodai close behind him.

'It comes, too early, but the Crystal calls. Quick, Jodai, put on the pack: you have not a moment to lose.' He fumbled awkwardly with the heavy knapsack, Lulu aiding him, but with her eyes so full of tears that she was more hindrance than help. Clem stared at the ground, unable to look at any of them.

Once Jodai was finally laden, Ehlana moved towards Lulu and wrapped her arms around the other's neck, her fingers hidden while they worked with the clasp of her chain.

'Hold tight through the pain,' she whispered in Lulu's ear. 'Though you think it unbearable, it will pass, and Jodai depends on your support and your hand now. Farewell and love long, my dearest sister and friend.' She stepped back and found herself in Clem's strong embrace. It took Lulu and Jodai a moment to fully understand what she had done. Ehlana picked up the bag containing the package of seeds that she had wrapped herself and thrust it into Lulu's already fading hands. 'Hold tight to the bag and to Jodai, lest you lose them as you journey: for it will be you that carries both. Think of us once the plants are grown. Good bye, my dear ones. Never doubt that I do anything other than what I want most. I claim this man as my reward.' She reached behind her head to touch Clem's face and felt the tears that ran there. Turning in his arms to face him she continued, more for him than them. 'Did you truly dream that I would choose to leave you? Once, two years from now I promised you that I would stay if it was what we both truly desired – ' Clem stared at her blankly. ' – or at least I would have promised it when you asked. Once again, there is no choice – but I chose it to be so. Now you have me wholly, whether you desire it or not.'

In answer he held her tight against him and buried his face in her long red hair. By the time either thought to look up they were alone.

Epilogue

Oxford, February 2311 AD

*T*he phone rang, tearing his attention away from
the photograph he held.

'Sorry to disturb you,' he heard, 'but there's a
gentleman here insisting that he delivers a letter to
you personally. I said I was capable of that, but he
wouldn't have it.'

'Don't worry, I'll be across in a moment,' he
replied. He strode briskly across the snow-filled
quad and went into the Porter's Lodge. Apart from
Jones, there was only an elderly cleric. 'You're
looking for me?' he asked the priest.

'Professor Andrew McGregor?' was the reply. He
nodded. 'I am Brother Matthew of the Order of St
Patrick. Three hundred years ago a package was
entrusted to our care, with the promise of delivery
to your good self at this place and time. We never
knew if we would be able to discharge this trust or
if it would prove to be no more than an aged
eccentric's ramblings. My brothers will be heart-
ened to know that we have not been misled. Should

you wish it, I can be contacted at this address and show you documentary evidence we have kept since first receiving the parcel.' The cleric handed him a package wrapped in brown paper, doffed his hat and left.

McGregor walked back through the quad to his rooms. He unwrapped the parcel to find a small box and two envelopes. The box he opened first and found a large translucent crystal set in a plain metallic ring. The thicker of the two envelopes contained a pass book and key number code to a bank account in London. Finally, he opened the second envelope and drew out a letter.

Professor McGregor,

My deepest condolences on the recent loss of your wife and my apologies for intruding at such a sad time. Unfortunately, this is the only address I could recall for you. So few records survived by the time I was born and, whilst I can now be considered something of an expert on the late twentieth century, I regret that I paid only little attention in class to your early life.

I appreciate that you are likely to consider me deluded: so many do, and all those who knew differently are no longer here.

Although I write from the past, I was born in the distant future, one of a small group of survivors who owe their lives directly to you. More madness, you insist. Yet if that is the case, how can I know for sure that in two years' time mankind will fire the galaxy with the heat of its own ignorance. Like yourself, I am no physicist and yet another of the things I failed

267

to learn as a child was why the solar reaction was so much stronger than had been expected. I know you will try everything in your power to stop the dumping, but I know that you will fail. However, I also know that our lone city of Nucassel grew two miles from the entrance to the bunker that you built. The only thing I can offer as physical proof is the ring enclosed with this letter. It came from a Crystal of many thousands of carats, formed in the earth beyond the safe harbour you created – it is my only link with my own time – and I am told that its qualities are completely at variance with any crystal known now: a quartz-diamond compound never seen before. Other proof than that, I regret I do not have. However, I have left my estate in trust for you, in the hope that the money it provides might be of some value. Finance was one of the many things I never truly understood, but I hope that with nearly three hundred years of compound interest it will be a useful amount.

Much ridicule awaits you, I know, but do not forget that you are our only hope.

I remain, and will become, a grateful survivor,

Lulu Grant.

NO LADY – Saskia Hope
ISBN 0 352 32857 6

WEB OF DESIRE – Sophie Danson
ISBN 0 352 32856 8

BLUE HOTEL – Cherri Pickford
ISBN 0 352 32858 4

CASSANDRA'S CONFLICT – Fredrica Alleyn
ISBN 0 352 32859 2

THE CAPTIVE FLESH – Cleo Cordell
ISBN 0 352 32872 X

PLEASURE HUNT – Sophie Danson
ISBN 0 352 32880 0

OUTLANDIA – Georgia Angelis
ISBN 0 352 32883 5

BLACK ORCHID – Roxanne Carr
ISBN 0 352 32888 6

ODALISQUE – Fleur Reynolds
ISBN 0 352 32887 8

OUTLAW LOVER – Saskia Hope
ISBN 0 352 32909 2

THE SENSES BEJEWELLED – Cleo Cordell
ISBN 0 352 32904 1

GEMINI HEAT – Portia Da Costa
ISBN 0 352 32912 2

RUDE AWAKENING – Pamela Kyle
ISBN 0 352 33036 8

GOLD FEVER – Louisa Francis
ISBN 0 352 33043 0

EYE OF THE STORM – Georgina Brown
ISBN 0 352 330044 9

WHITE ROSE ENSNARED – Juliet Hastings
ISBN 0 352 33052 X

A SENSE OF ENTITLEMENT – Cheryl Mildenhall
ISBN 0 352 33053 8

Published in February

ARIA APPASSIONATA
Juliet Hastings

Tess Challoner had landed the part of Carmen in a production of the opera which promises to be as raunchy as it is intelligent. But to play Carmen convincingly, she needs to learn a lot more about passion and erotic expression. Tony Varguez, the handsome but jealous tenor, takes on the role of her education. The scene is set for some sizzling performances and life begins to imitate art with dramatic consequences.

ISBN 0 352 33056 2

THE MISTRESS
Vivienne LaFay

It's the beginning of the twentieth century and Emma Longmore is making the most of her role as mistress to the dashing Daniel Forbes. Having returned from the Grand Tour and taken up residence in Daniel's Bloomsbury abode, she is now educating the daughters of forward-thinking people in the art of love. No stranger to fleshly pleasure herself, Emma's fancy soon turns to a young painter whom she is keen to give some very private tuition. Will Daniel accept her wanton behaviour or does he have his own agenda?

ISBN 0 352 33057 0

Published in March

ACE OF HEARTS
Lisette Allen

Fencing, card-sharping and seduction are the favoured pastimes of Marisa Brooke, a young lady who lives by her wits amongst the wealthy hedonistic elite of Regency England. But love and fortune are more easily lost than won, and Marisa will have to use all her skill and cunning if she wants to hold on to her winnings and her lovers.

ISBN 0 352 33059 7

DREAMERS IN TIME
Sarah Copeland

Four millenia from now, two thousand people remain suspended in endless slumber, while others toil beneath a hostile sun for the means to wake them. Physical pleasure and desire are long forgotten, until Ehlana, a historian and time traveller, discovers that her own primal memories are the key which unlocks the door to another world – and her own sexual awakening.

ISBN 0 352 33064 3

To be published in April

GOTHIC BLUE
Portia Da Costa

A handsome young nobleman falls under the spell of a malevolent but irresistible sorceress. Two hundred years later, Belinda Seward also falls prey to incomprehensible and uncontrollable sexual forces. Stranded in a thunderstorm at a remote Gothic priory, she and her boyfriend are drawn into an enclosed world of luxurious decadence and sexual alchemy. And their host, a melancholic, lovelorn aristocrat, has plans for Belinda – plans which will take her into the realms of obsessive love and the erotic paranormal.

ISBN 0 352 33075 9

THE HOUSE OF GABRIEL
Rafaella

Journalist Jessica Martyn is researching a feature on lost treasures of erotic art for a glossy women's magazine. Her quest takes her to the elegant Jacobean mansion of the enigmatic Gabriel Martineaux, and she is gradually drawn into a sensual world of strange power games and costumed revelry. She also finds trouble, in the shape of her arch-rival Araminta Harvey.

ISBN 0 352 33063 5

If you would like a complete list of plot summaries of Black Lace titles, please fill out the questionnaire overleaf or send a stamped addressed envelope to:-

Black Lace
332 Ladbroke Grove
London W10 5AH

WE NEED YOUR HELP . . .
to plan the future of women's erotic fiction –

– and no stamp required!

Yours are the only opinions that matter.

Black Lace is the first series of books devoted to erotic fiction by women for women.

We intend to keep providing the best-written, sexiest books you can buy. And we'd appreciate your help and valued opinion of the books so far. Tell us what you want to read.

THE BLACK LACE QUESTIONNAIRE

SECTION ONE: ABOUT YOU

1.1 Sex (*we presume you are female, but so as not to discriminate*)
Are you?

Male ☐
Female ☐

1.2 Age

under 21 ☐ 21–30 ☐
31–40 ☐ 41–50 ☐
51–60 ☐ over 60 ☐

1.3 At what age did you leave full-time education?

still in education ☐ 16 or younger ☐
17–19 ☐ 20 or older ☐

1.4 Occupation _____

1.5 Annual household income
   under £10,000 ☐   £10–£20,000 ☐
   £20–£30,000 ☐   £30–£40,000 ☐
   over £40,000 ☐

1.6 We are perfectly happy for you to remain anonymous; but if you would like to receive information on other publications available, please insert your name and address

_____

_____

_____

_____

SECTION TWO: ABOUT BUYING BLACK LACE BOOKS

2.1 How did you acquire this copy of *Dreamers in Time*?
   I bought it myself ☐   My partner bought it ☐
   I borrowed/found it ☐

2.2 How did you find out about Black Lace books?
   I saw them in a shop ☐
   I saw them advertised in a magazine ☐
   I saw the London Underground posters ☐
   I read about them in _____
   Other _____

2.3 Please tick the following statements you agree with:
   I would be less embarrassed about buying Black
   Lace books if the cover pictures were less explicit ☐
   I think that in general the pictures on Black
   Lace books are about right ☐
   I think Black Lace cover pictures should be as
   explicit as possible ☐

2.4 Would you read a Black Lace book in a public place – on a train for instance?
   Yes ☐   No ☐

SECTION THREE: ABOUT THIS BLACK LACE BOOK

3.1 Do you think the sex content in this book is:
    Too much   ☐   About right   ☐
    Not enough   ☐

3.2 Do you think the writing style in this book is:
    Too unreal/escapist   ☐   About right   ☐
    Too down to earth   ☐

3.3 Do you think the story in this book is:
    Too complicated   ☐   About right   ☐
    Too boring/simple   ☐

3.4 Do you think the cover of this book is:
    Too explicit   ☐   About right   ☐
    Not explicit enough   ☐

Here's a space for any other comments:

SECTION FOUR: ABOUT OTHER BLACK LACE BOOKS

4.1 How many Black Lace books have you read?   ☐

4.2 If more than one, which one did you prefer?

4.3 Why?

SECTION FIVE: ABOUT YOUR IDEAL EROTIC NOVEL

We want to publish the books you want to read – so this is your chance to tell us exactly what your ideal erotic novel would be like.

5.1 Using a scale of 1 to 5 (1 = no interest at all, 5 = your ideal), please rate the following possible settings for an erotic novel:

Medieval/barbarian/sword 'n' sorcery ☐
Renaissance/Elizabethan/Restoration ☐
Victorian/Edwardian ☐
1920s & 1930s – the Jazz Age ☐
Present day ☐
Future/Science Fiction ☐

5.2 Using the same scale of 1 to 5, please rate the following themes you may find in an erotic novel:

Submissive male/dominant female ☐
Submissive female/dominant male ☐
Lesbianism ☐
Bondage/fetishism ☐
Romantic love ☐
Experimental sex e.g. anal/watersports/sex toys ☐
Gay male sex ☐
Group sex ☐

Using the same scale of 1 to 5, please rate the following styles in which an erotic novel could be written:

Realistic, down to earth, set in real life ☐
Escapist fantasy, but just about believable ☐
Completely unreal, impressionistic, dreamlike ☐

5.3 Would you prefer your ideal erotic novel to be written from the viewpoint of the main male characters or the main female characters?

Male ☐   Female ☐
Both ☐

5.4 What would your ideal Black Lace heroine be like? Tick as many as you like:

Dominant	☐	Glamorous	☐
Extroverted	☐	Contemporary	☐
Independent	☐	Bisexual	☐
Adventurous	☐	Naive	☐
Intellectual	☐	Introverted	☐
Professional	☐	Kinky	☐
Submissive	☐	Anything else?	☐
Ordinary	☐	_____	

5.5 What would your ideal male lead character be like? Again, tick as many as you like:

Rugged	☐		
Athletic	☐	Caring	☐
Sophisticated	☐	Cruel	☐
Retiring	☐	Debonair	☐
Outdoor-type	☐	Naive	☐
Executive-type	☐	Intellectual	☐
Ordinary	☐	Professional	☐
Kinky	☐	Romantic	☐
Hunky	☐		
Sexually dominant	☐	Anything else?	☐
Sexually submissive	☐	_____	

5.6 Is there one particular setting or subject matter that your ideal erotic novel would contain?

_____

SECTION SIX: LAST WORDS

6.1 What do you like best about Black Lace books?

_____

6.2 What do you most dislike about Black Lace books?

_____

6.3 In what way, if any, would you like to change Black Lace covers?

_____

6.4 Here's a space for any other comments:

_____
_____
_____
_____

Thank you for completing this questionnaire. Now tear it out of the book – carefully! – put it in an envelope and send it to:

> **Black Lace**
> **FREEPOST**
> **London**
> **W10 5BR**

No stamp is required if you are resident in the U.K.